DROP OF HOPE

THE OMNI TOWERS SERIES BOOK 4

JAMIE A. WATERS

Drop of Hope © 2018 by Jamie A. Waters

Cover Art by Deranged Doctor Designs
Editor: Beyond DEF Lit

ISBN: 978-0-9996647-3-5 (Paperback Edition)
ISBN: 978-0-9996647-7-3 (eBook Edition)

Library of Congress Control Number: 2018907714
First Edition *October 2018

THE OMNI TOWERS SERIES

Drop of Hope

PROLOGUE

ARIANA RAN toward the priority elevators and plugged in her earpiece. She could hear the child's screams in the background. "Paul, talk to me. How bad is her condition?"

"It's worse than we expected. We're trying to stabilize her now," Paul explained, the worry in his voice indicative of the precariousness of the situation. "The transport team is working on her, but we've got burns covering about thirty percent of her body. Are you in your quarters?"

"I just left. I can meet you in the training room."

"No, it'll take too long," Paul argued, pausing for a moment to issue some instructions to someone. "Can you head directly to the medical ward? We'll have to meet you there. I've sent instructions to have a clean room ready."

Ariana swallowed, praying to whatever gods might be listening they wouldn't take an innocent life far too soon.

"I'll be there in a few minutes," she informed him and disconnected from the commlink call.

"Ari?"

Ariana glanced down the corridor to find Alec hastening toward her, but she couldn't stop while a child's life was in jeopardy. Pressing a button on the elevator, she said, "I'm sorry, Alec. I can't talk right now. I have to hurry."

His blue eyes were marked with concern. "What is it? What's wrong?"

"It's Mira," Ariana managed, pressing the button again and willing the elevator to arrive faster. She needed a blasted override code for these situations. Realizing who stood beside her, she grabbed his arm. Alec wasn't just a friend, he was also one of the High Council leaders.

"Alec, I need you to override the elevators. Mira's being transported to the medical ward right now. She was in an accident in the training room and burns are covering most of her body. I need to meet the medical team right away."

Alec paled and quickly entered in his code. "I'll go with you. She's the promising young fire channeler from the Gavron family, right?"

Ariana nodded as the doors opened. While Alec entered his code again to bypass all other floors, she said, "Yes. She's only eleven. I'm not sure what happened or why there wasn't a water channeler monitoring the situation, but I could hear her screaming over my commlink."

Ariana squeezed her eyes shut at the rush of emotion that went through her. She'd met Mira only a handful of times and was reminded of a bright, pixielike child with an insatiable curiosity and passion for life. The thought of not being able to prevent that precious light from extinguishing was more than she could bear.

The elevator shot downward, and she gripped the handrail tightly, worry for the young girl nearly overwhelming her. Desperate for a distraction, she opened her eyes to find Alec watching her. The depth of unspoken emotion and concern in his eyes spoke volumes about how much he cared for a little girl he barely knew. It made her respect and admire him even more. He'd always cared so much but rarely let anyone see his true feelings.

He had always fascinated her curious nature and made her want to learn more about him. She'd had a hard time keeping her distance from the moment she'd met him. Everything had changed since then, though, and she needed to remember some things happened for reason.

"I'm sorry for brushing you off," she murmured, casting her gaze downward and not wanting to reveal too much of her feelings. "Did you need me for something?"

"Don't ever apologize for something like that, Ari," he said, reaching over to touch her hand. A gentle caress of comforting air energy washed over her, stirring her energy to the surface. "You're trying to save a life. What I wanted to talk to you about can wait."

She bit her lip, lifting her gaze to stare at the descending numbers on the panel. The elevator wasn't moving fast enough. "Please distract me, Alec. Otherwise, I'm just going to worry about things I can't control. Once I'm in the medical ward, everything will change and I can focus on what needs to be done."

Alec searched her expression for a long moment, indecision clearly warring on his face. He rubbed the back of his neck. "I... I was hoping you might consider talking to Kayla again about training."

Ariana blinked up at him, surprised by the request. She had the feeling that wasn't what he intended to ask, but she wouldn't intrude by prying. Besides, her energy needed to be reserved for the little girl who desperately needed her help. "I thought Kayla *had* been training over the past few months. She hasn't?"

Alec hesitated. "Somewhat, but she's been distracted with the construction and river excavation. I know she respects you, especially after you healed her former camp leader. She's been working with me and her mother on her air and earth talents, but she needs to make training more of a priority. If you mention it to her again, I'm sure she'll listen to you."

The elevator doors opened, and they stepped out into the medical ward. It was too quiet on the floor, and the surrounding energy threads were moderately stabilized, so Mira must not have arrived yet. Turning back to Alec, she nodded. "Of course, I'll be happy to speak with her."

"I'd appreciate it." Alec paused, studying her for a long moment. As his eyes roamed over her face, her stomach did a neat little somersault at the intensity in his gaze. He took a step toward her. "Ari, I know this isn't the best time, but I was wondering if you'd be willing to have dinn—"

Voices and commotion exploded from the far side of the corridor as the medical team emerged from the service elevator with a stretcher. Even over the noise, she could hear the soft whimpers of a child in pain.

"I'm sorry, Alec, I have to go," Ariana called over her shoulder, running down the hall and toward the little girl who desperately needed her. She only hoped her healing gifts would be enough this time.

CHAPTER ONE

ARIANA DUCKED beneath the low-hanging beam and stepped into chaos. The heavy din of construction competed against a myriad of voices shouting to be overheard. She took a few steps forward, her soft, gray slippers leaving a trail of footprints in the construction dust. Someone bumped into a crate and it crashed to the ground, the noise not even beginning to mask the reverberations of the pounding and thudding that echoed throughout the building. It was a maelstrom of confusion, and Ariana was very much out of her element. She loved every minute of it.

A group of workers almost plowed into her, distracted by the heavy crates they carried.

"Watch it," someone snapped in her direction.

Ariana gasped and jumped backward, squeezing between a few stacked boxes so the workers could pass. She managed to voice an apology, but they were already halfway down the corridor before the words escaped her. They disappeared to whereabouts unknown. It was tempting to try to follow them to see where they were headed, but she doubted they'd be interested in trying to assuage her insatiable curiosity.

This time, Ariana was cautious before stepping out into the busy workroom. She had to remember to pay attention to her surroundings because a different set of rules applied here. The change was more than a little refreshing. Over the years, it had become commonplace for people to cater to her needs. Those workers weren't concerned with who she was or which tower she'd been born into. She'd been in their way, and they'd yelled at her.

She grinned at the thought and brushed the construction dirt off herself, hesitating as she caught a glimpse of her dusty dress. The casual dress she'd chosen that morning, with its soft grays and whites, was acceptable to wear within the Inner Sanctum of OmniLab's towers but clearly marked her as an outsider here. If she managed to get another opportunity to return, she'd have to try to blend in more. Maybe she could try finding someone to make her more functional clothing.

Ariana walked through the workroom area, avoiding the workers and observing their utilitarian-style dress. Even more impressive than their practical clothing was their streamlined efficiency. They somehow managed to all have a purpose, and no one was tripping over anyone else. It was like a carefully orchestrated dance, with the symphony of tools in the background playing as an accompaniment. A group of people argued loudly in one corner of the room, pointing to a design diagram and then upward at the structural members overhead. In the center of the cluster was the petite woman Ariana had been seeking.

Kayla stood with her hands on her hips, her green eyes flashing with anger as she argued with a tall, thin man wearing what looked like a permanent frown. "No, Leo, I don't care if you're the foreman. Get your head out of your ass and learn how to read the damn blueprint. The east area of this level is designated for the entire community. The offices go on the west side."

The annoyed man pulled off his helmet, the temporary lights reflecting off his balding head. His face had turned an angry, mottled red. "Dammit, girl, I know how to read a damn blueprint. I've been reading blueprints since before you were born. I'm telling you your plan is shit. What the hell are you thinking trying to put fucking Omni offices in the same space with the ruin rats? We'll kill each other. It'll be a fucking bloodbath. Omnis will be stringing up ruin rats by the rafters and we'll have a mutiny on our hands. It'll be slaughter. Fucking slaughter. They need to stay in their own damn tower."

Kayla scowled, tapping her foot impatiently as though waiting for him to take a breath. She caught sight of Ariana and paused, a wide smile spreading across her face in greeting. She held up a finger asking her to wait a minute and turned back to the foreman.

"It's not for the Omnis, Leo," Kayla snapped at him. "It's for the Coalition and ruin rat camp leaders, and one of those offices is yours. Now figure out how to build it and quit bitching at me."

As the man sputtered in shock at the announcement, Kayla trotted over to Ariana. "There. That should keep him busy for a while."

Ariana glanced over Leo, who had been Kayla's former camp leader. He'd swiftly regained his composure and was now almost giddy in his excitement as he began dictating orders to the other men. Ariana ducked her head and smiled. "I think you made him very happy."

Kayla shrugged, but her eyes shone with humor. "I've been dying to spring that on him all day. Come on, let's get out of here. It's too noisy." She linked her arm with Ariana and led her into one of the more finished rooms.

Ariana glanced around, once again surprised by how much they had accomplished in such a short period of time. It had only been three months since they started on the construction of the new tower. She'd heard rumors about delays, but based on what she was seeing, it was difficult to tell.

Ariana moved over to stand beside the desk where more images and diagrams of building plans were scattered. She looked down at them, trying to imagine how everything would appear once it was completed. According to the agreement between OmniLab and the Coalition, they only had a year to finish the construction. She didn't know how such a feat would be possible, but she was hardly an expert.

"I'm glad you could make it." Kayla reached into a small cooling unit and pulled out a couple of hydrating packs. "I didn't think you'd be able to get away from Jason or the Inner Sanctum. I can give you a partial tour, but we'll need to get you some UV gear to tour some of the open areas."

Grateful for the offering, Ariana accepted it and took a drink, trying to decide how to begin. She absently threaded the water energy from the hydrating pack into the carefully crafted metaphysical barrier around her, which was designed to protect against any outward stressors. Unfortunately, being in close proximity to so many people could be draining. The water was a welcome insulator.

Ariana considered Kayla for a long moment. Even though they were close in age and shared the same origins, their lives had been vastly different. Kayla was unlike anyone she'd ever known and much worldlier. Over the past few months, she had gotten to know Kayla better, and it had become apparent how much Ariana had been missing in her sheltered existence.

When dealing with Kayla, Ariana had found frank honesty was usually the best approach. Kayla didn't have much patience for anything else. It was rather refreshing compared to all the innuendo and double-talk within the Inner Circle.

"I didn't exactly get away," Ariana admitted, not wanting to think about how annoyed her brother would be when he discovered where she was. "I ran into Alec a few days ago on my way to help Mira, and he asked me to speak with you. Since you're over here quite a bit, I decided it would be a good opportunity to check out the construction tower."

Kayla raised an eyebrow, finished off her drink, and tossed the empty container into a recycler. "Mira's the little girl who got burned, right?"

Ariana nodded. "Yes, she's doing much better now. We were able to repair the damaged nerves and tissue, and it doesn't look like she'll have any scarring. It's a terrible lesson to learn, but I don't think she'll set any more fires without proper supervision. Her trainers will also be paying much closer attention now."

Kayla cocked her head. "This sort of thing happens a lot?"

"It's not usually this bad," Ariana admitted, remembering some of the other injuries she'd help treat in the past. "Most injuries are usually minor, and they typically happen outside the training facilities when our children aren't being supervised by their instructors. It helps reinforce our need to make sure all our people are properly trained."

Kayla wrinkled her nose. "Let me guess... the reason you're here is because Alec wanted you to give me a hard time about training?"

Ariana winced and put the hydrating pack on the edge of the table. "I'm not sure I would have put it quite so bluntly, but yes. I know you've been working with your mother on your earth talent, but Alec would also like you to explore your water abilities. I'm available whenever it's convenient for you." She bit her lip, unable to hide her excitement and added, "But now that I've relayed his message, I have to admit the whole truth. My reason for coming here was much more selfish. Everyone keeps talking about the construction, and I've been dying to see it for myself."

Kayla laughed and gestured to the drawings. "It's not much to look at yet, but we're getting closer every day."

Ariana ran her fingers over the graceful slope of the images. "It's wonderful, Kayla. You've managed to take an idea and breathe life into it. Your actions have merged so many different groups together to unite them under one cause." She lifted her gaze to meet Kayla's eyes. "Do you have any idea what you've accomplished? You've given all of us renewed hope for the future."

"Kayla has many talents," someone said from the doorway.

Ariana turned and recognized the Coalition ambassador. She'd only met him once before, during the Coalition's attack on the towers. Since then, she'd seen his image onscreen in various videos, but his physical presence was far more impos-ing. His blond hair was pulled back away from his face, emphasizing the strong lines of his jaw and drawing attention to his steely-gray eyes. He took a handful of steps into the room, his movements reminding her of a powerful predator.

His gaze caressed her intimately as he eyed her up and down. Ariana swallowed, her throat suddenly dry, unaccus-tomed to having this type of reaction to anyone outside the Inner Circle. The sheer magnetism of his presence was a force in itself. As though sensing her thoughts, the corner of his mouth twitched into a small hint of a smile.

"Kayla, you have the most interesting friends. We have met before, correct? I would never forget such a beautiful woman."

Kayla raised her eyebrows, a thoughtful expression on her face as she looked back and forth between Ariana and the newcomer. "Um, Sergei, this is Ariana Alivette. She's Jason's sister." Then she frowned and added, "You remember Jason, right? The zap-happy Inner Circle member who would love any excuse to send you into next week?"

Sergei's smile deepened as he moved even closer, his eyes dancing with amusement. Ariana had the sensation even the energy threads in the surrounding air parted in his wake. When he took her hand, the warmth of his skin against hers was like a shock to her system. She blinked up at him as he leaned over and brushed his lips across the back of her hand.

"It is my pleasure to see you again, Ariana."

She tilted her head at his accented words, studying him curiously. It was strange that someone with his compelling presence didn't accompany his gesture with the normal metaphysical greeting of their kind. It was just one more reminder he wasn't one of them. Even so, she couldn't help but be intrigued. How was she drawn to this man when he wasn't using energy to entice her?

Suddenly aware she hadn't responded, Ariana blushed at her lapse in etiquette. "Please forgive me, Ambassador. I didn't intend to be rude. I'm not accustomed to meeting someone and not experiencing their energy signature. I have to compliment you on your excellent grasp of our language. It's improved a great deal since I last saw you."

"You must call me Sergei," he insisted.

She smiled and lifted her head to study him. He returned her intent gaze, and Ariana was once more struck by his magnetism. Not only was he incredibly attractive, but there was something about him that called to her on an elemental level. She took a small step forward, lifted her hand, and pressed it against his cheek. He froze, his eyes widening the barest of a fraction at the contact. He remained still, though, except to continue watching her.

Ariana traced her fingers over his cheek and down the line of his jaw. The light stubble on his cheeks tickled her fingertips. Sergei was coiled with energy, but the sensation was unlike anything she'd ever experienced. He couldn't be a *Drac'Kin* like her, but there was something different about him from other non-sensitives. Her cooler water energy was drawn to the heat contained within him.

Itching to explore him further, she moved her fingers down his neck toward the open collar of his shirt. His Adam's apple bobbed as he swallowed, and his shoulders tensed. Ariana's eyes shot up to meet his heated gaze and she pulled her hand away, realizing her mistake.

"I shouldn't... I'm sorry..." she floundered, wondering what had come over her.

What was she doing touching a non-sensitive like that? Her brother would kill her, but before that, he'd remind her for the hundredth time why she shouldn't leave the Inner Sanctum. She glanced over at Kayla to find the former ruin rat barely suppressing her laughter. Ariana bit her lip. How on earth did they manage to get to know one another without exchanging energy? The entire thing was baffling.

Sergei captured her hand and brought it to his lips again, pressing a kiss against it. "Do not apologize, Ariana. You are welcome to touch anytime."

Ariana blushed again, still embarrassed by the social faux pas, but she didn't pull her hand away. She wasn't making the best impression, but this stranger was arousing every inch of her curious nature.

Kayla snorted. "Funny. I remember a time not too long ago when you said the same to me."

Sergei chuckled, but his gaze never left Ariana. "But that was a game. One you played very well."

His expression turned more thoughtful, and he reached up to brush Ariana's cheek with his hand. Unable to resist, she leaned into his hand, feeling his warmth once again brush against her cool water energy. If he was touching her, perhaps touch was just as accepted amongst their kind. She needed to better understand their ways. Sergei was almost reverent as he caressed her cheek.

"You do not play games, do you, *solnyshka*? Your heart shines in those beautiful silver eyes."

Entranced and curious by the foreign word, she parted her mouth slightly. Sergei leaned forward, and she lifted her head, caught by the intensity in his gaze. His mouth hovered just over hers, close enough she could feel his warm breath against her lips. Ariana closed her eyes, the awareness of his nearness heightening as his scent and heat surrounded her. It wasn't normal energy she was feeling, but some other sort of pull. Was he really going to kiss her? Excitement and apprehension flooded through her at the possibility.

Kayla cleared her throat and made a strangling noise. "Uh, Sergei? Not a good idea."

"What the fuck is going on?"

Ariana's eyes flew open when she heard the familiar voice. Sergei froze, his entire body tensing as he lifted his head. His face was an expressionless mask as he pulled Ariana behind him. She pressed her hands against his back, once more intrigued by his warmth through his shirt. Shaking her head to try to clear the distracting thoughts, she looked around him to see the newcomer.

Uh oh.

Her brother's expression was thunderous as he glared at the foreigner. Sergei, however, appeared unconcerned and leaned against the edge of the desk, positioning his body in front of her in a protective gesture. The only sign of his annoyance was a slight rigidity in his shoulders. Ariana wanted to reach up and touch his shoulders to ease away the tension. She frowned and flexed her fingers, reminding herself her energy wouldn't work as well on a non-sensitive. It was tempting to try though.

Sergei nodded at the other man. "Jason, it is good to see you again. I was making your lovely sister's acquaintance."

"Is that what you call it?" Jason snarled, clenching his fists and taking a step toward Sergei. "Get the fuck away from my sister, or I won't be held responsible for my actions."

Ariana moved to stand beside Sergei, refusing to hide behind a man she barely knew, especially against her twin brother. "Jason, that's enough. I came here to meet with Kayla. Sergei happened to come in a few minutes ago. I was curious."

She glanced again at Sergei to find him still watching her with that predatory gaze. Why that gave her a thrill, she wasn't sure. She reached out and touched his bare arm, intrigued by the energy just out of reach that called to her. Almost unbidden, she took a step closer to the fascinating man.

"I've never met anyone like him before. He reacts with the energy in the environment. I can sense his energy below the surface, but it's so different from ours. It calls to mine." She glanced at her brother. "Why can I sense him better than other non-sensitives?"

Jason squeezed his eyes shut and muttered a curse under his breath. Opening his eyes, he ran a hand worriedly through his dark hair. "Ari, you need to step away from him right now. He's not one of us."

Sergei's eyes narrowed at his words. Pushing away from the desk, he straightened his body to his full and imposing height. Ariana bit her lip and glared at her brother in frustration. Of course Sergei wasn't one of them, but there was something there. She just didn't know what it was nor was she willing to ignore it.

"Jason," Kayla intervened, "just chill out. There's obviously some attraction between them. Believe it or not, it can happen. I can't imagine my life without Carl in it, and he's not one of you. Maybe it's the same sort of thing."

"You're not my sister," Jason snapped at the petite brunette. "If you spent a little more time focusing on developing your own abilities and training, you'd understand the dangers of what you're suggesting. Your talents are nothing like Ariana's, and you cannot begin to understand our world with just a few months of exposure."

Kayla's mouth dropped open, and she looked ready to spit daggers at him, but before Kayla could launch into a verbal assault, Jason focused again on Ariana. She could feel every ounce of disapproval in his stare but also sense his underlying worry and fear.

"Ari, please. This is why we didn't want you to leave our tower. You cannot help him." He took a step toward her. "Let me take you back to the Inner Sanctum."

Ariana closed her eyes, remembering the warnings of her elderly teacher before she'd passed away. Was her psyche truly unable to withstand being around non-*Drac'Kin*? It didn't make sense. Something about her teachings wasn't right. Ariana had been trying to do some experiments on her own and expose herself to others in secret. She'd been careful, but this was the first time she'd really been drawn to one of them. She hadn't had the same reaction with anyone that she felt with Sergei.

As she hesitated, the air in the room started to crackle with frozen energy. Her awareness opened, and her eyes flew to her brother. Jason's worry and fear were quickly reaching a crescendo. The closer he came to his breaking point, the more his control started to slip. No matter what, she couldn't allow anyone to be hurt.

"All right," Ariana agreed in a rush, but she let Jason feel the warning snap of her energy in the air. "I'll return with you for now, but you would do well to remember you're *not* my keeper. You will not dictate who I decide to spend my time with. I'll consider your words, but my decisions and the consequences of those decisions are my own."

Jason's jaw clenched, but he nodded and held out his hand. She started to take it but hesitated. She couldn't leave things this way. Above all else, Sergei was an ambassador for another powerful group. He deserved their respect.

Ariana turned back to Sergei. "I apologize for my behavior and my brother's words. I'm glad to have met you and..." Her voice trailed off, and she frowned. Energized emotion vibrated around them, but she wasn't sure how to translate it into words. Nothing seemed sufficient. How did non-sensitives express their feelings when simple words weren't enough? She paused, wondering if Sergei could sense her energy the same way she could detect something within him.

Ariana took a step toward him and stood on her toes. Brushing a soft kiss against his cheek, she sent a wave of her energy over him and whispered, "Thank you."

With a small smile, she turned away and took her brother's outstretched hand, letting him lead her away from the room.

CHAPTER TWO

SERGEI WATCHED Ariana disappear with a mixture of emotions. She reminded him of another woman he'd once known and was easily one of the most exquisite women he'd ever met. Ariana was tall, with a graceful and willowy form. And those legs. They seemed to go on for miles. Her long, dark hair shone with a brilliance even the light seemed to be drawn toward. Her silvery eyes, however, were his undoing. Every emotion, every thought, had all been reflected back at him with a guileless innocence that was staggering. She was wholly feminine but had an innate curiosity and strength he found fascinating.

It had been a long time since he'd had such a visceral and immediate reaction to a woman. He'd been a hairsbreadth away from kissing her, all audiences be damned. Something about her made him forget himself. She was utterly captivating, and that alone made her extremely dangerous. He couldn't afford to be distracted while he was still technically in enemy territory. The Coalition's alliance with OmniLab was tenuous at best.

"Well, that was interesting," Kayla huffed and sat in her

chair. "I thought Jason was going to blast you for sure. Did you feel those little icicles in the air? He was definitely losing his shit. She got him out of here just in time."

Sergei glanced down the hallway again, but the two siblings were already gone. Part of him was tempted to go after her so he could touch her again. He rubbed his fingertips together, recalling the softness of her skin and her scent. She'd smelled like the flowers they had in the OmniLab greenhouses. He wasn't sure what kind they were, but he now had an almost fervent desire to figure it out. The scent had been subtle but seemed to act like some sort of drug, confusing and heightening all his senses at once.

He turned back to Kayla, wondering how much information he could glean from the former ruin rat. Kayla could be cagey when it suited her. "What do you know of her?"

"Ari?" Kayla mused with a shrug and began organizing the scattered design diagrams on the desk. "Not a whole lot, but I like her. Alec introduced us a few months ago so she could help train me. She's some sort of expert water channeler. Some of the Inner Circle people can be real assholes, but Ariana's just about as sweet as they come. Alec thinks the world of her too, but I don't think he feels the same about her brother. Jason's a handful."

"You were to train with her? Why have you not?"

Kayla glanced up and scowled at him. "Great, now you're going to start too? Alec's been a pain in the ass lately. That's why he sent Ari here. It's hard to say no to her, and Alec knows it."

When he didn't reply, she blew out a breath. "Look, I've just had my hands full lately between the construction here and helping to oversee the underground river excavation. I'll eventually get around to doing more training, but I'm kind of busy right now."

"These are excuses, Kayla. A weapon does not serve if you do not have the skill to wield it."

Kayla pursed her lips in annoyance. "Fine. I'll train with her. Sheesh. I swear, Alec must have put you up to this too." She was quiet for a moment and a sly smile crossed her face. "You seemed quite taken with Ariana. You know, if I decided to train with her... let's say... tomorrow..."

Sergei arched a brow, enjoying the deviousness of Kayla's machinations. It would give him the opportunity to learn more about these strange Omni abilities and more about the intriguing young woman. "You would need an escort?"

Kayla nodded and held up her hands in a helpless female gesture. They both knew the gesture was bullshit, but Sergei wasn't about to contradict her when she was plotting so well without his help. "Since I don't have the skill to wield my weapon and all that, I could really use a big, strong Coalition soldier to help protect me."

Sergei chuckled. "How much will your assistance cost this time?"

Kayla gave him a wicked grin and leaned back in her chair. "I think another bottle of that vodka would do nicely. Pay up and you get to play escort. I'll even look away if you want to get handsy with Ariana again."

"You have a deal," he agreed, and his smile faded as he remembered the reason he'd originally sought her out. "I need to speak with you about another matter."

When Kayla leaned forward and arched an eyebrow, Sergei asked, "What is the latest status of this river excavation?"

Kayla sighed. "I'm not sure. Carl's coming back soon to give us an update. When I spoke with him a couple of days ago, they were launching more probes to try to map the underground river. We're still having problems getting our equipment down to the ruins, so they need to try to find a more stable location to run the pipes. Between the original chasm, the ruin collapse sixteen years ago, and the more recent earthquake, the structural integrity of that area has been compromised."

"I see," Sergei replied, considering the implications. "I need to be updated as soon as you have more information."

Kayla cocked her head and studied him. "Your people are in trouble, aren't they?"

Sergei hesitated, debating how much to share with Kayla. Unlike many of the tower residents, she would understand some of the dangers his people were now facing. But there were boundaries he couldn't cross without severe repercussions.

"We have moved many of our people here to help with the construction and river excavation, but we do not have easy access to our stockpiled resources from other facilities. Transports are costly, and there have already been too many delays with the construction."

She frowned. "I know the delays have been worrying everyone, but I don't think anyone fully realized the scope of this project. We've had to make more adjustments than we first expected, and some of the materials we were going to repurpose aren't going to work. How bad is it on your end?"

"My superiors have some serious concerns," Sergei admitted. "At least two or three of our leaders are heading to the area to evaluate our progress and the situation."

Kayla's eyes widened. "They're coming to OmniLab? Does Alec know?"

"No," Sergei replied, leaning against the wall to keep himself from pacing.

If Kayla or anyone in the towers knew how dire the situation was, it could prove to be disastrous. He had to tread carefully to prevent the Coalition's position from weakening even more. The original agreement with OmniLab stated the

Coalition would withdraw from their forced occupation of the towers in exchange for the new tower construction being completed within a year. The new facility would provide a home to a thousand of their people, including many of the ruin rats.

Unfortunately, they hadn't anticipated all these delays. If they didn't make progress or turn things around soon, their entire alliance would be in jeopardy. The Coalition had too much invested to walk away empty-handed. Even now, there were rumblings about whether this agreement was truly beneficial to their people. Weapons were being shipped en masse to the surrounding camps in the event their alliance degraded completely. If necessary, they were preparing to retake the towers by force.

"Our leaders will not come to your towers," Sergei informed her. "They will stay in the outlying areas, interview our camp leaders, and make a determination. I have an appointment with Alec tomorrow, but I had hoped for better news before then."

"I can try to reach out to Carl later tonight," she offered. "Communication has been spotty since he's been spending so much time underground. But I'll get a message to one of our people on the surface."

Sergei nodded. It was the best they could do for the moment. He only hoped Carl had good news whenever he reached out to them. Otherwise, all Sergei's efforts to negotiate with OmniLab and preserve life might have been wasted.

———

ARIANA DOVE INTO THE WATER, her body cutting through the depths with the surgical precision of a knife. The cloud of emotion surrounding her fell away sharply until there was nothing but a peaceful serenity. The water encompassed her, caressing every inch of her skin, and she channeled the energy until she was one with it. When she could no longer remain submerged, she broke the surface of the water with a gasp and filled her lungs with air.

Even the air held the moisture she craved. While she could connect with the energy through the air, it wasn't until she was touching the water that she truly felt alive. She treaded water for a moment, each kick edged with power and infused with the elemental energy.

"Hey! Am I early?"

Ariana turned at the sound of Kayla's voice and gave her a wide smile. She'd been pleased when Kayla had contacted her about training, not just because Alec had requested it but because she genuinely liked the feisty woman. Ariana swam over to the edge of the pool with long, sure strokes and pulled herself out.

Wringing out her hair, Ariana said, "Not at all. I just needed to clear my head. I've never been able to resist diving into a completely still pool."

"I hope it's okay, but I brought someone with me to watch while we train," Kayla said and gestured behind her.

Ariana froze at the sight of Sergei. He walked toward her, his heated gaze traveling over her wet body, lingering on certain areas before moving on to others. She swallowed, suddenly feeling more exposed in her bathing suit than if she had been standing naked before him.

When he was inches away and close enough she could feel the heat from his body, he took her hand. Lifting it, he held her gaze with his and pressed a kiss on the back of her hand. His voice was low and husky as he said, "It is wonderful to see you again, Ariana."

"Oh!" She took a step backward, nearly slipping back into the pool.

Sergei's strong arms caught her, and he pulled her against him. She pressed her hands against his chest, the warmth of his skin under his shirt heating her flesh. Her fingers reflexively curled into his shirt, and she looked up at him.

"Thank you," she managed.

He pulled her tighter against him and leaned down to press a kiss against her forehead. "You do not need to thank me. I will not let you fall."

Ariana's eyes softened as she searched his expression. He was sincere. She could feel it, even without a metaphysical connection. The energy within him was still trapped below the surface, coiled like a serpent just waiting to strike, but she didn't sense any danger from him. At least, not to her. She sent a tentative thread of cooler water energy toward him, curious about his response.

The heated energy within him flared for a moment and then dimmed ever so slightly, as though she'd calmed some of the flames. He was regarding her with a question in his eyes. Had he sensed it? She bit her lip, wondering what would happen if she sent him more energy. Caution, she decided, was best for now.

Ariana glanced down at his darkened clothing and gasped, realizing she'd made another faux pas. "I'm so sorry. I've gotten you wet."

He gave her a wicked smile. "I have no complaints, Ariana. It is a small price to pay to have you pressed against me."

Ariana bit her lip but couldn't hide the smile his teasing words evoked. She glanced at Kayla, who was watching them with a knowing smile. The Coalition ambassador was too distracting, and Ariana had made a promise to Alec. She took a reluctant step away from Sergei, desperately needing some distance.

"If you're ready to start, Kayla, I think we should probably begin training."

Kayla grinned and gestured between the two of them. "You sure you two don't want some alone time? I could always go play by myself for a while if you guys want to play with each other."

Ariana blushed and covered her face with her hands. Sergei threw back his head and laughed as he put his arm around Ariana's waist. "Do not worry. Go train with Kayla. If there are no objections, I would like to watch. I would enjoy learning more about your abilities."

She peeked up at him through her lashes, weighing the sincerity of his words. Sergei was difficult to read, but she had the distinct impression he truly was interested in learning more about their ways. "All right."

With another gentle squeeze, he released her and took a step back. Kayla pulled off her overwrap and tossed it on a nearby bench. Putting her hands on her hips, she eyed the water with trepidation. "Okay, how do we do this?"

Ariana knelt and lowered herself back into the pool. She motioned for Kayla to come closer. "You can either join me or sit on the edge. It's shallow enough here that you can stand, but it's fine if you want to stay there. You just need to be touching the water to use it as a focusing object."

Kayla sat on the edge of the pool, letting her legs dangle over the side, and slipped into the water. She looked up at Ariana expectantly. "Okay. Now what?"

"Go ahead and reach out to the energy in the pool like we did last time," Ariana instructed. "You're not going to manipulate it yet. I only want you to refamiliarize yourself with the energy to determine which threads belong to the water element."

Ariana waited patiently while Kayla explored the energy threads in the pool. Ariana had only trained once with Kayla several months ago. They'd made arrangements to meet again, but unforeseen circumstances had cut their planned training sessions short. By the time the attack on the towers had ended, most of OmniLab was reeling from the news that the new tower was being built and a treaty had been brokered with the Coalition.

Part of Ariana was inspired by Kayla's courage to embrace the unknown. Up until that solitary training session, Kayla had never even seen a pool, but she'd willingly jumped into it, determined to learn about their ways. It was difficult to imagine what it must have been like for her growing up on the surface. Ariana wasn't sure she would have been able to manage her talents without the calming sensation of immersing herself in water. But then again, their abilities were a bit different.

Sergei moved closer to watch them. Ariana glanced at him and then turned back to Kayla, determined not to look at him again. She needed to focus on teaching, not ogling the enigmatic foreigner.

Once Kayla appeared to be finished exploring on her own, Ariana said, "I'll need you to create a small connection with me. We won't be sharing power, but you can use the connection to follow along while I manipulate the water. Once I've shown you what we're trying to accomplish, I can guide you through emulating the energy flow."

"Easy enough," Kayla agreed, and Ariana felt her reach out with her energy threads.

Accepting them, she intertwined them and felt Kayla's careful exploration along their new bond. In some ways, it was like teaching a curious child. Usually, when sharing a metaphysical connection, exploring it was akin to tugging on someone's hair, lifting their skirt, or blowing on their ear suggestively. It was only through years of practice that they learned the different nuances of manipulating energy and forging bonds. Kayla had missed all those experiences with her untraditional upbringing.

Ariana cupped her empty hands and held them out in front of her. Gathering the energy threads around her, she used them to tease some of the water out of the pool and into her outstretched hands. Once the water had filled her hands, she released the remaining energy threads.

Kayla watched in rapt fascination. "That's incredible! Is it my turn?"

Ariana smiled. "Yes, but do you mind if I reach out across the bond to correct your energy manipulations? Alec warned me you were sensitive to power fluctuations, and I don't want to do anything to make you uncomfortable."

Kayla shrugged. "No, that's okay. If I'm expecting it and know what's going to happen, it should be fine."

Ariana nodded and motioned for her to go ahead. With an undeniable natural ability, Kayla swept in and began manipulating the water into the air. Her technique was a little off, so Ariana offered some mild verbal corrections while adjusting the energy threads.

"That's very good, but you'll want to use thinner and longer threads for more accuracy. If you're trying to manipulate a large quantity quickly, you can use the other ones. Over time and with practice, you'll gain more control."

Kayla frowned in concentration but managed to do as instructed. When her hand filled with water, she grinned and let out a loud whoop. "I did it!"

Ariana laughed at Kayla's enthusiasm and glanced over at Sergei. Curiosity, wonder, and unmistakable desire was etched on his face as he gazed at her. Her stomach fluttered, and she wondered, not for the first time, what it would be like to touch him and kiss him. Aware her expression mirrored his, she lowered her head and took a deep breath, trying to regain her composure.

Kayla's laughter distracted her, and she jerked her head up. The former ruin rat was perched on the stairs of the pool and darting her gaze back and forth between her and Sergei. Mortified, Ariana clamped down on their shared connection. Her hands flew to her face which must be turning several shades of red. She debated whether to try living underwater for the next year or so. Maybe by then she'd remember she was supposed to be the teacher in this scenario instead of daydreaming about their observer.

"What is wrong? What happened?" Sergei's concerned voice broke through her embarrassment.

His question brought on another wave of laughter from Kayla. Ariana sighed and admitted, "I forgot about the shared connection with Kayla. She picked up on a few things she shouldn't have and didn't have the grace to pretend otherwise."

Sergei arched an eyebrow and leaned forward. "Oh?"

Kayla snickered and pretended to fan herself. "Oh yeah. Let's just say I'm going to need another dunk in this pool to cool off after we're finished. Ariana's not quite as sweet as she appears."

Ariana gaped at Kayla. Did she really just tell Sergei that? Her eyes narrowed on the former ruin rat.

"I'm not sure you need to wait," Ariana admitted and grabbed Kayla's wrists, yanking hard. Kayla tumbled forward, splashing into the cold water. She came up sputtering and wiped the hair out of her face. The two women stared at each other for a moment, and Kayla grinned.

"Okay, I totally deserved that."

Ariana nodded and splashed at Kayla, who shrieked and dove toward her. A splashing and giggling mini-war ensued for the next several minutes until they were leaning against the side of the pool, holding their sides and breathing heavily from laughter.

"Well, I must say, the entertainment is definitely top notch," a man said from the side of the pool.

"Carl!" Kayla jumped out of the pool, rushing over to him and soaking him with her embrace.

He bent down, wrapping his arms around her, and kissed her soundly. Ariana watched them for a moment, their unmistakable love and desire for each other staggering in its intensity. She'd thought only their kind could share energy bonds, but some force almost as powerful drew the two of them together.

When Carl finally released Kayla, he glanced over at Sergei and Ariana. "Too bad I didn't get to see the whole show."

Sergei leaned over the pool and held out his hand to Ariana. She accepted, and he lifted her easily, pulling her out of the water and against him once more. He wrapped his arm around her, and she looked up into his gray eyes, wondering if there was more to these non-sensitives than she ever imagined. Sergei was studying her intently in return, and she reached out to him again with her power. He was all heat compared to her coolness.

"Yes," Sergei murmured, his gaze lowering to her mouth. "It is too bad. The show was quite enjoyable."

Carl cleared his throat, and Ariana looked over just as Kayla poked him in the side and shook her head. Carl raised an eyebrow at Kayla but didn't comment.

"When did you get here?" Kayla leaned against him. "I wasn't expecting you back in the towers for another few days."

"About an hour ago," Carl replied. "We've had another little snag at the underground river. I'm about to go meet with Alec to discuss it. I thought you might want to come along and hear the details."

"Dammit. So much for good news," Kayla muttered with a

frown and glanced over at Sergei. "Yeah. I guess we need to take care of it. It would be nice if something went our way for once."

Sergei hesitated and looked down at Ariana again, regret etched in his features. "My apologies, but I must also attend. Any issues with the river affect my people too."

"Of course," Ariana said with a small frown, sensing his unease. He was difficult to read, but she was able to pick up on some of the stronger emotions. He was extremely worried about whatever news Carl had brought from the surface. "I hope you're able to get the situation resolved. Kayla, any time you want to train again, please let me know. It was a pleasure."

Kayla grinned. "Yeah, you just want a chance to dunk me again."

Ariana returned her smile, not bothering to deny it. "Of course. That's just an added benefit."

CHAPTER THREE

ARIANA GLANCED around the immaculate executive offices of OmniLab. It had been years since she'd last visited this part of the towers. As a child, she'd occasionally accompanied her father, but that changed once her specialized abilities began to emerge. Now it was her brother walking beside her, and Ariana found herself comparing her memories of the offices they passed with the reality. More had changed than had remained the same, but she supposed that was true for most things.

"I don't have a good feeling about this," Jason murmured in a low voice.

Ariana made a noncommittal noise, acknowledging his words. She didn't want to verbally agree and give weight to Jason's concerns, but the request made her uneasy too. Alec knew she didn't venture out of the Inner Sanctum often, and his request had been something of a surprise. Although there were a large number of *Drac'Kin* on this level, there were also quite a few non-sensitives. Their emotions were already beginning to affect her, and she threaded energy through her internal shields to reinforce them.

"I'm sure it's fine," she said, trying to minimize his fears.

Sometimes it was better to fake it for Jason's benefit than to give in to her worries. It didn't matter that Jason was one of the most talented energy channelers in the towers. His control seemed to slip when it came to her. If she was upset or feeling threatened, it was even worse. Unfortunately, that was one of the drawbacks to their complicated relationship.

"Alec probably just wants to find out how the training session went with Kayla yesterday," she added.

Jason frowned as they passed the corridor which led to their father's office. It was noticeably empty. Their father had been called away for some impromptu meeting in one of the upstairs conference rooms. His absence was probably for the best though. He wouldn't be pleased to see her in this part of the tower, and she wasn't in the mood for another argument.

"Then why didn't he meet us in our family's quarters?" Jason obviously wasn't buying what she was trying to sell. "He wants something, Ari. I find the whole thing rather suspicious. Father gets called to some random meeting and suddenly we're asked to meet Alec here?"

Ariana squeezed her brother's arm and sent a wave of soothing energy over him. Although she'd spent a lifetime learning how to block Jason's emotions, his unease still affected her. Part of her was tempted to grab a drink from her father's office to have on hand if she needed to quickly reinforce her metaphysical shield, but it would probably make things worse with Jason. If he thought she was in distress, he'd demand they return to their family's quarters. Besides, she needed to try to stop using water as a crutch; it was terribly inconvenient needing to carry a drink around with her. It required a bit more concentration and effort to pull moisture from the air, but it was much more discreet.

She glanced over at Jason and frowned. Over the past few weeks, he'd become increasingly agitated. His normally playful and fun-loving nature had disappeared almost overnight. His energy was more chaotic, and it was requiring more and more of her conscious efforts to soothe him. When she'd asked him what was bothering him, Jason was quick to brush her off.

Ariana hadn't wanted to push, so she'd left it alone, but now she wondered if that had been a smart decision. He was getting worse.

"Don't be so quick to distrust Alec. He has a lot on his shoulders right now with leading the High Council. He's been doing a wonderful job, but it's hard on him. We can't expect him to come running every time he needs a word with us."

"I can when he wants something," Jason argued. "I'm not about to become the High Council's errand boy. Not only that, but now that he's no longer bonded to Kayla, I'm not sure I trust him when it comes to you. Father has concerns about him as well. Our family isn't prepared to align with his until we're sure of his intentions and agenda. Until then, it's better if you keep your distance."

Ariana laughed at the absurdity of his comment. "I swear, I'm amazed you and Father ever find time to come out of the study. Every time I turn around, you're in there strategizing and analyzing something else. It hasn't been that long since his bond with Kayla was severed. I'm sure Alec's still adjusting. Besides, we're friends. Nothing more."

She lowered her gaze, making a point to keep an eye on the ground in front of her. It was better than allowing Jason to know she was trying to hide her true feelings on the matter. There had been a time when she'd thought, and even hoped, Alec felt something for her. But when nothing ever came of it and he met Kayla, she realized her infatuation with Alec was pointless. Instead, she'd focused on burying her attraction for the council leader and on being the friend he sorely needed. After everything he'd been through, Alec deserved to be happy.

Jason took her arm and took an unexpected detour, steering her down an empty side hall. He stopped suddenly, glancing around to make sure they were alone and said in a low voice, "You're wrong, Ari. You need to remember Alec is one of the few people who knows something about your abilities. He would have pursued you a long time ago if Kayla hadn't come back into the picture. We don't know his intentions, and I don't like his newfound interest in you now that they're no longer bonded."

She frowned. "What are you talking about, Jason?"

"Father and I have been discussing potential bondmates for you. He warned me to keep Alec away from you. He's still too new to his position, and we need to make sure he's nothing like his father."

Ariana jerked back at his words, shock and anger roiling through her. "Are you serious? Regardless of what you and Father have plotted, I won't be bought and sold. I will *never* enter into any bond unless I determine it's right for me and not just some sort of coup for power."

Jason reached for her, but she pulled away from him and snapped, "I'm not as fragile as you all would like to believe. I've agreed to many of your requests for my own safety, but neither one of you shall *ever* dictate how I live my life."

Jason clenched his fists and squeezed his eyes shut. "Dammit, Ari. If you were different, it wouldn't matter as much. You could have the freedom to live your life however you want. But you have the power to change the entire direction of our family and race." He opened his eyes and sighed, rubbing his temples as though warding off a headache. "You know it's not a coincidence we're twins. You were given this rare and precious gift that leaves you vulnerable, and my talents are designed to protect and defend. Maybe it's because of my talents or the fact you're my sister, but the need to protect you is just part of who I am. How can I do that if you won't let me?"

Ariana looked away, wondering if he was right. Was she trying to force him to go against his instinctual nature because she wanted to rebel? Guilt flooded through her, and she took a step toward her brother. He was in pain, both physically and mentally. She sighed knowing she couldn't change her nature any more than he could change his.

Placing her hand on his arm, she enveloped him in a soothing wave of healing energy. His shoulders relaxed as it washed over him. There had to be a way to make him understand.

"Jason," she began, weighing her words carefully, "there's a difference between protecting someone and being overprotective. You're right in that I'm more vulnerable than others, but I try to minimize the impact by keeping my abilities suppressed whenever possible. I'm extremely grateful you're willing to protect me when it becomes more than I can manage. But please remember, I'm also an adult. In many regards, I'm your equal. You need to let me live my life and make some mistakes."

Jason took her hands in his as his forehead creased with worry. "And what if your old teacher was right? What if one of those mistakes fractures you and we can't bring you back? It's not just a matter of you being my sister, Ari. You're too important to risk losing."

Ariana couldn't make any promises, and he knew it. They couldn't be sure of anything. Her father and teacher had poured over thousands of records trying to find out more information about her talents and how to circumvent the problems associated with them. Historical records were limited, and whoever held the pen always controlled the message. What if their perspectives were skewed and she was living her life based on a lie?

She was just so tired of living in a gilded cage. Every day seemed to wear on her a bit more. It couldn't be wrong to want to stretch her wings and fly.

As though sensing her reluctant acceptance of his words, Jason dropped his arm around her shoulders and pulled her in for a hug. "I love you, Ari-bella," he whispered, using his childhood nickname for her. "I'll try to give you some space, but I can't stop worrying. I don't want to lose you."

Her objections melted away, and she nodded. It was impossible to keep arguing with him when he was speaking from a place of love. Jason only wanted what was best for her; they just had different ideas on what that entailed.

Ariana looked away. "Let's just get this meeting over with and go home."

His relief blanketed the air, and Jason took her arm once again. As he escorted her back down the corridor, her footsteps felt more weighted than they had when she first entered.

When they approached Alec's offices, a smart-looking older woman stood and gave them a brief bow. "Master and Mistress Alivette, please, go right in. Master Tal'Vayr is waiting for you."

"Thank you, Sheila," Jason murmured and opened the door.

Ariana took a few steps inside and paused, not bothering to hide her surprise at the motley group assembled within Alec's office. Kayla was sprawled out on one of the couches surrounded by tablets and building diagrams, while Sergei leaned against the nearby wall. Brant, an Inner Circle Shadow and Alec's half-brother, stood on the far side of the room listening while Alec spoke quietly to him.

She swallowed, suddenly even more unsure about this

meeting and wondering if something else was happening. The last time they'd all been in a room together had been during the attack on the towers.

Ariana looked toward Alec, tentatively reaching out to sense the mood of the room. Alec glanced up and smiled, his eyes filled with genuine warmth at the sight of her. She couldn't detect any outward signs of stressors, but Alec had always been good at hiding his feelings, even from her. She wouldn't dare risk prying further, even if the thought was tempting.

Alec crossed the room and approached her, making her breath catch at the sight. From the moment she first saw him, she'd been captivated. Her reaction wasn't any different now. He was tall and athletic, with a swimmer's physique that made her wonder if he might actually offer her a challenge in a race. Instead of wearing his golden hair cut short or tied back like many others in the towers, he left it just grazing the top of his shoulders. It was an erotic and sensual statement that he didn't give a damn what others in the towers thought.

Alec nodded at Jason before taking Ariana's hands in his. He bent down and kissed her cheek before sending a small pulse of light, teasing energy over her. Alec's power was distinctive and alluring, one of the things that had first attracted her to him. She couldn't help but respond with her own welcoming metaphysical embrace.

Alec's smile deepened, and he gave her hands a slight squeeze. "Thank you both for agreeing to come here."

Jason huffed, crossing his arms over his chest. "Not like we had much of a choice. When the High Council leader says jump, you jump. Your position is going to your head a bit, my friend."

"Jason," Ariana admonished. She turned back to Alec, but the High Council leader merely grinned. Without releasing Ariana's hand, he tucked it against him and drew her closer.

"I see your brother is in his usual solicitous mood. As such, he can fend for himself. However, it would be my pleasure to offer you a drink. Would you like something?"

"Try the scotch," Kayla called out without looking up from her diagrams.

Ariana smiled up at Alec. "I suppose I'll try the scotch then. Perhaps with a splash of water?"

"Wise choice," Alec agreed and led her over to the bar area.

Jason followed and grabbed a bottle from the opposite side of the bar. As Jason began fixing his drink, he and Alec began arguing good-naturedly about the qualities in crafting a superior beverage. Ariana glanced over to where Sergei was standing nearby and met his intense gaze. She gave him a shy smile, and he winked at her, his eyes twinkling with amusement.

Deciding to take the opportunity to say hello to him while her brother and Alec were still engrossed in their debate, she walked over to him.

"Hi," she offered with a wide smile. "I wasn't expecting to see you here. I hope we didn't interrupt anything."

Sergei arched an eyebrow and trailed his fingers down her arm. "You are never an interruption, *solnyshka*. You brighten the room just entering it." When she shivered at his touch, he chuckled. "You are much more appealing than any business."

Her face flushed in response. Before she could say anything else or ask him about the foreign word he'd used, the door opened and a ghost from the past stepped in.

"Well, fuck," Lars muttered, sweeping his gaze over all of them. "I didn't realize it was going to be a blasted party in here. Alec, don't you ever do any work?"

"When it suits me," Alec replied and gestured to the audience. "I believe you know everyone here."

Jason picked up his drink from the bar. "So Lars finally decided to join the rest of society and climb out of his cave?"

Lars's eyes narrowed. "Ah, Jason, if I had known you were going to be here, I probably would have stayed where I was."

Jason laughed and moved forward to shake hands with the former exile. Lars clapped him on the back and then his eyes fell upon Ariana.

"Ari," Lars whispered, his eyes softening as he gazed at her. She hadn't seen him since the tower attack, and even then, it had only been for a few minutes. So much had happened that night. When he hadn't sought her out after it was over, she'd thought it best to give him space. But now he was here, and the memories came rushing back.

Ariana's eyes welled with tears as she rushed over and threw her arms around his neck. Lars pulled her into his embrace, nearly crushing her, and buried his face against her hair. Emotion and memories flooded through her, and she felt his raw pain like a sharp stab wound in the gut. The image of Anne, his younger sister and her childhood best friend, surfaced in her mind. She stifled a sob at the almost debilitating sense of accompanying loss.

"Lars," she murmured against his chest, "I'm so sorry."

"It's all right," he whispered.

But it wasn't all right. She could feel his pain like a dark chasm threatening to consume him. Power bloomed within her, and with it, an almost desperate need to ease his suffering. Without stopping to consider, Ariana gathered the energy threads around them and weaved them together in a complex pattern. She enveloped Lars in her energy like a powerful caress, and he pulled her even closer, inhaling deeply as though memorizing her scent. As her cool energy rushed over him and began strengthening the precious and treasured memories, his breath hitched. The more painful memories were diminished, muted by the love-infused energy she wove around them.

She would never remove the darker memories completely because without some level of pain, you couldn't appreciate the better ones. But she could alter his focus and help him heal. He'd been suffering so much and for so long. When the tension in his body slowly began to dissipate, Ariana once more surrounded him with another healing wave tempered with love, comfort, and understanding. As Lars tightened his arms around her, she felt his rush of heated air energy meet hers. He understood what she was doing and was gifting her with an infusion of gratitude and affection. She threaded her power with his, strengthening and fortifying both of them with their combined emotion in a tribute to his lost sister.

It wasn't a bond in the traditional sense, but there were some ties forged of love and understanding that could be just as powerful.

Lars pulled back slightly and cupped her face in his hands. His blue eyes scanned over her with a look of wonder and reverence. "By the gods, Ari. Anna told me she suspected, but I had no idea. You are a gift beyond compare. I can't... I don't know how..."

"Shh," she whispered, pressing her fingertips against his lips. "I'm so sorry I wasn't there for you sooner. I would have come to you if I had known."

He dropped his head, pressing his forehead against hers. In a pained voice, he said, "I wasn't... I wasn't sure if some wounds are meant to be healed."

Ariana reached up to touch his cheek, sending another wave of soothing power over him. "No, Lars, wounds *should* be healed, and they do, eventually. We all carry scars, but those are reminders. Anna wouldn't have wanted you to keep hurting and punishing yourself."

"She loved you," Lars admitted in a quiet whisper. "After

we were exiled, we didn't speak much of the towers. It was too difficult. But you were one of the exceptions. I think it was the memory of your friendship that helped her get through the worst of it."

Lars lifted his head to look into her eyes once more. A tear trailed down her cheek at the raw emotion in his expression. He caught it with his finger. "Don't cry, sweet Ari. Out of all of us, you should never have a moment of pain. You heal and give us peace, but what can we possibly offer you in return?"

She gave him a sad smile. "I don't have any secrets left, do I?"

"All women do," he whispered and pressed a kiss against her forehead. "But I swear you will never need them with me. I won't ever betray you."

Jason cleared his throat and put his glass down with a *clank*. "Well, Alec, if the point of this meeting was an ambush, I'd say it was successful."

"Not so much an ambush as a necessity," Alec replied quietly, not looking away from Ariana and Lars.

He walked over to Ariana and held out a glass of amber liquid. Somewhat shaken, she accepted the drink and took a sip, the liquid warming her from within as she swallowed. Alec had added a splash of water to the drink, and she quickly pulled on the water energy threads and used them to reinforce her fractured shields. Healing Lars had taken more out of her than she'd expected.

Lars frowned at Alec and gave Ariana another long look. He reached over to squeeze her hand, using the combination of touch along with his power to convey his gratitude. Sadness and longing were still within him, but it was different now, far less jagged and raw. With a reluctant sigh, he stepped away and crossed the room. He leaned against the wall, focusing on the outside world and what lay beyond the tinted window.

Ariana resisted the urge to go to him and soothe the remainder of those rough edges, knowing he needed time to reconcile his emotions with the past. That was the hardest thing she'd had to learn over the years: time was the most powerful healer of all.

"Ari," Alec said in a low voice, drawing her attention back to him. "Thank you for helping him. I should have warned you, but I wasn't sure he would even come."

She nodded and looked down at her glass, uncomfortable with being the center of attention. Everyone had kept her abilities quiet for so long, but it appeared more and more people were becoming aware of her gifts. Only time would tell if that was a blessing or a curse. For every person she helped, there was another who needed her. Her teacher had warned her about stretching herself too thin, but it was impossible to refuse someone in need.

Alec touched her hand, entwining his energy with hers and letting it drift over her in a gentle caress. "He wouldn't have asked for help on his own. I didn't want to see him suffer any longer, and I didn't think you would either."

She shook her head and glanced again at Lars. "No, I'm glad you asked me to come, Alec. There's been too much suffering and pain already."

Alec's thumb ran over the back of her hand, and he smiled at her. At his touch, Alec's mental words formed in her mind. *"Lars is right, Ari. You're a wonderful gift to all of us. I hope you know how deeply you're treasured."*

Ariana looked into his eyes and was taken aback by the intimacy in his gaze. Alec was normally extremely skilled at keeping his emotions hidden from everyone, but he was allowing her to pick up on some of them. She opened herself slightly to the energy threads surrounding him, and her mouth parted in surprise at the feelings of tenderness, affection, and desire emanating from him.

Clutching her glass, she took a half-step backward, confused by Alec's words and emotions. Her brow furrowed, and she glanced back and forth between Alec and Kayla, who was still lying on the couch watching them with a small smile. Ariana didn't understand Alec and Kayla's complex relationship, except that their bond had been broken. It was no secret Kayla was in love with Carl. For the past few months, they'd been traveling back and forth from the towers to the surface, usually together, alternating between focusing on the construction and underground river excavation.

Neither Alec nor Kayla seemed bothered by the fact they no longer shared a permanent bond. The two seemed friendly enough, but Ariana had never heard of a permanent bond being broken. No one had. Such a thing had never happened before. She couldn't help but wonder whether there were still residual feelings between them. But even if there weren't, Alec had never given any indication he felt anything more than friendship for Ariana.

Glancing down at Alec's hand still holding hers, she allowed him to sense some of her confusion and doubt through her energy threads. *"I don't understand, Alec."*

Alec paused, his eyes widening in surprise and then he considered her for a long moment. *"My apologies, Ari. I thought — I didn't intend to make you uncomfortable. Obviously, my choice of timing is poor. My only excuse is that I momentarily forgot myself and our present company. I hope you'll give me a chance to make it up to you."*

Sensing the sincerity of his words and his desire to put her at ease, Ariana nodded. He lifted her hand and brushed a kiss against the back of it. This time, the wave of energy he sent over her had the flavor of an apology but also a hint of a future promise. She tilted her head, intrigued by his uncharacteristic behavior but still remaining cautious.

"Have you finished manhandling my sister?"

Alec chuckled and released her hand before turning back to her brother. "Now, Jason, don't tell me you're jealous. After all, you must be used to the lack of attention when compared to the breathtaking beauty of your sister."

Jason snorted. "Oh, I get plenty of attention. If you'd like some tips, I'm sure I can throw some your way."

Lars leaned against the window and muttered, "Laying it on a bit thick, aren't you, Alec?"

Kayla propped up her feet and leaned back, interlocking her hands behind her head. Diagrams and schematics were still scattered around her. If there was any semblance of order, only Kayla knew what it was.

"Man, you can almost smell the drama in the air," Kayla said with a grin. "I could have made a fortune charging credits for this show."

"Kayla," Brant warned in a low voice.

Kayla wrinkled her nose at him. "Fine. I'll be good."

Alec frowned at them before turning back to Jason. "Although verbally sparring with you is highly entertaining, Jason, I did have a reason for asking you and Ariana to come to my office. I was hoping you might be able to provide some assistance with a problem we're having on the surface."

Jason's eyes narrowed in suspicion. "What sort of problem?"

Alec glanced at Sergei. "It's about the underground river Kayla discovered. Trader Carl Grayson and his team have been on the surface running tests and handling the excavation of the area. Kayla's been coordinating these efforts as well as handling issues with the construction of the additional tower."

"Trying," Kayla muttered and glared at the diagrams scattered on the couch. "The implementation is proving rather damn tricky."

"Yes, well," Alec continued, "Trader Carl reported to the towers yesterday with some distressing news. His crew attempted to launch more probes into the river to get more accurate readings. Unfortunately, our equipment is being destroyed. The rapids are hazardous in some areas, and our sensitive equipment can't withstand the force or damage from the rocks. I brought you here in the hopes the two of you would consider going to the surface. We need someone skilled with water energy manipulation to help guide the cameras as far as possible through the water so we can discover the river's origins or at least give us a better area where we can drill. With your combined abilities, you have the best chance of all of us."

Ariana's eyes widened at Alec's words. Out of all the things she might have expected him to ask, this possibility hadn't even dawned on her.

Jason shook his head and crossed his arms over his chest. "Absolutely not. You are not taking my sister down to the surface. Are you insane? Do you have any idea what could happen?"

Kayla stood and put her hands on her hips. "I lived down there most of my life, Jason. I'd say it's far more dangerous here. I had more attempts on my life in the short time I was in the towers than I ever did on the surface. Carl's been down there coordinating almost everything, and we've got all sorts of structural supports in place. It's crawling with people who are constantly making improve-ments. I'd say it's a hell of a lot safer than the towers right now."

Jason glared at Alec and gestured toward Kayla. "Well, it appears Kayla just made my case for me. That cave is crowded with non-sensitives. You know how dangerous that could be to Ari. You are not taking my sister down there completely unprotected."

"She won't be unprotected," Alec argued. "Your sister's welfare is one of my highest priorities, and we'll take every possible precaution. If you two are successful, you could help make that river a viable water and power source. Our alliance with the Coalition and the surface dwellers is dependent upon tapping into that resource and others as quickly as possible. We're not only in desperate need for the water but also for the power the river can generate to operate some of our equipment. We can't afford any more delays if we're going to meet our deadlines."

Ariana fisted her hands, trying to rein in her temper. She was so tired of everyone making decisions without bothering to ask what she wanted. Forcing herself to take a calming breath, she announced, "I'll go."

Jason slowly turned toward her, his stunned shock almost comical.

Alec gazed at her with a combination of surprise and approval. "Thank you, Ari. I meant what I said. We'll make every effort to make sure you're as protected as possible. All non-essential personnel will be cleared out and contact will be kept to a minimum. In addition to your brother, I'll accompany you as well."

"As will I," Lars offered.

Ariana swallowed, trying to push aside her fears, and nodded. If Kayla had managed to live on the surface all these years as a spirit channeler, she could handle a brief foray onto the surface. Yes, their abilities were different, but there were similarities too. There wasn't much information about spirit channelers either. Maybe it was time to embrace the possibilities and start taking more chances.

It was worth the risk if she could help the people who needed it most. Besides, the chance of getting another opportunity to see the world beyond these walls was slim. If her family had their way, she'd be locked in the towers for the rest of her life.

"If you believe I can help, I'd like to try. When did you want to do this?"

Jason approached her with a frown. The energy around him was infused with panic, worry, and fear. The stifling effect made it difficult to breathe. She instinctively threaded soothing energy bands around him, trying to alleviate the worst of his emotions.

"Ari, please reconsider. There are too many unknowns." He turned to glare at Alec. "You didn't bother to run this past the council, did you? My father has no knowledge of your machinations, does he?"

Alec's entire body stiffened, and he didn't respond immediately. Instead, he clasped his hands behind his back. "Ariana is an adult. She can make her own decisions. The council does not need to concern themselves with matters such as this. No one is ordering her to do anything. I simply asked."

"You're a real bastard, Alec," Jason swore, clenching his fists. "You know Ari would give her right arm if it would help someone. I swear, if anything happens to her, I'll kill you myself."

Brant stiffened in his place against the wall where he was acting as sentry.

"Jason," Ariana warned, infusing her energy with a calming influence. She could sense Alec's tension as well and spread her energy outward to encompass both of them. Alec was much more composed, but sometimes it felt as though her brother had more of a fire temperament than water. It was exhausting.

Suddenly weary from the efforts to soothe Lars's pain and the ups and downs from the tumultuous energy circulating in the room, Ariana's shoulders slumped. She put her drink on the table and rubbed her temples to ward off the impending headache. Not even a little splash of water was enough to help her now. She'd need to completely submerge herself in the pool when they were finished or she'd never make it through the rest of the day.

"There's no need for threats. Alec is acting in the best interests of the towers. He asked, and I agreed. Please, just leave it alone. I want to do this. Besides, you'll be with me the entire time."

Her words and energy had the desired effect. Jason turned away and headed back over to the bar, muttering under his breath.

Sergei had been quiet up until this point. He moved to stand beside her and touched her arm. "Are you well, Ari?"

She shook her head, the motion making her feel queasy. "No. I mean, yes. I'm all right. I'm just tired. It's been a long day."

Alec frowned and took a step toward her, his expression worried. He took her hand in his and sent a fortifying wave of energy over her. She closed her eyes and sighed in relief as it chased away the worst of the fatigue.

"Thank you," she murmured.

"You give too much of yourself to keep everyone's emotions in check," Alec said in a quiet voice. "Sometimes these things need to play out naturally."

She nodded, knowing what Alec was saying was true. But she'd seen what could happen when her brother's temper ran unchecked.

"I know, but Jason..." Her words trailed off, and she sighed. Sometimes it was better to leave the past in the past.

Alec squeezed her hand. *"I understand your concerns, but what happened with Doval was several years ago. That wasn't your fault."*

Ariana looked away, not wanting to discuss it. That entire

ordeal had cost her family dearly, and the cloud still hung over them. Jason had lost his temper defending her and used his abilities to attack one of their own. Unregulated duels were usually severely punished, but her father had made several deals to keep Jason out of trouble. But ever since then, she lived with the constant worry it could happen again.

Sergei put his arm around her waist, pulling her gently but firmly away from Alec. The High Council leader's eyes narrowed, but Sergei ignored him. "Ariana needs rest. If her brother wishes to remain, I will escort her back to her rooms."

Still standing at the bar, drink in hand, Jason looked over and scowled at the sight of Sergei's arm around her. "Take your hands off her, Sergei. What the hell is with all of you pawing my sister? She's off limits. I'll see to her myself."

"Then accept responsibility and stop acting like a child," Sergei snapped. "Ari is not feeling well, and you pay no attention when your sister suffers."

"You self-righteous bastard," Jason hissed and stalked toward him, his anger lashing out like an energy whip.

A sharp pain shot through Ariana's temples as her natural shields weakened even more. She winced as the tense emotions in the room continued to escalate. Forcing herself to draw upon her reserves, she coated Jason in a blanket of soothing energy. "Please, Jason. Sergei's right. I need to go."

Jason hesitated and frowned. He must have finally realized the effect everything was having on her because he grabbed a bottle of water from the bar area and handed it to her, encouraging her to drink. Gratitude rushed through her as she took a long sip. The cool water trailing down her throat helped a bit. It wasn't the same as submersing herself completely, but it allowed her to once again sense the cool moisture in the air. She tried to gather some of the additional moisture to insulate herself from the overpowering emotions, but she was too tired to be more than moderately successful. She didn't have the ability to focus enough to weave her usual complex threads.

"I'm sorry, Ari," Jason said, his expression filled with guilt. "Is that better?"

Brant took a step forward. "Do you need me to call for a medic?"

Ariana shook her head and glanced at the others who were also regarding her with concern. "No, that's not necessary. I'm all right. I just need to reinforce my shields a bit."

Alec frowned. "We were planning on going to the surface tomorrow, but we can delay those plans as long as you need."

She shook her head, too tired to explain. "No, tomorrow is fine. I just need to go for a swim and take a nap. I'll be fine by morning."

Realization dawned in Alec's eyes, and he nodded. "The water. Of course. I hadn't realized..." His voice trailed off as he considered her. "Hopefully, the proximity to the underground river will help if you feel any distress when we're on the surface. I'll also arrange to have additional resources brought with us."

Ariana gave him a small smile. "Thank you. That should help. Since Jason's already been to the surface, he can give you some ideas about what I'll need."

Jason frowned, still clearly displeased by her agreeing to go to the surface, but he remained silent. Instead, he offered her his arm. "Let's head back, Ari. I'll send him a list. I'm sure Alec can make whatever arrangements are necessary on his own."

Ariana nodded, said her farewells, and let Jason lead her back to her family's quarters.

————

ALEC WATCHED THEM LEAVE, questioning whether he should have pushed Ariana into making this trip. He'd wanted her to agree, but not if it put her at risk. There was too much damn secrecy around her to know how dangerous this could be for her. As soon as her abilities emerged years ago, her family had circled the metaphorical wagons. They weren't talking, and no one knew enough about her talents to even guess. Hopefully, he could learn something by reviewing the list Jason had agreed to send him.

Sergei tapped his fingers impatiently against his leg in an uncharacteristic movement. Something other than the resource issue was weighing on the normally stoic Coalition military commander, and Alec couldn't help but wonder if Ariana had something to do with it. He'd barely resisted the urge to hurt Sergei when he'd put his hands on Ariana. It was one thing for Sergei to play those sorts of games with Kayla, but it was completely different when it was someone like Ariana.

After several minutes, Sergei straightened and announced, "I need to check in with my people. If you have no other need for me, I will speak with you tomorrow when we head to the river."

"That's not necessary," Alec began. "We'll forward the results to you, but it may be better to limit the number of people attending."

Sergei's eyes narrowed, and he held up his hand to stop any further discussion on the subject. "No. I am the Coalition ambassador. I will represent our interests and accompany the group to the river. You will notify me when you are ready to depart."

Alec frowned but gave him a curt nod. Sergei quickly disappeared, heading in the same direction Ariana had gone.

"Stubborn and difficult. I swear, this alliance becomes more of a pain every day," Alec muttered and went over to retrieve his drink from the bar. Trust wasn't coming easily to any of them, Omnis and Coalition alike. Several hundred Coalition citizens were already living in the towers and even more were on the surface in the surrounding areas. When they'd originally made their agreement, no one had anticipated the widespread economic, cultural, and social considerations of such an alliance. Every day, more reports were coming across his desk with a wide variety of issues that needed to be addressed. With these additional delays in harnessing the river, things between their people were even more strained.

Alec sat on the couch across from Kayla and stretched out, desperate for a few minutes of relative peace. He swirled his glass and took a sip.

"Lars, are you going to stare out the window all night?"

"For fuck's sake, Alec," Lars swore and turned his head toward him. "Jason was right. You ambushed me... not to mention poor Ari. She couldn't help herself." He shook his head. "I swear, that woman is more potent than any drug. I didn't even realize what she was doing at first. I was just so damn happy to see her. But then I felt her energy signature and... It was like this blanket of power settled over me. I've never felt anything like it. She's always been so damn sweet, but that energy of hers is fucking hot."

A laugh bubbled out of Kayla at his description. "What did she do? I gotta tell you, watching the energy around you two was crazy. I took a peek using the connection I created with her the other day, and there was so much going on. It makes the stuff she's teaching me look like amateur hour."

"There's no comparison," Brant admitted, relaxing from his formal bodyguard stance and taking a seat next to Kayla. While shadowing her here and on the surface, the two of them had developed a close friendship. "I was able to pick up on some of what she was doing too, and I'm not even sure how she managed it. I've never seen anyone wield power like her."

Kayla scooted over to give Brant more room on the couch. "You haven't spent much time with her?"

Brant shook his head. "No. Her brother or father usually act as her escort when she's out in public. She's never asked for our services, and now I understand why. I had no idea she was that powerful."

"All I know is, while I was standing there basking in the glow of some of the most irresistible energy I've ever experienced, she was tearing me apart and rebuilding me in a matter of seconds," Lars said and scrubbed his hand over his face. "So yeah, if I want to look out the window all night while I catch my breath, I'm entitled to that. She rocked my entire world, Alec. I don't know how the hell she even managed to walk out of here, much less try to temper her whirlwind of a brother." He flexed his fingers and rolled out his shoulders. "Fuck, that woman knows how to get under your skin. I don't know how the hell you've managed to keep your hands off her for so long."

Not easily, but Alec didn't intend to advertise that fact. He knew more than most, but even he wasn't certain of the full extent of Ariana's abilities.

Kayla leaned forward eagerly. "So wait, what exactly did she do to you? I'm getting bits and pieces, but the big picture might be nice."

Alec swirled his glass again and nodded. "That was part of the reason I invited you here, Kayla. You need to understand more about our culture and abilities. Even more importantly, you need to back off on encouraging Sergei to pursue Ariana. I know you invited him with you to training the other day, but he's becoming a little too interested in her."

Lars spun around to face Kayla, his eyes wide in shock.

"You're fucking kidding me. You're trying to set Sergei up with Ari? Are you *insane?*"

Kayla's brow furrowed, and she leaned back, wrinkling her nose at them. "What's the big deal? They both have the hots for each other. He might not do any of the woo-woo stuff, but Sergei's got it going on. He's also really sweet with her. I mean, you saw him just now. He's really protective of her. Ten credits say he followed her to make sure she got back to her quarters okay."

Alec's grip tightened on his glass. As it was, he'd had a hard enough time getting a few minutes alone with her. How the hell had Sergei gotten to know Ariana well enough for things to develop between them so quickly? Ariana hardly left the Inner Sanctum. Other than Kayla bringing him to the training session yesterday, there shouldn't have been any other interactions.

Lars shook his head. "Kayla, I may not agree with Alec on most things, but encouraging a relationship between them is dangerous. Sergei is a ruthless killer and intensely loyal to the Coalition. He would destroy Ariana in a heartbeat."

Kayla rolled her eyes. "I think you guys are being a little dramatic."

Alec finished his drink and placed it on the table next to him. "No, Kayla, Lars is correct. What I'm about to tell you does not leave this room. I wouldn't even share it with Lars, except he already knows."

"What?"

"Ariana is a very strong dual energy channeler, possibly the most skilled I've ever met. I suspect she may even be able to channel a third element. Unlike other dual talents, though, she can channel water and earth equally. Water is her brother's element, so that's the one she claims publicly. Very few people know about her talents with earth energy."

He paused for a long moment, remembering when he'd

first learned about her skills. Seara had shared the information with him and made him promise to keep it secret. He had, up until now. The danger that had kept Ariana in seclusion had been eliminated by his hand. But there were other threats that could emerge if the rest of the towers learned about her talents. No one could understand the nature of those threats as much as the people in this room.

"To give you some idea of her power level, I'd say Ariana may even exceed yours. She could definitely offer most people within the towers a challenge. Fortunately, that's not her nature. Ariana's one of the least power-hungry individuals I've ever met."

Kayla's eyes widened. "Okay, so she's got mad skills. What does that have to do with Sergei?"

Alec paused for a moment, trying to decide how to explain. "The combination of water and earth is extremely rare. They can both be nurturing elements, particularly when paired together. When that happens, the wielder tends to possess very few defenses against other more dominant elemental abilities. This is part of the reason Jason is so protective of her. Jason possesses powerful offensive and defensive skills, whereas Ariana is a remarkable and gifted healer. She can heal physical *and* mental injuries. When you were seriously injured and brought to the towers," Alec gave Lars a pointed look, "Ariana was the one we called for help. She has talents and abilities our most skilled physicians can't duplicate with technology. But it's the mental aspect of her talents that has proven to be the most beneficial and most challenging."

Lars walked over to the bar and poured a drink. "Just call it what it is, Alec. She's a fucking empath. She reads emotions and thoughts, and then shifts the energy currents around her to heal whoever needs it. If someone's angry, she lessens it. If someone's hurt, she softens it. Whatever they need, she gives it to them, even at risk to herself." He lowered his head and stared down at his drink. "She's a walking miracle, and not one of us deserves the gift of her. Especially if we're going to risk putting her in danger tomorrow."

Alec's eyes narrowed at Lars. "Nothing will happen to her. We'll both be there to make damned sure it doesn't. If she shows the slightest hint of discomfort, we'll cancel the expedition and return to the towers. I'm not willing to risk her either."

Kayla frowned. "Okay, so wait. What's all the concern about her going to the surface?"

Alec turned back to Kayla. "First, you must understand... Ariana is unbonded. I suspect this is by her family's design. All potential suitors have been turned away and denied. Her family has kept her extremely isolated and her abilities kept quiet for many years. Only recently has she begun emerging more into society, usually with her brother as her protector or escort. That's why even Brant hasn't seen her manipulate energy until now."

Lars took a drink and cocked his head. "And just how would you know about her love life, cousin? Were you one of those denied suitors?"

Alec stood, snatching his glass from the table, and headed back toward the bar. He was going to need something stronger if they kept up this line of conversation.

Kayla's eyes almost bugged out of her head, and she nearly fell off the couch. "No shit. Seriously? You tried to date Ari and she said no?"

Alec scowled, putting his glass on the bar with a *clank*. "It was before I found you, Kayla. My father was still the High Council leader and Ari was... *is*..."

He paused, trying to decide how to explain. Things had been different back then, and words simply weren't sufficient to describe Ariana. Gods, she was beguiling, with those pouty lips and gorgeous silvery eyes that always saw too damn much. Staying away from her had been one of the hardest things he'd ever done.

Alec sighed. "Well, needless to say, I've always found her desirable. She's a remarkable and extremely beautiful woman. I spoke with her father about the possibility of courting her, but he refused. I understand now that his reasons were to keep my father and other councilors from learning too much about her abilities. She never had to suffer from wearing the bracelet because my father didn't believe she had much talent. I suspect the bracelets would have interfered with her natural shielding and could have possibly damaged her mind. Her parents did the right thing to protect her."

He frowned and poured more of the amber liquid into his glass. "I suspect there's also some concern about her talents if she becomes bonded. If she chooses to bond with a powerful fire or air channeler, one of her abilities may strengthen to serve as a stronger counterpoint to her mate's talents. I don't know how this would affect her healing abilities." Alec turned back around and considered Kayla for a long moment. "I wonder if a child from such a union could have the potential to become a spirit channeler like you. Your father was a powerful dual-energy channeler."

Kayla crossed her arms over her chest. "Well, that would suck for the kid. Trust me, it's no picnic. But besides that, I'm not seeing an issue with her and Sergei being together. You better not be objecting because you expect her to be some sort of broodmare. If so, I'll castrate you right here and now."

Lars laughed. "As interesting as that would be to watch, I think Alec's just speculating. We don't know enough about spirit channelers to understand how it happens." He arched his eyebrows at Alec and added, "But I find it fascinating you tried to court Ari and were refused. I guess I don't need to worry about you as competition if I decide to petition her father."

Alec glared at Lars, debating whether to pummel his cousin for even making the suggestion. "Keep in mind, it wasn't Ari who refused me. It was also a long time ago, when political circumstances in the towers were different. My father is no longer a threat to her. And after her reaction to me this evening, it's obvious she has no knowledge of my request to court her. Her father must not have told her."

Kayla arched an eyebrow and leaned forward. "Whoa. Are you saying you want to get it on with Ari? I thought you might be interested in her, but you never made a move after our bond broke."

Alec opened his mouth and then clamped it shut.

Kayla laughed, seemingly delighted by the possibility. "Uh huh. That's a definite yes. So what are you waiting for? Convince her to hop into bed with you and have some fun."

Lars rubbed his chin thoughtfully. "Well, that's a tempting thought."

At Alec's sharp look, Lars shrugged and added, "You can't blame me for thinking about it. Hell, I'm sure quite a few of us have. She's gorgeous."

Alec narrowed his eyes at Lars. With lightning-fast speed, he shoved a blast of air energy in his direction. His cousin stumbled backward, splashing some of his drink on the front of his shirt.

"Dammit, Alec!" Lars scowled at him as he shook the spilled liquid from his hand. Lars's air energy kicked up, and he wove it around himself to dry out his shirt.

Alec ignored him. "Kayla, Ariana isn't the type of woman you have a quick fling with. She's beautiful, and I think most men would agree she's, as Lars says, 'fucking hot'. However, based on her level of power, talents, and family's social position, there's no room in that scenario for a casual encounter.

There's only courtship. If that works out, it would proceed to marriage and entering into a permanent bond."

Kayla wrinkled her nose. "You guys are so ass-backward sometimes. What you're describing is archaic. Besides, you've had plenty of 'distractions'. There was that Celeste person, and that bitch Brianna, who tried to knock me off the beam. Those are only the ones I know about. You guys do the casual sex thing all the time."

Lars threw back his head and laughed. Alec scowled at him. "Go ahead and laugh, cousin. We can talk about your sexual exploits next."

Lars's expression quickly sobered.

Alec smirked. "Those women, my dear Kayla, never had any potential of being anything more than casual. I told you we're drawn to people who can wield our same level of power or exceed it. None of them could come close to what I want."

Lars sat on the couch and threw his arm over the back it. "Ari definitely could. You wouldn't think so at first glance because she's so unassuming and subtle. But she's something else. I don't think I'll ever forget the way she felt." He frowned and looked toward the window again, his expression thoughtful. "I wouldn't be surprised if she keeps energy constantly in reserve because she's worried about needing to bail out Jason."

Alec nodded. "I think you're right. I've been trying to pay more attention to the interactions between the two of them over the past few weeks. I'm starting to wonder if Jason may be a problem. Ari seems to spend an extraordinary amount of power keeping him in check. I don't remember him ever being this hot-headed before."

Kayla frowned and looked back and forth between the two men. "What do you mean? Jason's gotten into arguments a few times with some of the guys in the crew, but nothing serious. I think I've gotten into worse fights."

"It's probably nothing," Alec admitted. "I just want to keep a closer eye on him. We used to be good friends, but I had to keep my distance because of my father. He's changed since then, but I suppose that's true of all of us."

Brant leaned forward, resting his arms on his knees. "I don't know much about Ariana, but I've had more than a few run-ins with Jason. He's a problem and has been for the past several months. It's been getting worse lately though. I'd say we get a few security complaints every week, and they're escalating in frequency and severity. Most of the complaints come from some of the gambling halls or nightclubs."

Alec frowned. He hadn't been aware of Jason's proclivities. Over the past month, Alec had been trying to reach out to Ariana more, but she'd been his primary focus, not Jason. In her messages, she was always polite and friendly, but his efforts to meet with her alone hadn't gone well. Jason had been annoyingly persistent in accompanying her to every briefing, making it a point to direct the conversations back to tower business. Beyond that, Alec hadn't paid much attention to him.

"I'd like you to send me a report with the list of complaints and the corresponding establishments. Do you know if Ariana is aware of this?"

Brant shook his head. "No idea. I've never had any reason to monitor her. She's very good at staying under the radar. We've had to notify Jason's father, Devan Alivette, several times, though, to retrieve his son from our holding areas."

"Be careful, Alec," Lars warned. "You're already playing a dangerous game by asking Ariana to go to the surface and circumventing her father. Devan Alivette isn't someone to cross lightly. He holds a lot of influence with the Council, and he's very good at playing their game. If he learns you're insinuating yourself in his private family matters, you may provoke him into taking action against you. He can be one ruthless son of a bitch."

"I'm well aware of Devan's reputation," Alec admitted. "But if Jason's activities affect Ariana in a negative way, I *will* intervene on her behalf. That's secondary though. First, we need to see how she does tomorrow on the surface being surrounded by so many non-*Drac'Kin*."

Kayla cocked her head. "What are you talking about? She lives in the towers. You guys have thousands of normal people living here."

"Yes," Alec agreed, "but there's a reason we have two separate towers, Kayla. OmniLab was created to preserve our race and bring it back to its former glory. Already, we've seen huge shifts in the nature of our abilities. Every generation, new and greater talents emerge. We believe it's from so many *Drac'Kin* living in close proximity to each other within this tower. As a result, though, some of our kind have developed certain sensitivities. We can be easily affected by those 'normal' people, as you call them. That's one of the reasons Ariana never visits the public tower and only rarely travels to the public sectors."

"From what I've seen, Ariana's been fine around Sergei and other people."

Alec nodded, still troubled by Sergei's interest. "Yes, for short periods of time. There are some rare individuals who don't affect her at all, but that's not typical. Most humans have some sensitivities to energy threads. They can't use them like we can, but they react with them. Ariana naturally emits a type of healing aura. It's one of the reasons people are drawn to her and are protective of her. It's not something she ever completely shuts off. I don't believe she can. Unfortunately, if she's around humans, she'll expend energy trying to heal them without success. She'll push past the point of exhaustion and drain herself. That's when she's most vulnerable, and it could possibly damage her mind."

Kayla blinked. "So she's like a circuit board with a built-in battery and no off switch. She'll burn out? There isn't any way to shut it off?"

Alec shook his head. "Not that we know of. That's why the bracelets were so dangerous to her and why Brant and the rest of the Shadows haven't had any interactions with her. Her family wasn't willing to risk putting her in a situation where her energy could be cut off." .

"Wow," Kayla murmured. "So she could die just from being around humans for too long?"

Alec nodded. "I'm afraid it's a possibility. If she uses her ability around another *Drac'Kin*, she's better able to control the flow because there's a conscious merging of energy threads. We can also offer our power to supplement her own. It's a temporary measure to restore her to stasis until she can naturally repair her shields. I believe she attempted too much tonight. Healing of any sort is always difficult, and she wasn't prepared. That was my fault. Lars offered her a small amount of energy, and so did I. Without a bond, though, we can't do more than that. She'd be much more protected if she had a bonded mate."

Lars leaned forward. "Now do you see why it's dangerous to push Sergei and Ariana together? He's damaged, Kayla. I have nothing but respect for the man. He saved my life, and I owe him a great deal, but Ari would want to heal him. She might kill herself trying, without even realizing she was doing it. It's too dangerous to pair them together."

"Well, crap," Kayla muttered. "Apparently, I suck at this whole matchmaking thing. But I gotta tell you, energy aside... there's some serious chemistry going on between the two of them. Sergei looks at her like he's starving and she's the last meal around. I'll stay out of it, but I really haven't done much to push them together. Sergei's the one who's been in hot pursuit. I just gave him the opportunity he wanted. I mean, you saw him just now. I don't think he's going to be discouraged that easily."

Alec and Lars exchanged a look, neither of them willing to give voice to their fears. If Sergei was that drawn to her, it was possible Ariana's abilities were already affecting him. Her tiredness tonight might be an indication she'd been using her energy to try to heal Sergei without realizing it.

Lars stood. "If you'll excuse me, I think I need to have a word with Sergei. If Kayla's right and he's that focused on her, we may have a serious problem."

Alec nodded and watched him go, part of him hoping they were right but also dreading they were wrong. If Sergei's attraction to Ariana was something far more elemental than energy, that could be a problem too. Alec had let Ariana go the first time because it was the best way he could protect her. If he had to jeopardize his alliance with the Coalition to keep her this time, so be it. He wouldn't lose her again.

CHAPTER FOUR

SERGEI SLIPPED into the empty corridor and pulled out the security keycard he'd cloned weeks before. The Omnis were secretive by nature, and he'd found that doing his own investigations typically revealed more than they were willing to share. Swiping it over the locking mechanism, he slipped inside when the door slid open.

From his visit the previous day, he'd determined there was a back entrance to the Alivette quarters through the pool area. Judging by Jason's attitude earlier, he doubted a front door reception would be welcome. He didn't trust the man, especially not with Ariana's welfare. Over the years, Sergei had learned quite a bit about the Omnis' ability to channel energy. However, they still managed to hide a great deal. Ariana was obviously suffering from complications related to the energy channeling, and he was determined to discover the cause.

A loud *crash* halted his movement. It sounded like something metal had fallen. Sergei ducked into one of the small dressing areas and listened.

"Dammit, Ari, going to the surface is a mistake," Jason

argued, his voice accompanied by a small scraping noise as though he was restacking whatever had fallen. "Look at you! You're a mess right now and that was just from healing Lars. How are you going to handle being surrounded by dozens of people who've suffered a lifetime of misery? You won't be able to help them, but you're going to keep throwing energy around and trying."

"I have to go, Jason. I can't keep living in this bubble. I've spent the past several months trying to expose myself to others. I need to learn how to keep my balance, and I can't do that by avoiding everyone and everything. I'm not foolish enough to believe this isn't risky, but it's still something I need to do. If we can help utilize the river as a water and power source, we have to do it. We were given these gifts for a reason."

"Look, I get it. Testing your limits is great in theory, but the risks are too high. If you want to go to the other tower and try a controlled test, we can do that. Or even better, we could stand on one of the bridgeways while people walk by and see how that goes. But traveling to the surface completely outside the safety zone is too much. It's too dangerous, Ari. What are you going to tell Father?"

There was a long pause before Ariana replied, "I don't plan to tell him anything. I know he has my best interests at heart, but this is my decision. I'll discuss it with him afterward, but I've already made up my mind."

"You're putting me in a difficult position," Jason said with a long, drawn-out sigh. "I'm not sure our bond is enough anymore. I'm trying, but your abilities are evolving and growing stronger. Father and I believe a bonded mate may be the only way to protect you."

"What?" came Ariana's shocked reply. Sergei leaned forward and saw the two siblings around the corner. They were standing face to face just outside the door to their family's quarters.

"Kendra's cousin is going to petition Father for permission to court you."

Ariana shook her head. "Hayden? What are you thinking, Jason? I know he's your friend, but I hardly know him. Even if Father were to give his consent, I wouldn't agree to it."

"Would you rather it be Alec?" Jason took a step toward her. "He petitioned Father a couple years ago, and it doesn't appear his interest has waned. I don't know if I trust him with you, but he's more than strong enough to hold your bond."

Ariana froze, and her entire body tensed. "What are you talking about?"

Jason shrugged. "Father wouldn't allow him to court you back then, but he might consider it now, especially if he knew all the risky stunts you've been pulling lately. Hayden would be a better choice though."

Ariana looked away, and Sergei could make out the delicate features of her profile. She frowned and shook her head. "No, Jason. When I decide to give my heart to someone, it will be because it's right. I won't just accept someone on the off-chance a bond between us will protect me."

Jason's eyes narrowed. "Fine, but I think you need to get it out of your head that Sergei is a viable option. He's not. He's dangerous to you on more levels than you can possibly imagine. I've seen the way you look at him, and it needs to stop. You need to stay away from him."

Ariana clenched her fists and glared at her brother. "I will *not* discuss Sergei with you."

"He could kill you, Ari!" Jason shouted, grabbing her arms and pinning them to her side. "He could slowly drain away everything that makes you who you are, leaving you a shell. Is that what you want?"

"You don't know that!" Ariana retorted and pulled away from him. "All we have are speculations and guesses. There hasn't been another empath in over a hundred years. We don't know what caused her death."

"Are you willing to risk that on a guess?" Jason demanded. "Because I'm not."

Her shoulders drooped. She shook her head and wrapped her arms around herself. "Everyone has me so tied up in this neat little world, and I can't even begin to figure out the truth. I won't keep living like this, Jason. I can't live in fear, wondering if the next person I speak to will be the one who pushes me too far. What use is having these gifts if I don't learn how to use them?"

Jason threw his hands in the air in a show of frustration. "At least you'd still be alive! Don't think I haven't noticed you've been suffering more than usual lately. It's been getting worse. Dammit, Ari, I just... I can't reason with you. Sometimes I wonder why the hell I even bother. How am I supposed to protect you when you're determined to destroy yourself and take me with you?"

Without waiting for a reply, Jason spun around and stormed out of the pool area, slamming the door behind him. Ariana flinched at the sound and lowered her head for a long moment. When she lifted it again, Sergei noticed her skin was even paler than it had been in Alec's office. She turned and walked toward the pool, her gait slightly unsteady. It seemed as though the slightest draft would topple her.

Sergei straightened and prepared to go to her, but she paused. Ariana slipped the straps of her dress off her shoulders, letting the garment drift down and fall to her feet.

Sergei froze, unable to do anything but stare at the gorgeous woman in front of him. She was slender, with high breasts, a tiny waist and long legs that seemed to go on forever. He'd seen her in a bathing suit, but the full view was staggering. Ariana raised her hands and began removing the pins from her hair. It tumbled downward in a canopy of soft, midnight-colored waves, past her shoulders and halfway down her back.

Dropping the pins to the ground, she slowly stepped into the water. As she dove beneath the surface, Sergei shook off the lust-induced fog and approached the pool. Ariana moved like a mythical mermaid, her earlier unsteadiness a distant memory. Seeing her like this made it easier to understand her desire to be near the water. Her element surrounded her, protecting her and infusing her with strength. Here, she became part of the water. But Sergei also recognized the loneliness of her existence and the unmistakable need for something more.

He reached down and pulled off his shirt. The thought of entering the water wasn't altogether appealing, but it was what she needed. He kicked off his boots and removed his pants, pausing at his undergarments. Her innocence was unmistakable, and Sergei hesitated. She was curious about him, but he needed to be careful. This was about reassurance and connection. As much as he might be interested, he wouldn't push. Not now.

Sergei entered the pool, surprised to find it warmer than he expected. He wasn't sure whether she sensed his approach or the disturbance in the water, but Ariana broke through the surface with a gasp. Confusion and surprise crossed her face at the sight of him, and she looked around the room to see if he was alone before focusing on him again. Her brow furrowed as she treaded water in place, but she made no move to come closer to him.

"Sergei? What are you doing here?"

He frowned, noting the deepening water and trying to determine how far he could go until standing would be an issue. "To make sure you were all right. I was concerned."

"Really?" Her eyes softened, and she slowly swam toward him. She gave him a shy smile and then paused, suddenly becoming aware of her nudity. Submerging herself deeper into the water, she blushed, bringing a rush of color back into her cheeks. "Um, you shouldn't be here. I'm not— I thought I was alone."

He gave her a slow smile. "You have nothing to worry about, *solnyshka*. It is dark underwater, and I will not look if you do not wish it."

She cocked her head and her eyes narrowed. "You already looked, didn't you?"

"A man could no more manage to avoid looking at the sun if it were in front of him."

Ariana laughed, a light, musical sound that lightened his heart. She swam closer, her eyes trusting him to keep his word and not look again. He held her gaze until she was inches away.

"Hi," she whispered.

"Hello, Ariana," Sergei replied, brushing her wet hair away from her face and tracing the line of her jaw. She tilted her head, leaning into his hand. Her responsiveness was intoxicating, especially given her innocence. He brushed his thumb across her cheek, noting that even though her skin was cool to the touch, he could sense an inner fire within her. "I trust you are well?"

She nodded and hesitantly pressed her small hands against his bare chest. He forced himself to remain still as he suffered from the heady aphrodisiac of her touch. "I'm glad you came."

Sergei placed his hands over hers. "I heard what your brother said. I am not a good man, but I will not risk hurting you. Is he correct? Am I dangerous to you?"

Ariana closed her eyes and lowered her head. He pulled her against him gently, enjoying the sensation of her body pressed against his. She didn't resist. If anything, she seemed to crave his touch.

Her voice was a soft murmur when she answered. "I don't know. I should be upset you were eavesdropping, but I'm not. The truth is, we don't know anything for sure." She bit lit her lip and looked up at him. "There's something about you that calls to me. If you were dangerous to me, would I be drawn to you?"

"Like a moth to a flame," he murmured thoughtfully, searching her face for some clue as to how she was feeling. She seemed more like herself and less affected by whatever the energy had done to her earlier. If he had a negative effect on her, he couldn't see it. But then again, the water might be acting as a barrier. "You will tell me immediately if you begin to feel unwell."

She blinked at the command in his voice and nodded.

At her agreement, he relaxed slightly. "Do you need to swim?"

Ariana shook her head, trailing her fingers over his chest in exquisite torture. "No, I usually only need to spend a few minutes in the water to completely reinforce my shields." She tilted her head and smiled. "I would imagine it's not as comfortable for you as it is for me."

"No, but I will not complain about having your body against mine."

Her eyes widened, and she looked down to where she was touching him. Ariana started to draw away, but he pulled her close again, not willing to let her go yet. If she had any idea how tempting she was to him, she'd do more than just try to pull away.

Instead, he cupped her face and pressed a soft kiss against her forehead. She closed her eyes as he tilted her head back, the inky darkness of her lashes contrasting with the fairness of her skin. He leaned forward and kissed her forehead again, trailing light kisses downward and brushing the edge of her mouth. Her lips parted a fraction, and he hesitated, desire and duty warring within him. If he didn't stop now, he wasn't sure he'd have the willpower in another few minutes.

Her eyes fluttered open, and that was the deciding factor for him. Pure and complete trust shone in their depths. He wanted her, but he didn't deserve that level of trust.

Sergei ran his thumb over her lips. "You are far too tempting, *solnyshka*. If you are finished with your swim, I will exit first and get you something to cover yourself. I do not trust myself with you, not like this."

Ariana tilted her head to study him and reluctantly pulled away. She pointed toward a small closet against the wall. "There are some large wraparound cloths on the shelf by the door."

Sergei nodded and turned away, exiting the pool. He was probably a fool for not pressing his advantage, but sometimes the chase was just as fun. He smiled, feeling the heavy weight of Ariana's gaze on him, just as he'd watched her earlier.

———

Ariana admired the firm lines of Sergei's body as he climbed out of the pool. There were several scars on his back from some sort of old trauma. They had already healed, but she still felt the desire to trace their path downward with her fingers until they disappeared into his waistband. She moved closer to the edge of the pool, keeping her body submerged.

He grabbed a couple of the large wraps and headed back toward her. When he was close enough, Sergei closed his eyes and held out the cloth, waiting expectantly. She stood and slowly exited the pool, the water running down her body but the effects leaving her restored. As she moved closer to him, he remained motionless with his eyes closed. True to his word, Sergei didn't peek.

But she did. He stood in front of her wearing nothing but his wet undergarments which left very little to the imagination. Her eyes traced the lines of his muscular body and her fingers flexed, wanting to follow the same path as her gaze. Water dripped down his body, and she could almost sense the energy contained within those small droplets as they traveled downward.

She took one of the cloths from his outstretched hand and wrapped it around herself. Once it was secured, she stood on her toes and brushed a kiss against his cheek.

He opened his eyes and glanced down at her. "Better?"

"Much," Ariana agreed and bent down to pick up their discarded clothing. "If you'd like to use one of the drying tubes, they're in the dressing area."

He glanced over at the small rooms. "Do you use them?"

"No. The drying tubes take away too much of the moisture. I usually just let my skin dry naturally."

Sergei considered her words for a moment and wrapped the other cloth around himself. "I will not risk it."

Ariana paused, touched by his offer. Not only had he come all the way to the pool area to make sure she was okay, but now he was refusing the comforts of a drying tube simply for her benefit. Shaking her head, she wondered how he could possibly think he wasn't a good man. She held the bundle of clothing to her chest, not wanting him to leave just yet but unsure of the normal protocol.

"Would you like to come in for a bit? My family's quarters are right through that door."

He paused, studying her for a long moment before nodding. "I will not stay long though. You need to rest for tomorrow."

She led him through the side entrance of her family's

quarters and glanced back at him. He moved like a confident predator, taking in every small detail at once. Her family's quarters were one of the larger ones, since they'd been one of the original families aligned with OmniLab. As such, her personal quarters consisted of several rooms where she could live as independently as she wished while remaining under the protection of her family. Her brother's rooms were directly across the hall from her, and her parents lived at the opposite end.

Ariana pressed her hand over the palm plate next to the door to open it. Sergei strolled in, prowling through the main living area and studying each object carefully. Fascinated by his movements, she placed their clothing on the table by the entrance and watched him explore. She loved her home, but she didn't often have visitors, preferring to keep her living space private. She'd never considered how her home would appear to someone unused to living within the towers.

She'd chosen to decorate with dark blues and cool whites, with subtle hints of earth tones thrown in for balance. Numerous plants were around within the room, while a marble fountain stood in the corner making soothing gurgling noises. In a way, she supposed it reflected her alignment with the elements. The decorations were relatively simple compared to some, but she found her home peaceful and relaxing.

"You have a beautiful home." He leaned over to examine one of the more exotic plant specimens more closely. "I have not seen this plant before. What is it?"

She smiled and moved to stand beside him. Reaching out, she held her hand over one of the closed blooms and infused it with a trace of earth energy. A swirl of color exploded as the bloom opened, giving the appearance of a bird in flight.

"It's called a Bird of Paradise. It's not native to this area, but I fell in love with some images I saw of it. Jason was able to procure some seeds from the vault so I could grow it."

Sergei's eyes widened, and his gaze darted from the plant to her and back again. "Your energy can grow plants?"

Ariana hesitated, her hand trembling slightly. She was so unused to being around outsiders that she'd momentarily forgotten to suppress her more astounding abilities. She began to pull her hand away, but Sergei grabbed it. His expression was serious as he studied her.

"Ariana, you must tell me. You can do this with all plants?"

She swallowed and nodded. "Most plants. It's an earth talent. That's how we grow most of our food in the towers. We cultivate the plants and procure more seeds to store in the vault. There might be some plants that don't respond to me though. I don't know. I'm not registered as an earth talent. I thought because you were in Alec's office today... I thought you knew."

He was silent for a long moment, studying the flowering plant. "No. We suspected you had ways to grow food without genetic modification. We just did not know how. Your people are not forthcoming with information."

Ariana paled, astounded the Coalition hadn't known, and she wondered if this was supposed to have been kept a secret. If she had just betrayed her entire race in a moment of thoughtlessness, she'd never forgive herself.

She swallowed, wondering how Lars and the other exiles could have lived with them for so long and not shown them. "What are you going to do?"

Sergei looked at her and arched an eyebrow. "What do you think?"

"I don't know," she admitted with a frown. "I can't read your emotions very well right now."

Sergei placed his hands on her waist. With a gentle but firm grip, he pulled her closer and pressed a soft kiss against her forehead. When he eased back, his gaze was tender. "I will do nothing that will put you in harm's way. However, I must consider the implications and possibilities for my people. I have no choice when so many suffer on the surface."

Ariana bit her lip. "I know my people can be secretive, but please don't hold that against us. For centuries, we've been persecuted, studied, tortured, and killed simply for being different. Trust doesn't come easily to any of us, especially with outsiders. But this alliance between our cultures is a beginning. Please don't let me be the reason it falls apart."

"A heart such as yours is impossible to resist," Sergei murmured and ran his fingers through her damp hair. "Do not worry. We are still learning about each other. I can be a very patient man."

Her shoulders slumped in relief, and she let out a pent-up breath. She hadn't realized how much she'd feared his reaction. "Thank you, Sergei."

Sergei caressed her cheek. "I will travel with you tomorrow to the river. For now, you should rest. Can you sleep now?"

When she murmured her ascent, he nodded and pressed another kiss against her forehead. "Good. I will change and let myself out. Sleep well, Ariana. I look forward to seeing you tomorrow."

CHAPTER FIVE

ARIANA PRESSED her hand against her stomach, trying to stem her excitement and breathe through the equally intense emotions around her. In an effort to distract herself, she peered out of the protected and darkened window. The landscape was mostly barren, with a sprinkling of abandoned or collapsed buildings before more large stretches of nothing. It was a beautiful but harsh world, almost alien in comparison to life within the towers.

From the moment she'd awakened that morning, there had been a whirlwind of activity. Since she'd never been to the surface, they'd outfitted her with all the necessary gear to protect her from the harmful rays of the sun. On the plus side, she now owned clothing that would allow her to better blend in if she visited the construction site again. On the opposite end of things, the clothing was hot, bulky, and more than a little uncomfortable.

She was given a quick tutorial on how the equipment worked and how to use the communication devices. There was some sort of emergency drill she no longer quite remembered. It was all a jumbled mix of procedures and unfamiliar terminology which had made little sense when she was listening and even less now. If there were some sort of emergency, she was well and truly screwed. At least she'd have an exciting experience while it happened, and if she survived it, an even more amazing story to share.

After the condensed introduction to all things surface-related, she'd been escorted to the caravan. Alec had explained that due to the size of their party, they had to rely on the slower-moving ground transports. Ariana had gone along with all of it because there really weren't any other options. She'd agreed to help and wasn't about to back out now. It was more than just the promise of the adventure though. If they weren't able to harness the power of the river, it wasn't just her and her family that would be affected. There were thousands of people depending on this resource.

As the caravan bumped and jostled them along, Jason groaned, looking a little green around the gills. Ever since they'd fought last night, Jason had hardly spoken to her. The tension between them was palpable, and she gripped the edge of her seat tightly. His anger and motion sickness leeched into their bond and tainted the energy in the air with an almost sour stench.

Ariana tried to divert her attention again to the outside world. Sandwiched between Alec and Jason, her view out the windows was somewhat limited. Sergei, Lars, and Kayla were sitting across from her, but unlike her brother, none of them appeared fazed by the motion of the vehicle. That was a small blessing because the rest of the group's growing excitement, worry, and nerves grew stronger with each passing minute. She tightened her grip on the edge of the seat, trying to block it out.

A wave of nausea hit her, and she squeezed her eyes shut, willing it to recede. It was either an echo from her brother's misery or the escalating emotions in the vehicle were proving too much to handle.

Alec leaned toward her. "Are you all right, Ari?"

She could do this. She had to do this. Oh, hell, she couldn't do this. Now their worry and concern was out of control, threatening to suffocate her. There were too many people in close quarters. It was too much strong emotion all at once. The farther away from the towers they traveled, the more intense the emotion seemed to get. If she could just manage to breathe through it, maybe it would be okay. But even breathing was becoming difficult with the stupid helmet on her head.

Before she could respond, the caravan halted. Overhead, there was a loud beep signaling they'd enabled the UV guard.

Sergei's voice came from her right. "Lean forward. Put your head between knees." A hand pressed against her back, forcing her into position.

Someone removed her helmet, and her unbound hair fell forward, covering her face. She'd forgone braiding her hair that morning because she'd been told it would uncomfortable with a helmet. She was now grateful for the suggestion because her hair acted as curtain to hide her discomfiture. Someone pulled off her gloves and eased off the restrictive jacket. A cold, wet cloth was placed on the back of her neck and more were wrapped around her wrists. When a cool mist sprayed into the surrounding air, she nearly whimpered in relief.

"Make her drink," Jason instructed with a groan. "My shielding isn't doing shit for her. I think I'm making the situation worse."

Alec put his hand against her bare arm. She flinched at the sudden contact, wary of any additional emotions that threatened to invade her senses. Her shields had shattered in the past few minutes, and she'd given up trying to reinforce them. But Alec was shielding himself, trying to protect her from his emotions. It wasn't complete, but at least they were somewhat muted.

"Can you drink something, Ari?" Alec's voice was gentle.

"Yes," she managed and tried to sit up. Another wave of nausea struck, and she wondered if she could manage to keep it down. If she could drink, she could reinforce her emotional barrier enough to heal her brother. That might make it easier to get through this hellish trip. There was something really wrong in the universe when you had to worry about your brother's motion sickness becoming contagious.

"Easy," Sergei advised and helped keep the cloth around her neck in place.

Alec handed her a hydrating pack, and her hands shook as she tried to open it.

"Fuck," Lars muttered, leaning forward to open the hydrating pack for her. "This was a mistake, Alec. We need to get her out of here. I didn't realize it would come on this suddenly or be this bad."

Ariana shook her head and drank the cool liquid. It was a soothing balm against her throat. She wove the water energy around her to better insulate herself. She could still sense everyone's emotions, but it was more of a dull roar than a pounding bass. The fact the caravan had stopped and Jason's stomach was beginning to settle down also helped tremendously.

Alec pressed a button on his commlink. "Thomas, I need to know how quickly you can get an aircraft transport out to our location."

"No," Ariana said in a hoarse whisper, shaking her head again. "Alec, wait. I just need a minute."

"I won't risk you, Ari. It's not worth it. We'll find another way," Alec declared.

She closed her eyes and took a deep breath of the moist

air. The energy threads around her strengthened and solidi-fied even more. She continued to weave them into her shields, reinforcing the weakened areas. Once she was satis-fied, she turned to Jason and pressed her hand against his bare skin. Healing energy poured out of her, calming his stomach and his unease. He groaned in response, slumping back in relief.

"It's a bit better now, but I'll need another minute," she admitted sheepishly. "It was a combination of everyone's emotions and my excitement. I don't think Jason's stomach likes riding in a caravan very much either."

Jason made an answering grunt but didn't open his eyes.

Kayla chuckled. "Motion sickness at its finest. I think it's worse being inside a caravan. If you're in the open air on a speeder, it's not so bad. This sucks, even for me."

Sergei murmured his agreement.

Alec frowned. "Are you sure you want to continue, Ari?"

She nodded. "I want to do this. I don't want to cause problems, but I want to try to help if I can."

Alec sighed and placed his hand over hers. He spoke into his commlink and canceled the order for the aircraft before turning back to her. "What do you think would help the most? We can keep the moisture fans running, but I don't think you'll get the benefits if you're in protective gear. The UV shields on the caravan can't operate while the vehicle is in motion, and it's too dangerous for you not to wear your gear without the UV shield activated."

She paused, considering the best option. "The closer we get to the destination, the stronger everyone's emotions become. It's harder for me to ward against it. If everyone can try to suppress their excitement a bit, it would help."

Alec nodded. "That makes sense. We're about thirty minutes out. To be on the safe side, we'll stop every ten minutes. I think we pushed too far, too fast."

She nodded. It might be better if they took more frequent breaks. She glanced up to find Jason frowning. At least he wasn't arguing with her, but he still looked unhappy. Ariana sighed and started pulling her gloves and jacket back on, and then accepted her helmet from Sergei. This long trip was going to get even longer, but she was determined to see it through. Maybe on the way back, she could ride on a speeder like Kayla mentioned. Now *that* would be fun.

ALEC LEANED FORWARD and spoke a few words to the driver before announcing, "We're only a few minutes out from the base camp. The equipment has already been set up, and they're expecting us. Once we arrive, we'll go straight to the lift, which will take us down into the ruins. We need to do this quickly because our protective gear can't be removed until we're in the cavern. The lift can only accommodate three of us at a time. Ariana needs to be taken down first to keep her isolated from everyone in the base camp. Jason and I will escort her, and the rest of you will follow."

Alec sat beside her again and put his gloved hand over hers. "Ari, I know this is highly irregular, but I'd like you to consider forming a connection with me. It would need to be strong enough that we could communicate telepathically without touching and be able to transfer a significant amount of energy at will."

Her eyes widened at the request, and her face heated in embarrassment. She looked away and bit her lip, focusing on a small spot in the corner of the moving vehicle. What Alec was proposing was a shared intimacy usually only done in the most private of moments. Not only had she never done such a thing, but the fact he was asking her in front of everyone was akin to suggesting they both strip naked with an audience.

"You've got to be kidding me," Jason muttered and dropped his head in his hands. "For fuck's sake, Alec. She's my sister. I can't listen to this."

Lars made a strangled noise. "Smooth, Alec. Very smooth."

"Enough. Both of you," Alec snapped. When they fell silent, he turned back to her. "Ari, the last thing I want to do is make you uncomfortable or take advantage of you. I swear I won't violate your trust, but if the bond you share with Jason isn't enough, we won't have any other options until we reach the river. Please. I'm asking you to trust me with this."

She lifted her gaze to meet his. Was it wrong she'd daydreamed about sharing this type of connection with him for a long time? Granted, her fantasies had been in a far more private setting and without an audience. His reasoning was sound, but a part of her wished his request was for a different reason.

Her biggest fear was that he'd be able to really see her. All the emotions and thoughts she'd kept suppressed or hidden would come bubbling to the surface. She'd longed for that sort of connection with someone, but the reality of it was terrifying. If she had enough problems shielding emotions without a connection, she wasn't sure what would it be like with one. Although, when she really thought about it, there wasn't anyone else she trusted enough to form that intimate of a connection. If she were really going to do this, she wanted it to be with Alec.

Ariana nodded and lowered her gaze, feeling surprisingly vulnerable. "All right."

He let out a long exhale and squeezed her hand. "Thank you. Your trust means a great deal to me. Once we stop, I'd like you to try to drink a little more and reinforce your shields. We should be there any minute now."

Sergei leaned forward, his eyes narrowed on Alec. "This is not one of those permanent bonds, is it?"

Alec paused, considering Sergei for a long moment. "No, it's not permanent, but it's not something that's done casually either." He gave Sergei a pointed look and added, "Ari needs to be protected, and only one of our kind can offer that to her."

"So you claim," Sergei said and leaned back, holding Alec's gaze in a silent challenge. Alec glared at him but didn't respond.

A moment later the caravan came to a jarring halt, and a loud beep signaled it was safe to remove their protective gear. While Lars retrieved another hydrating pack, Ariana removed her helmet and slipped off her gloves. Once she pulled off her jacket, Alec turned on the cool misting fan and sat back down beside her.

He glanced around the caravan. "If you all could step outside for a few minutes, I'd appreciate it. We'll be with you shortly."

Jason swore under his breath and was the first to jump up. Ariana leaned back and closed her eyes, listening to the sounds of everyone exiting. Gods, this was humiliating. Someone stopped in front of her, and she opened her eyes as a gloved hand brushed against her cheek.

"All will be well, *solnyshka*," Sergei murmured. With a hard look at Alec, he added, "It is fortunate that an unwanted bond can be eliminated."

Alec stood, his body rigid as he met Sergei's glare. "Ariana has nothing to be concerned about. But you would do well to remember OmniLab has also learned a great deal over the years about eliminating unwanted threats." He gestured to the exit. "We will join you outside shortly."

Sergei smirked and then turned, exiting the caravan and closing the door behind him. Once he was gone, the silence was deafening.

Alec sighed and sat beside her, scrubbing his hands over his face. She could sense his tension and residual anger from Sergei's parting words. Ariana hesitated for a moment and then placed her hand on his arm. Sending a soothing wave of energy over him, she said, "It's all right, Alec. I trust you."

He looked over at her, searching her expression. Whatever he saw made him relax, and his expression softened. Alec brushed her hair away from her face and trailed his fingers over her cheek, almost as though he was trying to replace the memory of Sergei's touch with his. A light trace of his energy trailed over her skin and accompanied his gesture. He brushed his thumb across her lower lip and hesitated, his gaze lowering to her mouth. Her heart thudded at the look of longing on his face. She'd never thought to see that look from him again.

"I wouldn't have offered to do this with just anyone, Ari," he admitted.

She swallowed and whispered, "I've never done this before. I don't... I'm not..."

"Shhh," Alec murmured. He lifted her hand and pressed a kiss against the back of it. "Just close your eyes. I'll guide you. It's just a connection. It'll be a little stronger than others you've created. We don't have to exchange energy. This is only a precaution."

Trusting his word, she did as he asked and closed her eyes, opening herself to the energy threads around them. His warm air energy brushed against her skin in a soft and tender caress. It was light and coaxing, holding a thousand promises if she would only accept him.

Something within her awakened. A long-dormant need rose from within her, and she reached out with her energy. As she connected her threads with his, Alec accepted all she offered and enveloped her in his energy, holding her tightly in a metaphysical embrace. Awareness shifted, and she became part of him as he became part of her. Thoughts and emotions were shared and became something more than separate entities. In that moment, their connection was absolute and pure, something designed by the gods in their infancy when they'd sought a connection of souls.

"Alec," she whispered and opened her eyes to meet his.

Unable to resist, she reached out to touch him. She pressed her hand against his chest, but it wasn't enough to only touch him through his jacket. She needed to feel his bare skin. Ariana pressed her hand against his face, entranced by the sensation of the duality of touch. What she was experiencing went far beyond picking up emotions she normally read through energy threads.

She could sense Alec—the *real* Alec. The man behind the façade he presented to the world. It was more intimate and eye-opening than she'd ever imagined. For the first time, Ariana felt as though she'd found what she'd been seeking her entire life. She hadn't even realized the extent of her loneliness until that moment.

Ariana looked up into Alec's eyes and realized he understood. He knew how miraculous the connection between their kind could be, and he ached from the loss of it.

"Oh, Alec," she whispered, weaving her energy around him to let him know he was no longer alone. Healing energy rushed through her as her fingertips moved over his skin. Desire and a need for him unlike anything she'd ever known unfurled inside her, and she wasn't sure if it was coming from him or if it was the cumulation of their emotions.

She'd imagined touching him like this for so long, and even more. She lowered her gaze to his lips, wondering what it would be like to kiss him. Ariana froze, her eyes meeting his, and she realized he could read her thoughts. Through their connection, she could sense his surprise and elation. Before she could pull away, Alec wrapped his hand around her wrist, holding her to him.

"Ari," he murmured, his gaze tender. "I'd hoped you felt the same, but I wasn't sure after everything that's happened. I've wanted you for so long." He reached up to caress her cheek, and she leaned into his hand, entranced by the intimacy of their connection and wanting more.

"Gods, you're breathtaking," he whispered, his thumb grazing over her lower lip. She parted her mouth slightly, and his eyes darkened with desire. He leaned forward, his mouth hovering just over hers and then he paused. With a muttered curse, he pulled away slightly and shook his head.

"Not here. Not like this." Alec's expression was pained, and his voice filled with regret. With a sigh, he brushed her hair back from her face as though he didn't want to stop touching her. Lifting one of her hands, he pressed a kiss against it. "I wish the timing were better. I really want to explore this with you."

Ariana took a deep breath, trying to center herself. Alec was right. Even through the caravan doors, she could sense everyone waiting for them. Their impatience was escalating, and the energy threads around them were becoming stronger and more demanding.

"Is that what it normally feels like for you?" Alec asked in wonder, glancing toward the door.

Her eyes widened. "You can feel them too?"

He nodded and frowned. "I had no idea. You can block part of it, right?"

"Yes," she said, reaching over for the hydrating pack Lars had left for her. Ariana had been so distracted by Alec that she'd begun to let her internal shielding slip. She took a long drink and reinforced the protective barrier around her. The emotions from the others immediately muted. She could still sense them, but it was more like a low murmur rather than loud voices demanding attention.

"I can't turn them off completely," she admitted and bit her lip. The thought of Alec suffering from the effects of her empathic ability bothered her. "I've gotten used to ignoring them whenever possible."

Alec put his hand over hers. "That's all right. My focus is on making sure you're comfortable. I'll be fine. Are you ready to do this?"

She took a deep breath and nodded. It was now or never. "I'm ready."

He stood and handed her gloves to her. Lifting her hand one last time, he pressed another kiss against it. "You won't be alone, Ari. I'll be with you the entire time."

───────

THEY EXITED THE VEHICLE, and Ariana did her best to avoid the knowing looks everyone was throwing their way. The sunlight was nearly blinding, with the UV guard around their vehicle doing little to combat the brightness. She squinted through her helmet at the expansive base camps that had been set up. They were temporary structures, but the size of them made it obvious they'd been conducting extensive excavations for a while.

Alec wrapped his arm around her waist and ushered her toward one of the tents. It was slightly darker here, but this area was filled with complicated equipment. Two technicians glanced up from their displays when they entered, but Alec ignored them. He led her over to a large metal lift, waved Jason over to them, and then stepped onto the platform.

With a nod to one of the technicians, the platform immediately began its shaky descent. Ariana gripped the safety bars tightly as the platform lowered them into the recesses of the earth. As they moved downward, parts of the building became exposed, and she could see the remnants of old rooms and living quarters where people had once lived. She swallowed, wondering what had happened to all the people who had once been here and whether `any of them had survived the destruction.

Alec's gloved hand covered hers, and he spoke into the headset, "This area was evacuated before the war. Most of the people were long gone before these buildings fell into this chasm. Kayla was scavenging nearby when she discovered the underground river."

Ariana leaned forward slightly to get a better look. It was hard to imagine coming to the ruins every day and hunting for supplies. She wondered if Kayla would consider showing how she went about scavenging for lost items. Such a thing would be fascinating to experience.

Something tickled at the edge of her awareness, but without lowering her tightly-wound shields, she couldn't tell what it was. Even so, she knew there was something significant about this area. "There are still valuable artifacts down here?"

"Most likely, yes," Alec agreed over the headset. "We've had stability supports installed to minimize the chance of any further collapse. There have been quite a few challenges to move all of our equipment down here though. We still have plans to excavate the area further, but it's going much slower than we would like."

Jason glanced over at her. "How are you feeling?"

"I'm okay so far, but there's something down here," she replied, peering into the empty and abandoned rooms as they continued downward. She knew spirit channelers could see echoes of the past, but what she was sensing was almost like an echo of emotions from a time before. It had a distinctly different flavor than the normal feelings she usually picked up. The lower they went, the stronger the echoes became. Love, hope, fear, grief—they all resonated around her in a whisper that begged for her to listen.

Jason sent her some additional energy to reinforce her shields and exchanged a worried look with Alec. "I can pick up something through our bond, but I can't tell what it is. Do you know what's wrong, Ari? Do we need to stop?"

She shook her head. "No, I'm all right. It's just this strange pressure. I must be picking up on residual emotions from the former inhabitants. It's very strong though. I've never had this happen before."

Alec frowned and squeezed her hand. "I sense something through our connection too. We're almost to the bottom. Once we stop, we'll have to travel a short distance through the ruins and into a cavern. That's where the river is located. Do you think you can make it?"

Ariana took a deep breath, steeling her resolve, and nodded. The whispers were pressing down on her, but it was manageable for now. She wished she could remove her helmet to pull the moisture from the air, but it was easy to see why that would be dangerous. Many of the walls and ceilings had partially collapsed. With the vibrating groan of the mechanical lift moving downward, it appeared as though the remainder of the building could go at any time.

A few moments later, the lift stopped abruptly. Ariana stumbled slightly, but Alec wrapped his arms around her and pulled her against him.

He gave her an apologetic smile. "Apparently, it's a bit of a rough landing. Sorry about that."

Jason cleared his throat and gave them a sharp look.

Alec hesitated for a moment before releasing her, and she experienced a small pang of disappointment at no longer being in his arms. He gave her a knowing smile and leaned forward to open the metal door of the lift.

Ariana blushed, mentally chastising herself, and stepped down onto the reinforced floor and into another world. Sweeping her gaze around the room, she couldn't help but wonder how long it had been since other footsteps had traveled these floors. It was easy to understand the allure of scavenging in the ruins. Not only was there an element of exciting danger, but there were hundreds of mysteries just waiting to be solved.

Alec issued the order for the lift to return to the surface. She swallowed, her throat suddenly dry. Until the next group arrived, they were trapped underground. There was nowhere to go except forward.

Alec motioned for her to follow while Jason trailed close behind them. Although most of the debris had been cleared out or pushed to the sides, Ariana was able to make out remnants of old furniture she'd only seen in videos. The walls were dilapidated, with peeling wallpaper or paint. Some areas had collapsed completely, leaving nothing but a pile of rubble blocking access to other parts of the building or the earthen walls of the chasm. Metal bracers and supports had been installed to secure the walls and flooring.

Ariana was so caught up in looking everywhere at once that she missed a small pile of rubble on the ground. She tripped and fell forward, managing to catch her balance at the last second. Alec spun around and grabbed her arm, but it was too late. The miscalculation on her part had distracted her from maintaining the metaphysical barrier, and the heavy threads of energy began to swirl around her.

Cries of anger and fear were emanating from deeper within the ruins. It wasn't the normal emotional energy she usually picked up, but instead, she could actually *hear* the voices.

"It's coming down. I can't hold it."

"There's no time. We've got to get out of here."

"Run! Get out now!"

An overwhelming sick feeling rose inside her at the panic and terror she was feeling from these voices. Unable to breathe, she started to pull off her helmet, but Alec grabbed her wrists. He sent a strong wave of energy through their bond, encouraging her to reinforce her shields.

"Ari, you have to fight it. We're almost there. Please. You have to block it out."

She trembled, using Alec and Jason's offered energy to weave into her barrier. Through their shared connection, the two men were suffering too. The steady roar of voices continued to pound against her fractured mental barrier, demanding to be heard. There was so much fear and hurt. Even over the span of years since they had suffered, their echo of pain was still vibrant and real.

Alec said something to Jason, but she wasn't paying attention anymore. Ariana shifted her energy slightly and sent a healing wave outward, with the promise she would hear their pleas. The ghostly energy wasn't sentient, and her attempts to pacify it were pointless. She couldn't focus over their cries. How could the echoes be so potent?

Another strong wave of Alec's energy surrounded her, drawing her attention back to him. He winced against the onslaught of echoing voices. "Jason, need to get her to the river or back to the lift! It's too strong."

Ariana couldn't go back. If she managed to get to the river, it would be enough to reinforce her mental barrier. Focusing on her feet, she tried to block out the emotional voices and took a step forward. Her vision blurred, and for a moment she could see the faces. Ariana gasped. She knew those faces. That's why the energy was so strong and called to her. The three of them were close to where the people had been buried under so much rubble.

"Jason!" Her knees buckled, and she pressed her hands against the ground as tears streamed down her face. "It was here. They all died. They *knew* they were going to die. The ruins collapsed on them, and they were trapped."

Alec swore and removed both their helmets, tossing them aside. He knelt beside her and pulled her into his arms, holding her tightly. Jason started to object, but a shake of Alec's head stopped him. Ariana wrapped her arms around Alec, burying her face against his neck. His energy flooded through her, encouraging her to reinforce her barriers.

"Just breathe, Ari," he murmured, tugging off his gloves and running his fingers through her hair. He threaded more of his energy into the movements, and she quivered from the sensation. It was enough to distract her from the voices and make her focus on Alec. Through their connection, she could feel his agony from the transfer of residual emotions. She had to get a handle on everything.

"Here." Jason handed her an open hydrating pack.

She accepted it and took a long drink, noting his hands were shaking almost as badly as hers. The water energy from the small drink wasn't strong enough to fully block the voices, but it was enough to lessen the impact. When she finished, Jason took the empty container.

Alec tilted her head back, searching her expression. A deep sadness reflected in his eyes and pulsed along their shared connection. Horror struck her as she realized her brief lapse in maintaining her mental barrier had caused him unnecessary pain. Through her, he'd heard his mother's tormented cries moments before her death.

Refusing to allow him to suffer a moment longer, Ariana yanked off her gloves and took his hands in hers. What she intended could be done without contact, but her energy was far more effective with it. She looked up at him and directed her calming energy to flow into him.

Alec closed his eyes and lowered his forehead against hers. "Ari," he whispered on a sigh.

She might not be able to soothe the emotions of the deceased, but the living could still be helped. Drawing upon the surrounding residual emotions, she ignored the echoes of fear and pain. Instead, she focused on strengthening a softer emotion—love. It was the love these people shared for their families that should be honored as their dying declaration. If she couldn't give them the peace they deserved, she would help the ones they'd left behind.

Somewhere nearby was a strong source of water, and she reached outward with her senses to locate it. It was closer than she thought, and she took hold of it, drawing upon its energy to amplify her abilities. Ariana took a deep breath, letting the power fill her as she focused on the love each person had felt for the family they'd left behind. She held it for a long moment and then flung it outward, filling the ruins from its deepest depths up to its highest point with her energy. Alec and Jason gasped, swaying slightly from the unexpected outpouring of energy, and then their shoulders relaxed as the energy in the ruins began to shift. She felt the others in various parts of the ruins experience similar effects. Even the non-sensitives weren't immune to the dramatic change.

"How are you doing this?" Alec looked down at her with a touch of wonder in his voice.

Ariana shook her head, not sure if she had the ability to explain.

"Lars is right," Alec whispered, shaking his head. "You are a gift, Ariana. I'm not sure any of us deserve you."

"It's not me," she admitted. "It's them. Their last

thoughts were of love and family. I only strengthened those thoughts and shared them."

Alec's eyes softened as he gazed at her. "No, Ari. You had the ability to reach beyond their pain and turn it into something beautiful. It was you, with your wonderful and sensitive heart, who could shift the energy and heal this place. You're the most beautiful and courageous woman I've ever known, both inside and out."

She looked up at him. His words touched something inside her, and a strange feeling began to blossom. Over the years, she'd heard countless warnings that her talents could be dangerous and she needed to keep them hidden. There were many people who would, if given the opportunity, try to use her skills for their own purposes. Manipulating thoughts and feelings could easily shift political agendas or intentions, especially in their world. Their people had always been obsessed with power, and she could be a means to capitalize upon such power. But that wasn't the case here. Through their shared connection, she sensed Alec's sincere gratitude and sense of wonderment.

"I understand your family's fears better than most," he said to her telepathically. *"Our skills, yours for shifting emotions and mine for influencing people, can be dangerous in the wrong hands. That's why I supported your family's decision to keep your talents hidden while my father was still alive. I won't ever take advantage of you, Ari. I promise."*

Ariana looked down at their clasped hands, her heart aching for what he must have experienced. She hadn't realized he'd lived through the very thing her family had always feared would happen to her.

He lifted her hands, pressing a small kiss against them. *"It's not the same, beautiful. Our abilities have similarities, but they're also very different. It would have affected you more to use your talents in a way that wasn't natural for you. Influencing people is more of a strong suggestion. I've never had to experience their emotions."* He paused for a moment. *"I wasn't aware you felt everything so deeply. I knew you could sense emotions, but I had no idea you lived them."*

Before she could respond, Jason reached over to pick up their discarded helmets. He held them out, forcing them to release each other's hands to accept the offering. "If you're feeling better, we should go. I hear the lift descending again, and I'd like to limit the number of people around you until we get to the river. I don't think any of us can afford to have your focus split right now."

She nodded and took her helmet from him. Alec stood and helped her to her feet, but he didn't release her. Instead, he tucked her close to his side. Jason's eyes narrowed at the gesture. Her brother huffed and walked ahead of them, making his disapproval obvious.

Ariana sighed but didn't move away from Alec. If this was her only opportunity to be close to him, Jason was just going to have to deal with it.

———

ARIANA GAZED around the underground cave in wonder. The moment she'd entered the cavern, she'd taken off her protective gear. Since she wasn't suffering from any ill effects, Alec had allowed more personnel to enter the area. With the water rushing through the rocky cave, she felt more at home surrounded by her elements than she ever had in the towers. There was a sense of rightness at the perfect union between earth and water. They needed each other, and here they'd found a way to co-exist in perfect harmony. But there was something more to it. There was a power within the cavern that called to her, but she wasn't sure if it was more of the echoes of the past. Given what had already happened, she wasn't willing to risk lowering her guard to investigate.

Sergei crossed his arms and eyed the piece of equipment in front of him. "You will need to explain. I thought this equipment could not be operated with energy."

"It can't," Alec replied. "Our hope is Ariana and Jason can control the rapids enough to direct the equipment down the river without hitting any of the rocks. Since Ariana specializes in water and earth, we have a better chance of success."

Ariana nodded at the explanation. The process should be fairly easy. She probably could have accomplished this without Jason, but together, they should be able to send the equipment much farther than either of them could alone. Jason didn't have her skills with earth energy, but their bond would help amplify her ability to channel both.

She studied the layout of the river again. "I should be able to get a sense of the location of the underwater rocks by connecting with the earth energy throughout the cavern. Then, it's simply a matter of guiding the movement of the water to carry the device. Depending on the number of jagged surfaces, I may need to slow down or redirect the current a bit to get the equipment past the rocks."

Carl leaned over and pulled out a diagram showing the areas they'd been able to map. He pointed to a few specific areas not too far from where they were standing.

"We know for a fact these areas are particularly treacherous. We've lost four cameras here. A few made it beyond that, but not far."

He tapped on the screen and pulled up an image of the underwater topography. Ariana frowned as she leaned closer. From her studies, she recalled most underwater surfaces were smoother. Over time, the water wore away the sharper areas.

"This river is new," she mused.

Alec nodded. "That's our belief as well. If it was older, we should have had an indication it existed on some of our pre-war maps. We suspect when the earth energy was manipulated to cause the cave-in, it redirected a much older river to this location."

Kayla pointed to another area on the diagram a short distance away from where they were standing. "This is where I was scavenging when I originally found the river. Based on the size of the rock formations there, it looked like there used to be a much smaller branch of the river in that location. The cave-in opened it up and made the entire thing larger and, unfortunately for us, much more treacherous."

Ariana studied the image. They hadn't been able to map much at all. "We don't know where the river originated or where it ends?"

"No," Alec admitted. "We hope to eventually explore it fully, but for now, we need to focus on finding the best place to drill without compromising the structural integrity of the ruins. If we can map far enough downstream, we should be able to find an area to run the pipes to extract the water."

Ariana nodded and lifted her head to look around the cavern again. "All right. I need a few minutes to get a better feel for the cavern and the river. Once I'm finished, we should be ready for the equipment to be lowered into the water." She turned to her brother, who was still studying the diagram. "Jason, can you help me manipulate the water energy? If you can slow some of the rapids, it'll make it easier to push the device."

Jason nodded. "Of course."

"How close do you need to be to the river?" Alec took her hand and led her closer to the water. Sergei moved to stand on the other side of her.

Ariana looked around, considering her options. Ideally, she'd need to touch the river in order to form a complete focus. She could use something as simple as a hydrating pack or the moisture in the air, but it wouldn't have the exact same composition. Even a slight difference might affect her abilities. Since there was so much riding on this endeavor, they needed to maximize their chances for success.

"Is there a relatively safe location where I can touch water *and* land? I don't need to submerge myself, but I need to engage with both elements for the best possible outcome."

Sergei pointed out a small outcropping not too far away. "The river slows there. We can use a harness for safety, but you can still touch both. I will remain with you."

She beamed a smile at him. "Perfect."

Alec frowned but motioned for one of the men to retrieve a harness. As soon as he returned, Sergei took it from him and proceeded to fasten it around her waist. "Are you feeling better? You have more color."

She rested her hands on his arms for balance as he adjusted the harness. "Yes, proximity to the water helps. The air is full of moisture here and acts as a buffer from the emotions. I actually feel wonderful."

"Good," he replied and leaned forward to kiss her forehead.

Alec's jaw clenched slightly, and he motioned for Sergei to step back. "You can monitor the equipment better from back there. Even if she's feeling better right now, this will require a great deal of energy and concentration. It's best to limit Ariana's exposure to others while we attempt this."

Sergei arched an eyebrow. "Of course, but who will monitor you around our precious Ariana?"

Jason scowled at both men. "For fuck's sake, I turn around for two seconds and you two are all over my sister again. Let's just get this over with. I don't want to be down here longer than necessary."

Ariana sighed and decided the best tactic would be just to ignore them. They were all acting like children. She knelt, placing one hand against the ground and dipping the other into the cold river water. Closing her eyes, she breathed in deeply and let the wild energy fill her. It was exquisite and unlike anything she'd ever experienced. It was untamed and free. The water rushed down whatever path the earth dictated. The sheer force of it was overwhelming.

"Oh, Jason," she murmured, "you have to feel this. The river is so primal. It's almost like touching raw energy."

Jason stopped bickering long enough to approach her. He bent down to touch the water and stumbled, his foot slipping on the slick ground. Ariana watched in horror as he tumbled forward, plunging into the rushing rapids. She tried to dive toward him, but the harness yanked her backward.

"Jason!" Ariana screamed, scrambling to find the buckle for the equipment around her waist.

"Get him out of there now!" Alec shouted.

Jason struggled and flailed, slamming into the first outcropping of rocks. His head bobbed at the surface and disappeared from view as he was pulled under by the force of the river. He only had precious seconds before he reached the next rocky alcove that had destroyed the equipment. He'd never survive being thrown against the rocks a second time. Ariana knew he was injured or else he would have manipulated the river to slow the rapids.

There was no time for finesse. Ariana had to act. Shoving her hand deep into the water, she yanked the energy threads from the river directly into her body. The water slowed, almost stopping its flow, but a river wasn't designed to stop completely. It was a source of power that was constantly moving, and Ariana had circumvented its purpose. There were consequences to every action, and everyone in the cavern would pay the price if she didn't act quickly enough.

Slapping her other hand against the earth, she pulled the energy threads deep from within the earth's core. The ground shook and rose up, halting Jason's progression. She wove a powerful dam of energy around her brother, redirecting the remaining flow of water she wasn't holding around him. Ariana trembled from the exertion of simultaneously holding on to the earth and the water.

As the river dried up and a path formed to the unconscious figure now lying on the ground, Alec shouted instructions. She barely heard him, intent on holding back the tidal surge that threatened to be unleashed if she made the slightest error in judgment. Sergei, Alec, Lars, and Carl jumped into the riverbed, scrambling over rocks to reach Jason. Kayla tossed a rope toward them, and they hefted Jason up, using the rope to pull him and themselves to safety.

Once he was out, Ariana slowly began to release the earth energy threads back where they belonged. Her body trembled from the increasing force of the water. Although she ached to just release the energy, the water from the river was far more dangerous to everyone in the underground cavern. One wrong move, and she risked drowning them all. Taking a steadying breath, she slowly allowed the water to trickle through her shields. Gradually, more filtered through and the pressure lessened. Her shoulders slumped from fatigue, but she couldn't stop. Alec's hand landed on her shoulder, and she felt a renewed rush of energy he shared through their connection.

The energy helped strengthen her resolve further, and she carefully released the remainder of the river, allowing it to once again flow naturally through the cave. She pitched forward, but Alec wrapped his arms around her and held her tightly against him.

"Jason," she managed. "Is he all right?"

"I'm sorry, Ariana," Alec said in a gentle voice. "It doesn't look good. I've called for an aircraft to transport him to the towers immediately, but we haven't been able to revive him. We have someone working on him now."

Her throat suddenly felt dry as darkness edged at the corners of her vision. Alec held her, preventing her from falling, and sent another strong wave through their connection.

"Please, Alec, I need to go to him."

Without arguing, Alec lifted and carried her to her brother's limp body. She could still feel Jason faintly through their bond, but their connection was dwindling fast. Although the medic had tried to expel the water from his lungs, Jason hadn't regained consciousness. He was dying.

Ariana leaned over her brother, reaching outward with her senses. Using the last of her energy reserves, she wove earth and water together and placed her hands against him. Alec reached out to her, sending additional energy to support her efforts.

With a powerful surge, she focused on assessing each of Jason's injuries. The large lump on his head that had rendered him unconscious was the most worrisome. There was too much intracranial pressure. She eased her healing energy into him, reducing the swelling in his brain. His spleen had ruptured and three of his ribs had broken when he hit the rocks, puncturing his lungs. She fused them back together and yanked the remainder of the water from his lungs. Jason coughed and sputtered, gasping for breath. The rest of his injuries were minor bumps and scrapes.

Sergei turned Jason onto his side to finish expelling the water while the medic assessed him. Ariana slumped to the ground in relief and exhaustion. Alec wrapped his arms around her again, and she dropped her head against his chest.

"Remarkable," the medic murmured and checked his device. He glanced up at Alec. "We need to do a full battery of tests, but it appears the worst of the injuries have already healed."

"His brain... Make them check... There was swelling," she whispered, unable to keep her eyes open. She couldn't remember ever being so tired.

"Shh," Alec murmured in her ear, stroking her back. "Just rest, beautiful. I'll take care of everything. Jason will be fine."

Trusting him at his word, she slipped into unconsciousness.

CHAPTER SIX

ARIANA SAT beside Jason's bed in the medical wing and held his limp hand in hers. He was still unconscious, but the doctors had assured her it was a necessary healing sleep. They expected him to make a full recovery and be released the following day.

She squeezed her eyes shut, guilt consuming her at the thought of how close she'd come to losing him. If she hadn't insisted on having him accompany her to the surface, Jason wouldn't have been hurt. Not only that, but they hadn't even been able to evaluate the river like they'd hoped. The entire endeavor had been a failure.

Alec dropped his hand to her shoulder and gave it a squeeze. A light band of soothing energy wrapped around her at his touch. "It's not your fault, Ari. You saved his life. That's far more important than anything else. No one else could have done what you managed and gotten him to safety. What you accomplished was a miracle."

She looked up at Alec, sensing his compassion and sincerity through their shared connection. "You, Sergei, Lars, and Carl took a huge risk as well. Thank you for trusting me enough to hold back the water and for saving Jason."

He sighed and sat beside her, taking her hand in his. "We need to talk about what happened."

Ariana looked away, her gaze falling once again on Jason's still form. She focused on her brother's deep breaths, the movement reassuring her he'd eventually awaken. Although the immediate threat in the cavern had been subverted, the resounding backlash from her actions was still imminent. In this case, she'd gladly accept the consequences if it meant her brother would wake up healthy once again.

"I know what you're going to say, Alec. Even though you cleared a lot of people from the area, there were too many down there. I'm sure even now the rumors are circulating through the Inner Circle about what happened." She lifted her head to face him. "I can't hide anymore, can I?"

"No," he admitted and glanced at Jason. "I don't think you should either. I understand why it was necessary when my father was in power, but things are different now. There are no bracelets, and no one will force you to do anything you're not willing to do. I swear I'll protect you."

"Don't make promises like that, Alec," she chided softly. "I'm not your responsibility."

Alec hesitated and then lifted her hand, pressing a kiss against it. A small wave of his energy enveloped her, offering comfort and the hint of a promise of something more.

"Ari—" He stopped abruptly as the door was flung open.

Her parents rushed in, taking in the scene and Jason's still form. Ariana immediately stood, moving to the side and away from Jason's bedside. Her mother turned to her, making a dramatic show of hugging her tightly. Ariana wrinkled her nose at the smell of liquor that hung like a heavy perfume around Marguerite Alivette.

When she pulled away, her mother darted a glance at Alec

and gushed, "My darling girl. We heard what happened. You're all right?"

Ariana resisted the urge to sigh. It was only in public that Marguerite made an effort to act the doting mother. Behind closed doors, her mother barely interacted with them. She wasn't a cold woman, just unhappy. Her parents' marriage had been a calculated arrangement to produce powerful offspring. Unfortunately, while that part of the arrangement had succeeded, it didn't coincide with a happy marriage. Her father took every opportunity to occupy himself in political machinations, while her mother immersed herself in whatever liquor happened to be handy.

"Yes, Mother, I'm fine. Jason will be too," Ariana assured her. "They're just keeping him overnight for observation."

Unlike her mother, her father insisted on trying to control and direct every nuance of his children's lives. At least, every nuance of *her* life. Jason had far more freedom. And now, Devan Alivette was about to unleash his full fury on the room for circumventing his will.

"Was this *your* foolish idea?" he demanded in an icy voice, his cold, gray eyes focusing on Alec. The chilling snap of her father's energy filled the room, turning it cold enough Ariana could see her breath.

"Devan," Alec stood and acknowledged the older man, "I understand you're upset, but this is not the time or place for this. You are in a place of healing."

"You have the audacity to dictate to me?" he challenged, his eyes turning even colder in an unmistakable warning. "Dozens of our people died in those ruins at the hands of your father. Was it your intention to carry on your father's legacy? Your actions nearly killed my son and daughter."

Alec stiffened, his eyes narrowing slightly, but he didn't back down. "Watch yourself, Devan. I will say this once, and you will not question my integrity again. It was never my intention to put either Ariana or Jason in harm's way. I deeply regret that Jason was injured."

Devan took a threatening step toward Alec, the freezing lash of his energy pummeling against the room. The temperature plummeted, and frost began creeping up the walls, webbing outward with its frozen fingers. "You expect me to believe your words when you intentionally bypassed the Council and led my children into harm's way? It's only by the grace of the gods they're both alive at all. You've overstepped yourself, Tal'Vayr."

"Enough, Father," Ariana declared, using the moisture in the room to insulate herself from his cold fury. She stepped in front of Alec, not willing to allow her father to keep attacking him when it had been her decision to go to the surface. "This was not a Council decision. Alec explained the hazards on the surface, but it was *my* choice. *I* was the one who talked Jason into accompanying me. If anyone is to be blamed for what happened, it's me."

Her father's eyes narrowed on her. "Then we'll make sure it doesn't happen again. You will *not* leave the sanctity of our quarters again for any reason. As a result of your foolish decision, everyone within this tower will know about your abilities by the end of the week. I will not risk you being harmed or coerced into an undesirable bond."

With this declaration, the chill in the room slowly began to retreat. Devan turned back to regard Jason, who was still unconscious in the medical bed. "You've risked everything, Ariana, including your and your brother's life, to prevent some silly piece of equipment from being broken. Your purpose is greater than that. If I cannot trust you to make reasonable decisions, I will make them for you."

Something inside her broke at her father's harsh words. Ariana refused to be shackled again and imprisoned in her rooms. After having the first taste of freedom in years, she'd be damned if she was going to relinquish it. Straightening her shoulders, she lifted her chin in defiance.

Gesturing toward the shuttered window, she said, "I went to the surface to try to help the thousands of people dependent upon our ability to find new resources. My parents taught me we have a responsibility to protect not only our race but all of mankind. I listened well to your lessons, Father. Or were those just fanciful stories?"

He turned back to face her, but the derision on his face only inflamed her.

"We *need* the resources the river provides," she said, taking a small step toward him. "Not only for our people, but our alliance with the Coalition and the surface dwellers depends on it. If my talents and abilities can help bring peace to our people, I will do everything within my power to make it happen." She clenched her fists. "What I will *not* do, is hide away in my family's quarters as though I'm ashamed of my actions. I am *not* a child, Father. You don't have the right to dictate to me any longer. I will make mistakes, but they will be mine to make."

Devan Alivette stared at his daughter as though seeing her for the first time. Her mother's eyes welled with tears, and she nodded at Ariana. "Ari, you've made your point. Go and get some rest. Your father and I will speak with you later, after we've had a chance to discuss things."

Ariana swallowed and gave her parents a curt nod before turning and leaving the room. Once she was outside, she pressed her back against the wall and tried to calm her racing heart.

What in the world has gotten into me?

She'd never argued with her father like that. In the past, she'd relied upon her abilities to soothe the tensions in the room. Instead, she'd stood her ground and refused to back down. Alec had told her she needed to let things play out naturally. She shook her head, wondering if he could be right.

"Ari? Are you well?"

Ariana turned to meet Sergei's worried gaze. *Was* she well? Not really, but if she analyzed things too closely, she'd fall apart before she made it back to her rooms.

She smiled hesitantly. "Yes, I'll be fine."

He frowned and studied her thoughtfully. "Your brother?"

She nodded and pushed away from the wall. With everything that had happened, her emotions were spinning. All she wanted was to take a long shower to clear her head.

"Jason's going to be fine. They just want to keep him overnight for observation. He'll be released tomorrow."

"Come here, *solnyshka*," Sergei murmured and pulled her into his arms.

She went to him willingly, leaning her head against his chest. She needed the comfort more than she thought possible, and for some reason, Sergei made her feel safe.

"You are stronger than you believe," he said, running his hand over her hair. "It takes great courage to do what you did today. You saved Jason's life."

Ariana buried her face against Sergei's chest, curling her fingers into his shirt, and breathed in his spicy scent. "It wouldn't have been enough. If you hadn't helped to drag him out, he wouldn't have survived." She lifted her head to look up at him. "Thank you for my brother's life, Sergei. It's a debt I'll never be able to repay."

Sergei pressed a kiss against her forehead. "You do not owe me any debts, Ari." He paused for a moment, and a wicked grin crossed his face. "Your brother is a different matter though. I shall enjoy reminding him of that often."

Despite herself, Ariana couldn't help but laugh. Jason would hate being indebted to him.

"Ari?"

She lifted her head to see a tall, dark-haired man standing in front of her. Recognizing her brother's friend, Ariana straightened and offered him a warm smile. She didn't know him as well as Jason did, but he'd been close with her brother for the past several years. She held her hands out to him in greeting. "It's good to see you, Hayden. You're here to see Jason?"

He hesitated for a moment, eyeing Sergei with distrust, and took her hands in his. "I actually came to see both of you." He frowned and took a step closer, putting his arms around her and hugging her tightly. Hayden's heated fire energy surrounded her and offered a measure of comfort. "By the gods, Ari, I heard what happened and came straight away. Are you sure you're well?"

She nodded, allowing her cooler water energy to brush up against him. "Yes, I'm fine. So is Jason. He's sleeping right now."

"That's good to hear. I'm assuming your parents are with him?"

Ariana gently pulled away from him and glanced at the closed door, hoping she hadn't left Alec in an even worse situation. Her father could be difficult in the best of situations. It was astounding he could appear so much like an older version of Jason but lack much of his son's casual humor and warmth. "Yes, but I'm sure they won't mind if you pay your respects."

"Perhaps in a moment." He fixed his gaze once again on Sergei. In a voice that was unmistakably cold, he asked, "Who's your friend, Ari?"

Ariana blushed, ashamed at her lapse in manners. "I'm sorry. I'm not feeling myself today. I hadn't realized you haven't met." She gestured to Sergei. "Hayden, this is Sergei, the Coalition ambassador and a dear friend. He was one of the people who helped save Jason's life." She gave Sergei another grateful smile and motioned toward the newcomer.

"Sergei, this is Hayden Gavron of the Inner Circle. I believe you may know his uncle, William Gavron from the High Council."

The two men assessed one another for a long moment as though weighing each other as potential opponents. Sergei gave the man a brief nod before turning back to her.

"Do not apologize, *solnyshka*. You have been through a great deal today."

Hayden frowned and made a show of taking Ariana's hands again. "Allow me to escort you back to your quarters, Ariana. I'm sure you'd like to get some rest, and it'll give us a chance to talk privately."

Sergei's eyes narrowed, but he didn't comment. Ariana shook her head, not willing to fuel whatever tension was between the two men. "No, that's all right, Hayden. I appreciate the offer, but I know you came to see Jason. It'll mean a great deal to him and my parents to know you were here for him."

Hayden hesitated and then nodded. "Very well. I need to speak with your father about another matter anyway."

He lifted Ariana's hand, pressing a kiss against it, and sent another warm pulse of energy over her. This time, his energy was flavored with unmistakable desire and intent. "I look forward to seeing you soon, Ari."

Jason's previous words about Hayden's desire to court her came rushing back. She swallowed, making a conscious effort to pull the moisture from the air to insulate herself from picking up on any additional wayward emotions. She couldn't deal with anything more today.

Giving him a polite smile, she slipped her hand out of his. "You too, Hayden."

Ariana turned to Sergei and stood on her toes to kiss his cheek. "Thank you for being here and for helping Jason, Sergei. I don't know what I would have done without you."

"It is my pleasure," he replied, kissing her forehead. "Rest well, Ariana."

Ariana gave him another smile before turning away and heading toward the priority elevators. She desperately needed a long shower and a large glass of wine.

———

ALEC EMERGED from Jason's medical room with a combination of frustration and relief. After Ariana had left, the conversation with her father hadn't gone as well as he'd hoped. Although he'd managed to elicit Devan's agreement, Ariana's father had made it clear he wasn't pleased with Alec's role in taking Jason and Ariana to the surface. Whether he'd managed to avoid the minefield of Devan Alivette's retribution remained to be seen, however.

Alec stopped just outside the door at the sight of Sergei and Hayden glaring at each other. He glanced between the two men. "Is there a problem?"

Hayden straightened and gave Alec a brief nod in greeting. "No problem. I was simply commenting on how they've relaxed the rules about who was allowed onto this floor. I wasn't aware the role of ambassador provided outsiders with special privileges."

Alec arched an eyebrow while Sergei merely chuckled and leaned against the wall. With one last irritated look at the foreigner, Hayden turned to Alec.

"I'm assuming Ariana's father is still here?"

"Yes," Alec replied, suspicion creeping over him at Hayden's question. "Her parents are visiting with Jason. I wasn't aware you were so well-acquainted with Ariana."

Hayden gave a smug smile. "Now, Alec, if you remember correctly, I've known her longer than you. Besides, I've had many years to develop a close association with their family.

If you'll excuse me, I need to have a private word with Devan."

As Hayden disappeared into the room, Lars stepped off the priority elevator and approached them. "The cavern site is secure. Kayla and Carl remained behind to keep an eye on things. On the plus side, Kayla's more determined than ever to keep training with Ariana. As she put it, she wants to 'kick ass and take names.'"

Alec sighed, making a mental note to have certain training areas reinforced. Kayla would most likely be causing all sorts of problems once she returned to the towers and started this new wave of training. "I'll reach out to Kayla tomorrow. We're going to need to find someone else to try to navigate our equipment down the river. Ariana was perfect for the endeavor, but I'm reluctant to ask her again so soon with everything that happened today."

Sergei nodded, crossing his arms over his chest. "I understand, but if you cannot make progress within the next week, my people will require payment in the form of additional resources to accommodate this delay. Our leaders are not pleased with these continued excuses, and we are already in danger of not meeting our goals."

Alec inwardly cursed. Sergei's demand was understandable, but OmniLab was having enough problems of their own without needing to provide additional support to the Coalition's forces. Just that morning, he'd signed off on additional mandatory water restrictions. The High Council and Inner Circle were going to be in even more of an uproar if he had to initiate the next stage, which involved requiring additional support in harvesting resources. Ever since the cave-in sixteen years ago, their people were even more reluctant to venture to the surface. They'd most likely not have much of a choice though. Even though Sergei hadn't said it outright, he'd alluded to these frequent delays causing strain on their already fragile alliance.

"We'll make every effort to assist your people," Alec promised. "In the meantime, I'll try to locate a powerful enough water and earth channeler who may be able to aid us. I don't know of any bonded pairs strong enough with that particular alignment, but we'll begin making inquiries immediately."

Alec paused, thinking of Ariana and the connection they'd forged. Her unmistakable ease in wielding both elements simultaneously and the awesome display of power left no doubt she could easily accomplish the task. Although everyone in the cavern had been witness to her dramatic display, he was the only one who'd had an unrestricted view of her abilities.

There was something different about her energy though, as if it possessed a quality he'd never seen before. Whatever it was, it called to the most primitive parts of him. More than anything, he wanted to explore their newly-forged connection. He'd promised not to take advantage of her, but the idea of sharing energy with Ariana was intoxicating.

Even if Jason didn't return to the surface, the connection Alec had created with her might be strong enough to protect her against the emotional onslaught. Although, if he were honest with himself, he was tempted to ask her again so he could form an even deeper connection with her. At least now he had a better idea of what needed to be done to safeguard her from most negative effects.

"If we can't find someone, I'll discuss the possibility again with Ariana. We'll need to take additional steps to safeguard her though. I won't allow another incident to happen that might put her at risk."

Lars frowned. "How are Ariana and Jason doing?"

Alec rubbed the back of his neck, considering the conversation he'd had with her father. "They're both fine. Ariana was able to heal him before the damage was too great." He turned back to Sergei. "Did you see Ariana leave? I was hoping to speak with her."

"She returned to her family quarters," Sergei replied and gave a nod toward the closed door to Jason's room. "I would suggest keeping a close eye on the man who just went in there. I do not like the way he looks at our Ariana."

Lars frowned. "Who are you talking about?"

Alec clasped his hands behind his back. Hayden had been looking at Ariana that way for a long time. As far as Alec knew, Ariana hadn't looked back, and he didn't intend to give her the opportunity to start. "Hayden was here just a moment ago asking after Ariana."

"He looks at Ariana as though she is his marked prey," Sergei said with disgust. "She is uncomfortable with his attentions. If you have an interest in her, you would do well to make sure he stays away from her."

Alec arched an eyebrow. "Are you offering me a warning, Sergei? Here I thought you had designs on Ariana yourself."

Sergei shrugged. "You confuse her, but you will do nothing to harm her. That man, however, has a long-standing agenda. There is something about him I do not trust."

Lars frowned. "Heed Sergei's words, cousin. I don't know Hayden, but Sergei has a remarkable ability to read people."

"I see," Alec mused. He'd already decided to keep a closer eye on Hayden and everyone else close to Ariana. "I suspect Hayden intends to court Ariana. After her powerful display earlier, he will probably be one of many."

Lars chuckled. "Too bad you've already been kicked out of the running. I was considering trying to court her myself, but I'm afraid I still think of her as my little sister's best friend."

Alec's jaw clenched at the reminder he had previously been rejected by Ariana's father. "On the contrary, I've just finished speaking with Ariana's father and indicated my intentions."

Lars stared at Alec and laughed loudly. "I'll be damned. You don't waste any time, do you?"

Alec shook his head. "You're wrong on that account, Lars. I waited too long already. I should have acted a long time ago. That's my fault, and I just hope Ariana forgives me for it."

When his cousin raised his eyebrows in question, Alec sighed. "It doesn't matter. If you'll excuse me, I want to make sure Ariana made it back to her quarters safely. I need to explain some things to her and apologize."

———

ARIANA SAT on the edge of the bed and dropped her head into her hands. The events of the day had finally caught up to her, and the shower had only helped a bit. Her energy reserves were utterly depleted, and the last vestiges of strength had been used to argue with her father. She replayed her words in her head, still stunned by her behavior. She'd never raised her voice to him before, always using her abilities and talents to ease tensions rather than fuel them.

What's happening to me?

A chime interrupted her thoughts. Ariana stood, wondering who could be at her door at this late hour. Hastily tying her robe around her waist, she rushed to the door, praying it wasn't bad news about her brother. If his condition worsened after she left, she'd never forgive herself.

Sliding open the door, Ariana felt a moment of panic at the sight of Alec. She clutched the side of the door. "Is Jason okay? Did something happen?"

Alec didn't answer right away. He slowly perused her up and down, his gaze darkening with unmistakable heat. He swallowed and shook his head. "I should have realized... I'm sorry, Ari. Yes, everything is fine. Your brother is still sleeping. I should have called first. I wasn't thinking."

Ariana glanced down at the translucent robe she'd thrown over her nightgown. Even if she hadn't seen it in his eyes, she could sense his desire and very male appreciation through their shared connection. She flushed. "That's all right. I just... I wasn't expecting company. Give me a minute to change."

"No," he said hastily and took her hand in his. "You're beautiful. You should be comfortable in your own home. I didn't think this through, especially given everything that's happened today. I just wanted to speak with you before you went to bed."

Ariana bit her lip and stepped aside, allowing him to enter her quarters. He took in the surroundings, his gaze lingering on some of the plants scattered throughout the room.

"Your home is lovely," he commented. "I've never seen it before. You've managed to artfully weave together your affinity for earth and water."

She gave him a small smile at the compliment. "Can I get you a drink?"

He hesitated and then shook his head. "No, please. Allow me. Why don't you sit down? I'm the one intruding here."

"All right." She sat on the couch, watching curiously as he headed over to the bar area. In all the time they'd known each other, he'd only been to her family's quarters once but never to her private ones. It was strange and a little surreal to have him here now, fixing a drink as though he were perfectly at home.

Alec glanced over at her. "Do you still like a splash of water in your wine?"

Ariana nodded and gave him a small smile. "You remembered."

He frowned and looked down at the wine he was pouring. "I'm remembering a lot of things. I'm regretting even more."

Before she could question him, he carried over both glasses and handed one to her. The energy around him was chaotic, as though an internal conflict warred within him. She took a small sip and set her wine glass on the table in front of her.

"What's going on, Alec? You seem upset."

He hesitated and then put his glass aside. Taking her hands, he carefully traced a pattern over her hands with his thumb.

"I'm not upset, Ari. Not exactly. I wanted to speak with you about what happened earlier. In particular, about the connection we formed."

She blushed and resisted the urge to pull her hands away. This was going to be an awkward conversation.

As though sensing her thoughts, Alec chuckled. "No, nothing like that. I just wanted to tell you how much your trust means to me. I meant what I said earlier. I wouldn't have agreed to form a connection like this with just anyone."

She looked down at their entwined hands. "I don't want to think about what would have happened if you hadn't been there to give me the additional power I needed to heal Jason. Thank you for that."

"You don't ever have to thank me," Alec assured her and then paused, a faraway expression on his face. "Do you remember a year ago when I gave you that book?"

She smiled at the memory and nodded toward the shelf along the far wall. "Of course I remember. It's one of my most treasured possessions."

Alec looked in the direction she indicated, his eyes widening slightly at its place of prominence. He turned back to her and frowned. "I'm a fool, Ari. I'm so sorry if I hurt you."

Ariana pulled her hands from his, suddenly uncomfortable

with the conversation. "It was a long time ago, Alec. Things happened the way they needed to happen."

He reached for her again, grasping her hand tightly in his. "No, Ari, you don't understand. The same night I gave it to you, I came back after the Council dinner. I spoke with your father and asked his permission to court you. He... Well, let's just say he refused and not so delicately warned me away from you."

Ariana lowered her head and squeezed her eyes shut. She hadn't doubted Jason's words, but hearing it from Alec hurt more than she wanted to admit. If she had known back then, maybe things would have been different.

"You knew?" Alec's tone held mild surprise.

She shook her head and looked up at him. "No, not then. Jason told me yesterday."

Alec sighed and stood. He began to pace the length of the room, stopping at the shelf to look at the book he'd given her. She hadn't been exaggerating when she told him it was her most prized possession. Most of the literary works circulating through the towers were digital copies that had been written before the war. The few remaining ancient books still in their possession were highly coveted. At the time, though, it had represented so much more than their lost heritage.

"I was angry when he refused," Alec admitted. "That was my own arrogance. It wasn't until the following day that I had a chance to speak with Seara. I told her what happened with your father. She tried to talk me out of going to you directly, but I wouldn't listen. It was then she told me about your dual talents and her suspicions about your empathic abilities."

Ariana picked at the silver threading of her robe. "My parents wanted me to gain some specialized instruction on my earth-based talents. My teacher had passed away, and Seara was the only one they trusted not to betray me."

He ran his fingers over the protective book covering and

nodded. "I know. Seara made me swear not to reveal your secret. When I realized how dangerous it could be if my father became aware of your talents, everything made sense. I'd like to think that was the turning point for me. I became focused on finding a way to destroy those bracelets. If we could remove them, I would be free to pursue you."

Ariana stood and went over to stand beside him. Placing her hand on his arm, she wove a comforting embrace of energy around him.

"Alec, what happened wasn't anyone's fault. My father warned me away from you as well. I never blamed you for keeping your distance. In some ways, it made things easier."

Alec turned to look at her and reached over to brush a tendril of hair away from her face. Unable to resist, she leaned into his touch.

"Gods, Ari," he murmured, taking a step closer to her. "You have no idea how hard it was for me to stay away from you. I thought about you every single day and wished things were different."

"Alec, why are you telling me this now?"

He paused, his gaze roaming over her face, and his eyes filled with some unspoken emotion. His warm air energy surrounded her, drawing her closer. "I need to explain about Kayla." When she stiffened slightly and started to pull away, he held her tightly. "Please, Ari. Just listen."

She paused and then nodded, not wanting to know but knowing he needed to share whatever was troubling him.

He let out a long, drawn-out breath. "My relationship with Kayla was mostly a lie. You know we formed our bond as a way to keep the bracelet off her. It was the only way I could think to protect her. I owed Seara so much."

Ariana nodded. She'd heard the story before and didn't blame Alec for his actions. But she'd also seen him and Kayla together and knew their bond wasn't merely superficial.

"It wasn't," Alec admitted, listening to her thoughts through their shared connection. "I still care deeply for Kayla, and I always will. She's incredibly important to me, but you need to understand I'm not in love with her. She's not in love with me either."

Ariana looked up at him and frowned. Shaking her head in denial, she said, "I felt both of your emotions, Alec."

He gave her a sad smile. "No, you felt our love, but neither one of us was in love with the other. It was the bond and circumstances that drew us together. Once we were free to have a choice, both of us realized we weren't right for each other." He chuckled and shook his head. "If Kayla and I had met the traditional way, we probably would have ended up strangling each other within a month. We wouldn't have ever considered forming a bond together. We're always at odds, but we taught one another quite a bit. She needed a protector within the towers, and I needed to be able to look outside myself and see the world in a different way."

Ariana cocked her head, intrigued by Alec's words. "What do you mean?"

Alec reached up to cup Ariana's face, trailing his fingers along her jawline. "I'm not sure I would have been good for you back then. I was selfish, arrogant, and manipulative. It took what happened with Kayla for me to realize I didn't want to be that type of person. What she has with Carl is beautiful and right. He was willing to sacrifice everything to keep her happy and safe, even if it meant losing her. When I look at them together, I see two people who complement and strengthen one another. It made me realize I wasn't worthy of that same type of relationship unless I learned to put *my* needs and wants aside for someone else. Love is unconditional and absolute. Kayla helped me understand that."

Ariana's eyes welled with tears at his words. She could

sense his love for Kayla and also the sense of loss from their bond. "Alec, I'm so sorry."

He shook his head and gave her a smile. "No, Ari. Don't misunderstand. A bond is a wonderful and beautiful thing. I feel fortunate to have shared that with Kayla, even if it was created out of necessity rather than love. I admit that I miss having that connection and closeness with another person." He reached down and lifted one of her hands, pressing a kiss against the back of it. "One day, I'd like to have that again. But this time, it will be for the right reasons and with the right person."

Her eyes widened slightly at the implication in his words. "What are you saying?"

Alec's eyes warmed. "I spoke with your father again tonight, Ari. I asked him for permission to court you." He paused for a moment and shrugged. "Well, I suppose I should say I informed him of my intentions. I didn't give him an opportunity to refuse me again. I wasn't willing to risk it."

A laugh bubbled out of her. "Wait a minute. Are you saying you *told* my father you were going to court me?"

Alec chuckled and nodded. "After the shock from you yelling at him, mine was a minor offense. He'll get over it soon enough, I expect. Although, I doubt I'm his favorite person right now."

Ariana shook her head and pulled her hands away. Although part of her wanted this more than anything, she wasn't sure she could trust it. Ariana turned and took a few steps away from him, wrapping her arms around herself.

"What is it? What's wrong?"

She glanced back at him. "I'm sorry, Alec. I can't agree to this. I don't want you to court me."

His brow furrowed, and his expression filled with confusion. He took a half-step toward her. "Why the hell not? I know you care for me."

Ariana threw her hands up in frustration. "Alec, for lack of a better description, you have a hero complex. This is what you do. You've never been selfish. I don't know how you ever got that idea into your head." Unable to remain still, she started pacing the length of the room. "You saw Kayla in trouble and dove in to rescue her by forming a permanent bond with her. Now you're doing the exact same thing with me. You created a connection with me this morning to protect me too. Now that my secret's out and the entire Inner Circle knows about my abilities, you're swooping in again to protect me. I don't want you to sacrifice yourself because you think I need a strong bondmate. I won't do that to you."

Alec gaped at her for a moment and then threw back his head and laughed. Ariana scowled and put her hands on her hips, glaring at him.

"Why on earth are you laughing?"

He stalked toward her, the look in his eyes almost predatory. "I'll tell you why..."

Alec yanked her against him and lowered his head, his mouth claiming hers. She gasped in surprise and he swept in, taking full possession. Pressing his hand against the small of her back, he pulled her even tighter against him and fisted his other hand in her hair. Her body melted against his, and she curled her fingers into his shirt as he plundered her with his kiss. Energy poured into her, setting her senses afire with passion and desire. Ariana could no longer tell where she ended and he began.

The sensation of being in his arms and having his mouth on hers was more than she had ever imagined. She whimpered and clutched him tighter, afraid she'd lose him again if she let go for even a moment. His kiss gentled, and he reached up to cup her face. Pulling back slightly, he searched her expression with a look of wonder on his face.

"By the gods, Ari," Alec murmured. "If I had kissed you back then, I never would have been able to walk away. How can you possibly think I'm simply being noble when it's always been a struggle just to keep my hands off you?"

"Oh..." She blinked up at him, trying to clear her head of the lust-induced fog. He'd managed to scatter all her senses with his touch. "If you promise to kiss me like that again, I'm okay with you courting me."

Alec laughed and lowered his head again, pressing his lips against hers. He was gentler this time, but no less potent. Instead, he took his time exploring and tasting rather than consuming. She let out a soft moan, wrapping her arms around his neck. He drew her against him again, his energy teasing and caressing her.

When he finally broke their kiss a second time, he cupped her face and murmured, "You taste even sweeter than I imagined."

She looked up at him, afraid this was too good to be true. "Tell me this is real, Alec."

His eyes softened as he wrapped his arms around her again. She laid her head against his chest, and he threaded his fingers through her hair. "I'm not going away again, Ari. I promise. This is real. For as long as you want it to be."

She nodded, listening to his heartbeat and sensing his sincerity through their connection. "I've missed you so much, Alec."

"I've missed you too, more than you'll ever know," he murmured, continuing to hold her. "Those days we spent in the library together and hiding out from your brother were some of my happiest memories."

Ariana smiled and traced a small pattern over his chest. She never thought she'd have the opportunity to touch him like this, and she didn't want to stop. After she and Alec met at Kendra's party, he'd found out about her love for reading.

While Jason would visit one of the recreational areas, she'd curl up with a book in the library and spend a few hours reading. At least, until Alec started going to the library. From that point on, they'd spend the time talking or visiting one of the nearby shops or museums.

"They were some of mine too. Jason used to get so annoyed with me. I don't think I've been back since then."

"I know," he said in a quiet voice. "I looked for you on the library surveillance. I'm sorry if I was the reason you didn't go back to your reading spot."

She shook her head. "Not exactly. My father became suspicious of my activities. He restricted Jason's funding so he wasn't able to access some of his financial accounts without my biometrics. I'm guessing it was another way for my father to prevent me from seeing you alone."

Jason had been more than a little annoyed when it happened, and it had caused some problems between them. Even though they were twins, they had vastly different interests and needed their own space. Their father eventually relented, but he'd made his position clear about her desire to go off on her own. To keep the peace, she'd gone along with it.

Alec was quiet for a long moment. "I think you're probably right. I wish things would have happened differently, but I'm glad to have this chance with you now. I should probably warn you, though, there's going to be some competition for your affections."

She frowned and looked up at him. "What are you talking about?"

"Hayden went to see your parents after you left. I believe he was also asking permission to court you."

Ariana sighed. "I barely know him."

Alec raised an eyebrow and tilted her head back to look into her eyes. "Ari, you're going to get many offers now that people know about your abilities. I suspect he's just one of the first and is using his ties to your brother to press his suit."

She frowned, hoping he was wrong but worried he might be right. Their kind were always drawn to power. Her parents were proof of that.

"I suppose it's too much to hope that my father refuses them. I don't want to have to deal with a bunch of people I barely know wanting to pursue me."

Alec chuckled. "I think he'll do what he can to protect you, to a degree. If the past is any indication, your father won't give his consent lightly. But I think it's clear your shared bond with Jason is no longer going to be enough."

Ariana sighed and buried her head against his chest. "Jason said the same thing. I suppose all things have to change. We suspected this eventually might happen. I should be thankful we were able to keep it quiet as long as we did."

Alec stroked her back, tracing small circles and weaving his energy around her. Ariana relaxed against him and inhaled deeply, breathing in his rich, earthy scent. It was intoxicating. The combination of his touch and energy stirred something deep within her. She wrapped her arms around him, sending an accompanying wave of energy trailing over his skin.

He inhaled sharply and gently eased away from her. There was a trace of regret in his voice as he said, "I should go before it's too late, but I'd like to see you again tomorrow evening. Will you be available?"

She looked up at him in surprise, disappointed he was leaving so soon. "You're going now?"

He gave her a rueful smile and nodded, once more giving her a slow perusal that made her stomach flutter in response. "You're far too tempting, Ari. Being this close to you and feeling your energy, especially when you're dressed in only a lounging robe... well, let's just say my willpower is sorely being tested."

Ariana flushed, but couldn't resist teasing as she said, "It's your own fault for not calling first."

"I'd do the exact same thing all over again, if given the opportunity. Especially if it meant I could kiss you again," Alec replied, his eyes twinkling with humor. He cupped her face and brushed another light kiss against her lips. "Can I convince you to see me tomorrow?"

She smiled up at him and nodded. "I'd like that."

"Good." He took her hands in his. "I'll come by around seven. Will you let me cook for you?"

Her eyes widened with surprise and delight. For some reason, she hadn't thought he would have bothered to learn. "I didn't know you could cook."

He grinned. "Seara taught me. She claimed it would help impress a woman one day. You'll have to let me know if it works."

Ariana laughed. "That sounds like something she would say. When she was training me with my earth skills, she dedicated several lessons to edible plants. I really enjoyed learning from her." She was tempted to ask what he was planning to make, but the surprise would be more fun. Although, since she'd never advertised herself as being an earth talent, she didn't have access to the same types of ingredients Seara had in her garden. "Should I have anything specific here? If you tell me what you need to cook, I can order it."

"No, beautiful," he murmured, "I'll take care of everything. You just need to be here."

"I will," she promised and then paused as her gaze fell on a nearby plant. "I need to tell you something before you go."

He smiled and raised an eyebrow. "Oh? What's that?"

She bit her lip. "It's about Sergei."

Alec's expression became more guarded. "Yes, I'm aware you've been spending some time with him. What about him?"

"He stopped by last night to check on me."

Alec's body stiffened. "He was here? In your quarters?"

She frowned, absently weaving a reassuring wave of energy over Alec. "Yes. He wanted to make sure everything was okay after I left your office. When he was here, he overheard an argument I had with Jason. Sergei became concerned his presence might be dangerous to me. I told him I didn't think so. We spoke for a while. But before he left, I may have done something that could cause you a problem."

Alec cocked his head and studied her. "What did you do?"

She gestured to the Bird of Paradise plant on the table. "He'd never seen some of these plants before. I encouraged one to flower so he could see it in full bloom." She bit her lip and looked up at Alec in concern. "I had no idea the Coalition wasn't aware we possessed that ability. I never would have done anything to betray us if I had known. I thought, since he was in your office that day with Lars, he knew about my talents."

Alec let out a relieved sigh, and his shoulders relaxed. "It's all right, Ari. It was only a matter of time before they found out. The only reason they didn't know before was because there weren't any earth channelers with that particular ability in Lars's group. If it makes you feel better, I'll speak with Sergei."

She nodded, grateful she hadn't jeopardized anything. "Thank you."

Alec paused, glancing at the plant again. "Out of curiosity, what did he say when he found out?"

"He was surprised, to say the least. He said they had suspected we had other ways of growing food, but they had no definitive proof." She tilted her head to study the plant, wondering how difficult it must have been for them to survive without any of their abilities. "He promised he wouldn't do or say anything that would cause me harm, but he did say he needed to consider the implications and what this could mean for his people."

Alec nodded. "Sergei will keep his word. If nothing else, you can count on him for that. I'll speak with him tonight and offer to let him see the gardens in the Inner Sanctum. I believe Seara will be more than happy to show him around."

"She'll like that," she agreed. "I wonder if she would allow him to see her private gardens? They're spectacular, and I think he'd really enjoy it."

"I'll speak with her about it," he promised.

Ariana smiled up at him and kissed his cheek. "It's been a while since I had the opportunity to spend much time with Seara. Her gardens are one of the most peaceful places I've ever known. One day, I'd like to have something like that."

Alec glanced around her living quarters. "It would seem you're well on your way."

She laughed. "Not hardly. What Seara has created is extraordinary."

"Hmm," he murmured thoughtfully. "We'll have to see what we can do to make sure you have the same opportunity. Your gifts shouldn't be wasted. Now that you're publicly acknowledging your abilities, you can use some of them more freely."

"I hadn't considered that," she admitted, stunned by the possibilities. "I could really have my own garden one day."

"Yes," Alec replied, taking her hand in his once again. "You already do a lot with healing in the medical center, but engaging all your talents would benefit the towers a great deal."

She beamed up at him. "I hope so. I'd like to be able to help more."

Alec pulled her close and caressed her face tenderly. "Gods, Ari, you have no idea how long I've wanted to touch you like this. Do you have any idea how beautiful you are?"

She blushed and looked away. He lifted her chin with his fingers, tilting her head back to gaze into her eyes. He searched her expression and pressed another kiss against her lips. "If I don't leave now, I won't be able to leave at all."

Ariana curled her fingers around his wrist, holding on to him. "I don't want you to go."

Alec closed his eyes and took a deep breath, pressing his forehead against hers. "As much as it pains me to say it, I want to do this the right way." He opened his eyes and gazed at her with adoration. "Let me court you, Ari. There's too much at stake to treat what's between us lightly. You mean too much to me. I need to prove my worth, both to myself and to you. You deserve nothing less."

Touched by his words, she nodded and reached up to kiss him again. "Then I'll see you tomorrow."

"Tomorrow," he agreed and sealed the promise with another kiss.

CHAPTER SEVEN

ARIANA WOKE up the next morning, rolled over, and smiled into her pillow. Excitement coiled within her as she recalled the way Alec had kissed her the night before. She pressed her fingertips against her lips, imagining it all over again. It still seemed like a dream, and if so, she wasn't willing to wake up yet.

She had a lot to do before she saw him tonight. Her thoughts drifted toward her brother, and she frowned. The doctors had seemed confident last night, but she wasn't willing to leave anything to chance. She needed to check on him and make sure he was well enough to come home today. They discouraged visitors first thing in the morning, so she'd have to take care of some of her other errands first.

After dressing, she started to reach for her home comm-link to call her father and then stopped. He wouldn't take kindly to her request for an escort to the public district after their argument yesterday. She bit her lip, debating her options. If some of her secrets were well and truly out, there *was* someone else she could call. Making the decision, she pressed the button and called Brant, the Inner Circle Shadow who had been in Alec's office yesterday. Ariana smiled at Alec's half-brother as his image came on the screen.

"Good morning, Brant. I'm sorry to disturb you, but I need to visit one of the public sectors this morning. My brother is still in the medical ward and is unable to accompany me. Would any of your men be available to act as an escort?"

"Of course, Ariana," Brant replied. "I'm actually not too far from your quarters right now. I can be there within a few minutes, if you'd like."

"That would be wonderful," she agreed, beaming a smile at him. Alec trusted Brant implicitly, and Ariana trusted his judgment. It made the whole situation a little easier knowing Brant would accompany her rather than someone she didn't know at all. "And please, call me Ari. I appreciate you doing this on such short notice."

After saying goodbye and disconnecting, she sent a quick message to her parents to let them know she needed to speak with them later. Now that her father had had a chance to calm down, she wanted to resolve any differences between them and make her intentions clear regarding any courtship arrangements. She wasn't about to be put on the auction block based on whichever match they decided was most advantageous.

The bell chimed a moment later, letting her know Brant had arrived. She met him at the door and gave him a warm smile. There was a slight resemblance between him and Alec, but only if you knew to look for the connection. Their bone structure and shape of their eyes hinted at their familiarity, but their coloring was dramatically different. Brant's short, dark hair, hazel eyes, and bronzed skin were a sharp contrast to Alec's blond hair, blue eyes, and fairer features.

The two half-brothers had gotten close since their father's death. Brant had been instrumental in assisting Alec with the merger to include the Shadows as members of the Inner Circle. Even though the Shadows now carried new titles and responsibilities, many of them still preferred to keep their former identities as special security officers. Brant was one of them, but Alec had elevated him to the position of overseeing the entire Shadow division of tower security. It was a little strange he'd offered to act as her escort instead of delegating the duty, but she suspected he'd agreed because of Alec.

"Did you have a particular destination in mind?" Brant asked as they headed down the hallway.

She nodded. "Yes, I was planning to visit the garden center on the twentieth level. I wanted to see about arranging a gift for the Coalition's ambassador."

Brant stopped short, the crisp scent of his surprise permeating the energy in the surrounding area. Ariana took a deep breath, focusing on blocking the distracting emotions. Brant quickly recovered and entered the priority elevator with her.

"I see. I'm sure that can be arranged." He paused for a moment, and the elevator began moving downward. "I wasn't aware you were close with Sergei."

"Sergei helped save my brother's life yesterday, and I want to give him something to show my gratitude. A few days ago, he expressed an interest in some of my plants. I thought it might be a nice gesture to give him something that originated from his homeland."

Brant arched an eyebrow. "That's a very thoughtful gift."

She smiled, watching the panel indicate their descent. "I'm hoping they're able to help me find something. I had some ideas, but I don't know what they'll have available."

The elevator door opened, and Ariana stepped out into the busy thoroughfare. She didn't frequently come into the public sector and had to make an effort to fortify herself against the sudden onslaught of emotions.

At her pause, Brant spoke softly, "Please let me know if there's anything I can do to make this easier."

She glanced around and gestured toward a beverage kiosk. "They sell herbal teas there. I'll grab something and then I should be fine. We shouldn't be here long enough for it to be a problem." At least, Ariana hoped it wouldn't be an issue. The experiments she'd secretly conducted over the past couple of months had somewhat erratic results. She was able to withstand being around humans in limited capacity, but she still wasn't accustomed to exposing herself to so many all at once. It usually left her drained and lightheaded afterward.

Brant nodded and led her toward the small beverage stand. Ariana glanced over the selection of herbs, using her energy to test them for potency and effects. The merchant leaned over, obviously pleased by the interest of an Inner Circle member. "Is there anything that interests you, Mistress?"

Ariana pointed to two of the small jars on the stand. "Yes, I'd like a mixture of equal parts of those two herbs."

He nodded eagerly and began to prepare the drink. "Would you prefer it hot or chilled?"

"Chilled, please." Although her preference was for hot tea, she couldn't risk psychically cooling the drink. She needed to conserve her energy. Ariana glanced over at Brant. "Would you like something?"

"No, thank you. I'm fine," he said, sweeping his gaze over the passersby, warning them away with a hard look. Many of the non-sensitives in the towers were curious about her kind. She couldn't blame them, but it made it even more difficult for her on the rare occasions when she traveled to the public sectors.

Ariana pressed her palm against the payment panel and accepted the beverage from the merchant. Taking a sip of the brew, she was pleased by the subtle mixture of flavors. She wove the energy threads from the water into the surrounding energy, helping to reinforce her emotional barrier.

Brant raised a brow. "Better?"

At her nod, he led her down the corridor and toward the garden center. Once they were inside, Ariana took a deep breath. The rich scent of the earth and plant mixture was like a soothing balm, easing away her tension. It was almost as calming as the water energy in her hand. As she started to browse, Brant took a few steps away to make a call on his commlink.

A young woman approached her and bowed deeply. "Welcome, Mistress. Is there anything we can assist you with?"

Ariana glanced over one of the displays and smiled at the girl. "Yes, I'm looking to order a seed packet, but I have specific requirements. I'll also need accessories, depending on the type of plant you have available."

The woman nodded eagerly and pulled out a small tablet, anxious to be of service. "Of course. What sort of requirements do you have?"

"I'm looking for something that was available in pre-war Russia. I'd like an edible plant, preferably some sort of fruit or vegetable. No trees. It needs to be something smaller and easily portable. Maybe a small bush?"

The woman entered her specifications into the tablet and showed her a list that populated the screen. "Unfortunately, many of these seeds are restricted. We would need special authorization to retrieve them from the vault. The ones I've highlighted are possibilities that might suit your needs."

Ariana tapped her finger against her bottom lip, considering the choices. None of the available options were quite right.

Brant cleared his throat. "Pardon the interruption, but Mistress Alivette's purchases have been approved by Master

Alec Tal'Vayr. This is to be registered as a diplomatic transaction in your records."

The woman's eyed widened as she nodded. "Of course."

Ariana looked over at Brant in surprise, a wave of gratitude and excitement unfurling inside her at the possibilities. Since she'd never publicly claimed herself to be an earth talent, she'd never been put on the approved list to receive the rare seeds. This was Alec's way of giving her the opportunity while still allowing her to keep some semblance of anonymity. At least, until word got out to the rest of the Inner Circle about what happened underground.

At Brant's encouraging nod, she grinned and eagerly studied the list again. "I'd like one of the arctic raspberry seeds and the supplies to go along with it."

"Right away," the woman agreed and entered in the order. "If you'd like to join me at the reception, you can pick out the accessories you'd prefer. The seed is being retrieved from the vault. It should be here momentarily."

Ariana followed the woman over to the desk and looked over the supplies listed on the screen. She made her selections and the merchant retrieved each item, placing them on the desk for inspection. The small pot was simple but elegantly crafted and perfect for her purposes. She didn't want anything that would detract from the plant itself.

Ariana moved on to the next item. She rested her hand on the small bag of soil, sending a thread of energy into it. The soil was fertile and vibrant, with the perfect composition for growing the particular plant she'd chosen. There was also a small light with a timer programmed to achieve maximum results. Ariana lifted her head and nodded at the woman, indicating her satisfaction with the items.

A moment later, a small, gold envelope appeared in a glass chute on the far side of the desk. Ariana pressed her palm against the console to unlock it, pulled out the envelope, and peered inside.

The solitary seed lay nestled in the envelope, so innocuous and unassuming, but its value was immeasurable. She surrounded the seed with her earth energy, sensing its readiness to germinate and grow. Lifting her head, she couldn't help the wide smile that crossed her face.

"It's perfect."

———

ARIANA HAD LEFT Brant once she'd finished in the public sector. He'd offered to accompany her on the rest of her errands, but she declined. Brant was very kind, but she'd never felt overly comfortable around the Shadows. She'd always kept her distance from them in order to keep her talents a secret in the past.

If she allowed herself, she could read their emotions as easily as any other Inner Circle members. Their ability to negate energy also didn't affect her in the same way it did others of her kind. Ariana suspected she could break through their barriers as easily as Kayla, but she wasn't willing to risk attempting it. Just because some of her secrets had been revealed didn't mean it was wise to change years of behavior on a whim. Sometimes, it was better to err on the side of caution.

Ariana shifted the priceless box in her arms and pressed the button next to the door. She bit her lip, unsure what sort of reception she'd receive at arriving unannounced. She'd wanted this to be a surprise, but maybe this wasn't the best idea. Before she could change her mind, the door slid open, and Sergei's eyes widened at the sight of her. He hastily moved forward to take the box out of her arms.

"Ariana? It is a pleasure to see you, but what is all this?"

She smiled at him and tucked her hair behind her ear. "A gift. May I come in?"

He moved aside, allowing her to enter, and carried the box over to a nearby table. She took the opportunity to study his living quarters. It was one of the few finished residential units in the construction tower. It would be several more months before the rest of his people began to move in.

Despite herself, she was curious about Sergei. The room he was staying in was small and the furnishings were sparse. It fit with the militaristic perception he presented, but she couldn't help but wonder about the man behind the façade. Who was he, and where were all the possessions that showed a glimpse into his real life? He was as much of a mystery now as when she first met him.

Ariana turned and met his gaze. His lips twitched in a small smile as though guessing the direction of her thoughts. "You are curious about me?"

She nodded. "You're hard for me to read, much harder than a lot of other people." Trailing her fingers on the back of a chair, she wondered if he frequently sat in it or if it just came with the space. He gave off the impression of constantly being in motion. It was hard to imagine him completely relaxed.

"Ah, but you must be disappointed," he commented and gestured to the room. "I do not spend much time here. It is simply a place to rest."

She cocked her head and moved closer to him. "Is there no place you call home, Sergei?"

He leaned back against the wall, watching her. "Not for many years."

Ariana frowned. It seemed a lonely existence. It bothered her more than it probably should. Maybe it was strange to feel this connection with Sergei given he wasn't a *Drac'Kin*, but something about him drew her in. A small scar on the back of his hand drew her attention and she reached out, taking his hand in hers.

He didn't object and merely continued to observe her as she turned over his hand, looking at his palm and the back of his hand. The softness of her skin was a sharp contrast with the hard calluses on his fingers. Whatever had happened had resulted in a serious injury. She traced over the scar with her fingertips, sensing the residual damage under the surface. It must have taken a long time to heal, and it still pained him on occasion.

"Will you tell me what happened?"

"An argument with a knife," he replied in a dispassionate tone, as though recounting something inconsequential.

Ariana frowned and instinctively wove a band of healing energy around him, calming the angry nerves in his hand. Her skills didn't usually work as well on non-sensitives and required more energy, but she couldn't sit back and let him continue to be in pain. As she wove her energy around him, she could sense his energy trapped beneath the surface. He responded to her healing better than she expected, but it was as though something was blocking or preventing her energy from reaching his.

"You have a delicate touch, Ariana." He lifted her hand, the ring on her finger glinting in the light. He studied it for a moment and then pressed a kiss against her hand. "That is a beautiful ring. It becomes you."

"Thank you. It's been in my family for generations." She adjusted her ring, making a mental note to take it into the jeweler. It was a little loose on her finger, and the rare deep-blue stone needed to be polished. The color had always reminded her of the calming sensation of water and the allure of Alec's blue eyes. It was almost an exact match.

Ariana looked up at him and smiled. "I'm sorry. You must be wondering why I showed up unannounced." She gestured to the box sitting on the table. "I wanted to bring you something. It's to thank you for everything you did yesterday and also a goodwill gesture between our people."

Sergei arched an eyebrow. "Now I am intrigued. Will you show me?"

She nodded and reached over to open the box. As she removed the contents, placing each item on the table, Sergei leaned over to investigate. "What is all this?"

Ariana turned to look at him, clasping her hands together. "Right now, it's just raw potential. But when we're finished, it'll be a plant. More specifically, a plant called an Arctic Raspberry. It's native to your homeland. The flowers are very pretty, but more importantly, it grows these small, sweet fruits that were considered a delicacy before the war."

Sergei studied the items and then focused on her. "You will grow this plant for me?"

She beamed a smile at him and handed him the pot. "Even better, you're going to help me."

Sergei stared down at the pot with a perplexed look on his face. He seemed so out of his element she was tempted to laugh. She didn't think he would appreciate it though, so she suppressed the urge and pointed to the bag of soil.

"Pour the soil into the pot. You're going to want to use the entire thing. It's already pre-measured."

He did as she instructed, pouring carefully as though the soil was a precious substance. In truth, it was. But the care and seriousness he was taking with the entire process touched her. "Now what?"

"You're going to poke a small hole in the dirt with your finger." She leaned over, taking his hand in hers, and demonstrated what she meant. Once it was the appropriate depth, she picked up the gold envelope. She took his hand and turned the envelope upside down, letting the tiny seed fall into the palm of his hand.

"It is so small," he murmured, studying the seed.

She nodded, continuing to hold her hands around his and embracing the small spark of hope that was contained inside. "Yes, but I can feel the life and potential within it. It'll grow into a strong plant for you, Sergei."

He lifted his head to meet her gaze. "You can sense it?"

"Yes," she admitted, looking down again at the tiny seed. "Not all earth channelers can manipulate plant energy, but some of us can. I can sense the life in the seed and call it forth. It's actually more of a coaxing than anything else. If the seed were dormant, nothing I could do would make it otherwise."

He considered her words and nodded. "I see. What do I do?"

Ariana showed him how to plant the seed and covered it with the soil. She reached over and picked up a hydrating pack, explaining what the young woman in the garden center had said about the care of the plant. "I brought you a light and the timer has already been set on it. Once I grow the plant, I'll come back every day to check on it until it's established. I don't think you'll have a problem though. Supposedly, these plants are very hardy."

Once the seed had been watered and the soil was sufficiently moist, Ariana said, "I'm not sure if you can feel the earth energy, but I'd like to try this with you. It may be that you just get the slightest tingle from it, but I want you to experience as much of this as possible."

When Sergei nodded, Ariana took his hand and held it with hers over the seed. Using the earth energy threads that surrounded them, she reached into the soil and connected with the energy contained within. The small spark from the seed called to her, and she answered in a wordless song, coaxing and calling it forth. The seedling began to sprout, unfurling itself from its long-awaited sleep, and she heard Sergei's sharp intake of breath.

The plant continued to grow, reaching and stretching outward as though awakening from a long slumber. Small buds formed and then burst to life in a flowering salute before bright-red berries formed on the ends like fingertips.

Ariana pulled back on the earth energy, satisfied the plant had received a strong start in its life. It would only continue to thrive under Sergei's guidance.

She glanced over at him and couldn't help but smile at the awestruck expression on his face. Reaching over, she plucked one of the berries from the limbs and held it out to him.

"Will you try it?"

He stared at the small, red berry and took it from her hand. Holding it up, he studied it from every direction as though unconvinced it was real. Ariana didn't stop the laugh this time.

"Go ahead and taste it," she urged, pulling off another berry and popping it into her mouth. Her eyes widened at the explosion of flavor on her tongue. It was even better than she had imagined.

He arched a brow at her, put the berry in his mouth, and closed his eyes as though trying to memorize the taste. When he swallowed, he stared at the plant with a look of wonder and then turned the same gaze on Ariana.

"Even after seeing, I do not understand how this is possible," he admitted.

She gave him a small smile. "There are many things in life we don't understand. Sometimes you just have to accept it."

He took a step closer to her. "I did not think one such as you could exist in this world. You create miracles."

She lowered her gaze, touched by his words. "I'm just thankful you accept me for what I am. You don't question me or try to dissect every small thing. You just accept my abilities. It's easy to forget myself around you. I don't have to pretend to be something I'm not."

He wrapped his hand around the back of her neck, causing her to look upward at him. "You should not pretend, Ariana. I told you I am not a good man." Before she could object, he shook his head. "It is true, *solnyshka*. I should not be here with you like this, but you offer redemption I do not deserve. I would be a fool not to take it. You are truly an angel, and a gift from God."

Ariana searched his expression, her heart aching from the pain in his eyes. She reached up to cup his face, wishing she could ease the rest of his hurts. "I don't believe that, Sergei. I see the good in you. Our past doesn't define us. Our choices in the future shape our destiny."

He gave her a small smile and brushed his thumb across her lower lip. "Tell me, Ariana, what do you see in your future? What do you want?"

She blinked up at him and blurted out the first thing that came to mind. "Alec asked to court me."

Sergei threw back his head and laughed. "Of course he did. He would be a fool not to pursue you."

She bit her lip, wondering if she was misreading the entire situation. "Are you pursuing me?"

His grin widened. "Would you object if I were?"

Ariana frowned. She'd never considered being with someone who wasn't one of her own kind. Her brow furrowed at the thought, and she sputtered, "But... but I'm not like you. I don't... I don't even understand how you communicate without energy."

He chuckled. "Explain it to me. Help me understand our differences."

She bit her lip, trying to find the words to explain. "I'm not always good with words. They seem to come secondary. We rely on our energy to show how we feel. Maybe that's wrong, but it's just a part of how we communicate. Sometimes, when I talk to outsiders, I feel like I'm speaking a different language." She looked up at him and tilted her head. "It's like there's an entire layer of communication that's missing. I'm only speaking in black and white, but when I communicate with other *Drac'Kin*, there are thousands of shades of color."

Sergei nodded. "I believe I understand. But there is an adjustment when learning a new language or culture. It takes time to understand all the nuances."

"I don't even hear the nuances," she muttered in frustration.

He chuckled. "You must learn communication is not only words." He gave her a long, slow smile and took a step closer. Lowering his head, he pressed a small kiss against her neck. He inhaled deeply as though smelling her skin, and the sensation of his warm breath against her neck sent a small shiver through her. Wrapping his arm around her, he drew her closer against him. "Thousands of nerve endings are in your body, Ariana. That is thousands of ways to communicate without words or energy."

She swallowed. She pressed her hands against his chest, and the heat of his skin beneath his shirt radiated against her palms. "What are you trying to tell me?"

He leaned back slightly but didn't release her, and a knowing smile crept over his face. "It is what you are telling me."

"What?"

He leaned forward, hovering just a hairsbreadth away from her. "You, your eyes, your body... everything tells me you want me to kiss you. Is that what you want?"

Was it? By the gods, she was a mess. She licked her lips and wondered what the heck she was doing. "I don't know. I agreed to allow Alec to court me. I shouldn't want to kiss you. Should I?"

"Do you have a permanent bond?"

When she shook her head, he moved the rest of her hair off her neck and nuzzled her once more. "Mmhmm. I have looked into your courtship ways. Have you made any promises?"

"No," she whispered, feeling his heated words against her neck.

No promises were supposed to be made for at least a month. Their ways were somewhat archaic, but it was designed to prevent challenges between bondholders. Sergei had obviously done his research, but even so, they weren't the same. He wasn't a *Drac'Kin*. He could never give her what she needed. They were too different.

He leaned back, cupping her face and searching her expression. "Then tell me, Ariana," he demanded. "If there are no promises between you and nothing holding you to him, what do you want from me?"

"I..." she floundered and blinked up at him. Gods help her, but she was curious. Was this what Kayla had seen in Carl? She needed to understand the differences between them. "I want you to kiss me."

The moment she uttered the words, Sergei lowered his head and took possession of her mouth. That was the only way to describe the sensory explosion. She could taste the berry on his lips. The accompanying sweetness was a sharp contrast to the heated edge of his kiss. She wrapped her arms around his neck, giving herself over to the sensations coursing through her.

He took his time tasting and exploring her. It wasn't just his lips either. His hands moved over her body, alighting her senses and caressing her with their teasing exploration. She leaned into him further, wanting to know more. He was an expert teacher, sweeping in and taking control of the kiss, showing her by example and demanding a response.

As his hand slipped beneath her shirt, brushing against her heated skin, the door pinged loudly. Sergei froze and slowly drew back, as though surprised he'd lost control and forgotten himself for a moment. Ariana looked up at him with the same sense of wonder she'd seen in his expression earlier.

He hesitated for a moment and then cupped her cheek. "I was right about you. You are far more dangerous than you appear, *solnyshka*."

As she pondered the meaning of his words, he pressed another kiss against her lips and turned away to answer the door. She leaned against the table for support, pressing her fingers against her swollen lips, and tried to figure out what had just happened. There was no doubt she was attracted to Sergei, but her feelings for Alec ran much deeper. She had the suspicion that no matter who courted her, she'd given her heart to Alec long ago.

"Good, you're here," Lars greeted Sergei and stepped inside, oblivious to her presence. "I need to speak with you about this nonsense with..." His voice trailed off as he spotted the raspberry plant, and then his eyes widened at the sight of Ariana.

Lars's expression grew alarmed, and his entire body stiffened. His gaze darted back and forth between her and Sergei. "I apologize. I wasn't aware you had company."

Ariana's face flushed, fully aware he had probably guessed what had transpired between them. She gave Lars a small smile and walked over to him. Pressing a kiss against his cheek, she sent a wave of her cool water energy over him in greeting. "It's good to see you, Lars. I just stopped by to bring Sergei a gift. I owe you a thank you for helping Jason yesterday as well."

Lars's jaw clenched for a moment, and he shot a dark look at Sergei before softening his gaze and looking back at her. He reached down for her hands and gave them a small squeeze, trailing his gentle air energy over her. "You owe me nothing, Ari. I can never repay you for your healing gift." Lars looked over at the plant. "You never fail to amaze me. Your talents have exceeded all expectations."

"Thank you," she murmured and glanced over at Sergei. He was still watching her thoughtfully but hadn't said anything since Lars arrived. There was a tension between the two men, and she guessed she was partly the cause, but she didn't want to invade their privacy by probing their emotions. "I should probably get going. I need to stop by the medical ward and check on Jason."

"Of course," Lars replied.

Sergei stepped forward, taking her hand and drawing her way from Lars. He wrapped his arm around her and pressed a kiss against her forehead. "I will see you soon, *solnyshka*. Thank you for the precious gift."

She nodded and gave him a small smile before leaving the two men alone.

———

"WHAT THE FUCK WAS THAT?" Lars demanded, switching to Sergei's native tongue the moment Ariana left. "What were you thinking?"

Sergei's gaze grew cold as he regarded his former companion. "You question me, Lars?"

Lars fell silent, and he began pacing the small length of the room. Sergei ignored him and reached into the cooling cabinet to pull out a bottle of vodka. After kissing Ariana, he needed that and a whole lot more. She'd stirred up more memories and emotions than he'd anticipated.

Fuck.

Taking a seat at the table, he poured the cold liquid into a glass and downed it. Leaning back, he watched as Lars ran his hands through his hair. In truth, he hadn't seen Lars this agitated since the entire debacle with Kayla. It mirrored how he felt at the moment, even if he outwardly appeared composed.

Sergei poured more vodka into his glass and stared at the plant. He was still having trouble getting his head around it. And her. God, she was potent.

"You need to stay away from Ariana," Lars said with a sigh and slumped into one of the opposite chairs. He grabbed an empty glass and pulled the bottle away from Sergei.

"I do not recall asking for your opinion," Sergei replied, keeping his tone neutral.

Even if he agreed with the former exile, he had no intention of admitting it. Lars, like the rest of these Omnis, had a tendency to ask too many questions, and there were some things he wasn't willing to discuss.

Lars finished pouring his drink and brought the bottle down onto the table with a *clank*. "No, you damn well didn't, but you need to listen in this case. Ariana needs the protection only one of our kind can offer. Not only does her natural resistance weaken when she's around others, but after that display yesterday, she's going to have just about every power-hungry *Drac'Kin* male in the towers after her."

Sergei took a drink and swirled the liquid in his glass, using the motion to test out the old injury in his hand. He'd been right. She'd done something to him when she touched him. His hand felt better than it had in years, but he couldn't help but wonder what it had cost her. "I am aware of the dangers."

"Then what the hell are you doing with her?" Lars demanded. "Fuck, Sergei, if Alec wasn't already trying to

court her, I'd be doing the same just to protect her. I understand the whole game thing with Kayla. Hell, I played it too.
But Ari's different."

Sergei drummed his fingertips on the edge of the table,
growing annoyed at Lars's continued warnings. "She was here
for some time today, Lars. I spent time with her yesterday
too, and the day before. She hasn't given me any indication
she was suffering from any ill effects."

Lars froze, his eyes narrowing on Sergei. "What are you
saying?"

Sergei shrugged. "Ariana was the one who sought me out.
She is curious about me, and I do not believe I am a danger to
her. She may suffer effects from being around others, but she
has not given me the same impression."

Lars took a large swallow of vodka and winced. "I still
don't know how you drink this stuff. After all these years, I've
still not gotten used to it." He stared at the half-empty glass
for a long moment before pushing it aside. "Let's say you're
right. Let's say you're safe for her to be around. But then
what? Fuck, Sergei, she's a complete innocent."

"There is that," Sergei agreed and refilled his glass. He
thought back to the softness of her skin and the way she'd
felt pressed up against him. Even her scent was intoxicating.
It was all just another reminder of what he'd lost. "It is difficult to be faced with such heart-wrenching beauty and remain
impassive. Could you do any less?"

Lars scowled at him. "I damn well could. You can't sit here
and tell me you didn't put your hands on her. I could see it in
her face."

Sergei stood from the table, leaning over it to glare at the
former exile. "You overstep yourself, Lars. I will not warn
you again."

"You're wrong, Sergei. In this, I'm not overstepping
anything," Lars retorted and pushed away from the table. "I

just got word that Hayden, the asshole from yesterday, asked Ariana's father for permission to court her. Her father agreed. Alec wanted me to look into Hayden's activities, and I don't like what I see. I came here to tell you that I think you're right about him being dangerous to Ari, but I need help proving it. Alec can't get involved without jeopardizing his chances with her."

Lars paused at the door and gestured to the blooming plant. "Think long and hard about what you're doing with her, Sergei. Ariana needs a future, and unless I'm mistaken, that's not something you're prepared to offer. If you toy with her, you could end up destroying her and all she represents."

CHAPTER EIGHT

ARIANA DIPPED her hand into the reflecting pool, letting the water trail between her fingers. She'd felt more lost in the past few days than she had in years. Her emotions were a jumbled mix, and she wasn't sure how to begin sorting them out. She was so used to being at the other end of the spectrum—offering a calming touch to ease other's burdens—it was strange she couldn't do it for herself.

"Ari?"

She turned at the sound of Alec's voice. His footsteps were quiet as he breeched the solitude of the meditation room.

"I didn't mean to interrupt your reflection. Do you want me to come back later?"

She shook her head and returned her gaze to the water. "No. I was just trying to make sense of everything, but it doesn't seem to be working."

He frowned and sat beside her. Ariana lifted her hand from the water, sending hundreds of droplets up into a pattern and giving them the appearance of dancing in midair.

She froze them in place for a moment before letting them fall back into the pool.

Alec placed his hand on top of hers. "Would you like to talk about what's bothering you?"

Ariana lifted her eyes to meet his. She offered him a small smile and wrapped a band of soothing energy around him, not wanting to worry him. "Jason's coming home in a few hours."

"I heard," he replied, studying her carefully. "I don't believe that's what brought you here though."

"No," she murmured and looked out at the water again. "Alec, do you believe we rely too much on our abilities?"

He frowned. "No. I'm surprised you would ask. You're a *Drac'Kin*, Ari. This is who and what you are. Manipulating energy is part of that."

She nodded and raised her hand, sending another wave of droplets dancing in midair. It was as natural as breathing, but no one outside this tower would agree. "I know, but do you think we've stifled our other senses by relying too much on our energy?"

His brow furrowed, and he lifted her chin so he could study her face. "What happened today? These aren't idle questions."

"I took a plant to Sergei." She frowned, placing her hand back in her lap. "I tried to explain how it was sometimes difficult to communicate with outsiders. There's so much emotion in energy. It's hard to remember to not use it when I'm dealing with them."

Alec rubbed his thumb over her hand and wrapped his energy around her, offering a comforting embrace. "There's nothing wrong with that. It's our nature."

She gave him a sad smile. "That's just it. We do it instinctively. It's like trying to speak to them using a handful of words instead of the full scope we can access. It's flat and one-dimensional."

"You were raised primarily knowing your own kind," Alec pointed out. "It's easier for some who regularly spend time in both worlds because they've already learned this other 'language.' You don't have the same experiences."

"I know," she admitted and sighed. "I told Sergei I wanted him to kiss me."

Alec froze for a long moment, and she felt a myriad of emotions rush through him. As he struggled to dampen their connection, she stood to distance herself from his emotional turmoil. It was hard enough to manage her own emotions right now.

"I want to understand, Alec. They communicate on a level we don't. I don't know if it's because we've become so dependent on our abilities that we don't pay attention to our other senses, or if it's because they've learned to compensate for not having energy. I want to understand why Kayla was drawn to Carl. Why would she willingly choose one of these outsiders over our kind? I don't understand."

Alec's eyes widened, and his mouth curved upward in a smile. "Wait a minute. Are you telling me you conducted a test on Sergei to see if he had the ability to... erm, arouse you as well as one of our kind?"

Ariana flushed bright-red. She covered her face with her hands and sank back down on the edge of the pool. "Gods, you're right. That's exactly what I did. What's wrong with me?"

Alec threw his head back and laughed. "And how did that experiment go?"

She leaned over and smacked him lightly. "Stop it. I'll have you know I enjoyed it a great deal. I'm attracted to Sergei."

Alec's expression quickly sobered. "I'm aware of your interest in him, Ari."

She looked at him. "Don't get snippy, Alec. I like him, but

I've only known him a handful of days. I've been half in love with you for almost two years."

Alec's gaze softened, and he reached over to take her hand again. "Only half?"

She laughed. "Aren't you greedy?" Her smile faded. "It's only half because I was trying to talk myself out of loving someone who could never belong to me."

Alec entwined his fingers with hers and sent a soft caress of energy through their connection. "And now that you know it's possible?"

She looked up at him, allowing him to see everything she felt. Her feelings for him ran deep, but she was afraid of losing everything he promised. "It's still too new to trust, Alec."

He nodded and leaned forward to kiss her. As he pressed his lips against hers in a silent acknowledgement of her words, their energy wove together in an intricate dance.

"I won't push you," Alec murmured as he pulled back. He paused for a moment, his eyes filled with determination. "But I won't back away either. I intend for you to be mine, Ari. I've wanted that since I met you, and I've always regretted the need to back away."

Ariana swallowed at the jumbled mix of emotions his words evoked. Their kind could be fiercely possessive, but it usually took some time for the feelings to form. Then again, they'd been dancing around each other for a long time. Reaching up, she touched his face, and the trace of his energy responded to hers.

"I don't want you to back away, Alec. I want to be yours."

He pulled her closer, burying his face against her neck and surrounding her with his power. "Gods, you completely undo me, Ari."

Ariana cuddled against him, enjoying the security he offered. She couldn't remember ever feeling so adored and protected. Tracing her fingertips over his chest, she asked, "Did you come here to feed me?"

"Hmm?" He rubbed a tendril of her hair between his fingers. "Yes, I did. I hope you don't mind, but I used my override to leave the food supplies in your quarters. The automated system told me you were here."

She laughed. "The High Council leader broke into my quarters?"

"I suppose I did." He pressed a kiss against her lips. "Just remember I wield great power. I have the ability to open all sorts of doors. You'll never be able to hide from me."

She smiled up at him, unable to imagine a time she'd want to hide from him. "Well, let's see your powers at work, great leader. I'm hungry."

He chuckled and stood, extending his hand to help her up. "By all means, let me feed you."

———

ARIANA TOOK a sip of her wine and leaned over to peek around Alec. He'd been chopping and mixing things together in a bowl but had set it aside in the cooling bin to let it marinade for a few minutes. Now he was stirring some other concoction together. It didn't look particularly appetizing, but she'd withhold final judgment until the taste test.

He chuckled. "I can hear what you're thinking, beautiful. It's much better than it looks."

"If you say so," she replied and wrinkled her nose.

Alec grinned and took her wine out of her hand. He put it on the counter and pulled the spoon from the bowl. Holding his hand underneath, he offered it to her. "Try it."

Ariana eyed the dark substance with skepticism, but she supposed it all came down to trust. Leaning forward, she opened her mouth to allow him to place it on her tongue. Her eyes widened at the complexity of flavors. It was rich and sweet, with an earthy undertone that complimented the bite of alcohol hidden within it.

"It's incredible," she said. "That can't be for dinner."

He chuckled and returned the spoon to the bowl. "It's actually for dessert. I have some fresh fruit and thought this would be a nice dipping sauce. It's a mixture of chocolate, brandy, and a few other things. Seara gave me the recipe when she found out I was coming here tonight."

"I think we should skip dinner." She reached over to dip her finger in the bowl.

Catching her wrist, he *tsked* at her. "Stealing from the chef?"

She laughed. "When it's that good, all bets are off."

Alec's eyes danced with mischief as he lifted her hand and put her finger in his mouth. Her lips parted on a gasp as he swirled his tongue around her finger, licking and sucking the chocolate sauce from the tip. The erotic images that formed in her mind at the thought of him doing the same to other parts of her body made her shiver in anticipation.

As though sensing her thoughts, he took his time licking the last of the chocolate from her finger before releasing her hand. He wrapped his arm around her, pulling her against him. "I'm thinking *you* might be better for dessert."

He reached over, dipping his fingers into the sauce, and brushed them across her lips. Her eyes widened, and Alec's gaze dropped to her mouth before he lowered his head, nipping lightly at her lips. He flicked his tongue against them, and she could taste the chocolate on both their lips. His touch was light and teasing, and his energy caressed hers, encouraging her to respond.

Ariana reached up, wrapping her arms around his neck, and opened herself to his kiss. Energy flared between them as he possessed her mouth, consuming both of them with an internal heat. He moved his hands upward, lifting her shirt to reveal her stomach, and she gasped as his cool air energy brushed across her bare skin. He traced its path with his fingertips, heating her with his possessive touch and sending small shivers across her skin.

She arched her back, wanting to feel him even closer against her. With a wicked grin, he took more of the sauce and smeared it across her midsection.

She gasped at the chill and laughed. "Alec, what are you—" Her voice broke off as he dropped to his knees, sweeping his tongue in and circling her belly button.

"Oh," Ariana murmured and threw her head back, fisting her hands in his hair as he nuzzled against her stomach. His mouth was impossibly warm as he licked and nibbled her overly sensitized skin.

"I was right." He pressed another kiss against her stomach. "You are better than any dessert."

She looked down and met his passion-filled gaze. He slowly moved upward, caressing her skin and brushing against the side of her breasts. She swallowed, desire for this man consuming her beyond all reason. He cupped her face and lowered his mouth to kiss her again.

As his energy filled her, something within her broke free. Ariana amplified his power, returning it threefold. At the sudden explosion of energy connecting them, his control suddenly snapped. He lifted her into his arms, deepening their kiss. Wrapping her legs around him, she pulled him closer and felt the hard evidence of his arousal.

Alec pressed her against the counter. Sliding his hands under her shirt to cup her breasts, her nipples tightened as he ran his thumbs over them. Desperate to touch his bare skin, Ariana lowered her hands to the hem of his shirt and tugged it upward. Alec pulled it over his head, tossing it aside. She spread her fingers against his firm chest, the heat and texture of his skin an exquisite torture.

He captured her lips again and stroked her skin, sending her to an even greater frenzy as his energy followed his touch. Power flowed around them, electrifying the air between them and sparking with every caress. Ariana removed her shirt, aching to be rid of the confines that separated them. The desire to have his bare skin against hers was overwhelming.

"Ari," he murmured, his heated gaze roaming over her partially nude body, "you're exquisite."

"Alec, please," she pleaded, entwining her energy around him, begging him to touch her again.

He complied, trailing his hand along the lines of her lace bra. Slipping the cup downward, he exposed one of her breasts. He took her nipple into his mouth and sucked, swirling his tongue in a pattern that left her whimpering. She gasped, clutching him even tighter as his mouth seemed to have a direct connection with her core.

Heat welled within her as she arched against him, demanding more. As Ariana's energy around him intensified, she felt his control slip even more. Relishing in the experience, they both became nothing more than sensation and need, exploring their long-suppressed desire for each other.

Alec pushed up her skirt and brushed against her panties. She gasped as he slipped his fingers inside the material, caressing her most intimate parts. He rubbed against the center of her pleasure, sending exquisite shockwaves through her, and she rocked against him, crying out as their energies met in an explosive union, binding them even tighter together.

Collapsing against him, Ariana dropped her head against his chest, trying to catch her breath. Alec wrapped his arm around her, pulling her tighter against him as though he didn't want to let her go. He brushed her hair away from her face, and she lifted her head to look down at him. They were sprawled on the floor with her on top of him. Her brow furrowed as she looked around.

"How did we end up on the floor?"

He chuckled and shifted her slightly. "No idea, but I'm not about to complain."

She giggled and lowered her head to his chest again. "I can't believe we just did that."

Alec kissed the top of her head. "Gods, Ari. I think it's safe to say sex is probably out of the question until the month is over."

She frowned and blinked at him. "*What?*"

He arched an eyebrow. "Check our connection, love."

Ariana opened her senses, and her eyes widened at the realization their connection was even stronger. Although it still wasn't a permanent bond, she'd attached herself even more to him. It would fade in time if they didn't continue to deepen it, but it went far beyond what was typically acceptable for a courtship. She swallowed, suddenly feeling unsure.

"Don't," he ordered, sitting up with her still on his lap. "Ari, don't doubt what's between us. What you just gave me was a precious gift. I want even more from you, but I don't trust my control around you."

"But you didn't..." She bit her lip uncertainly.

He chuckled and stroked her cheek. "No, and I won't until you're sure of us. You... your energy... Gods, Ari, you're incredible. It took everything I had just to hold back as much as I did. The amount of power you can wield is staggering. It was hard not to let myself match it."

She ran her fingertips over his bare chest, enjoying the sensation as her energy trailed along the same path. It was almost as though, now that their bond had deepened, his energy reacted instinctively to hers.

"How can you be so sure about us, Alec?"

He covered her hand with his. "I've had a long time to think about what I want. I've experienced a permanent bond and understand what's involved. I'm not perfect, Ari. I know I'll make mistakes and bad decisions. But when I think about the future, I can't imagine one without you in it. Even when I was bonded with Kayla and discovered what she was, you were the only person I trusted outside of Seara. Why do you think I asked you to help train Kayla? I've never doubted you, Ari. I only doubted myself when it came to you."

Ariana blinked, trying to hold back the emotion his words evoked. She wanted a future with him, more than she'd ever wanted anything. There had always been a connection between them. She'd been drawn to him from the moment they'd gotten to know each other.

His eyes softened as he gazed upon her. "If you keep thinking like that, I'm not sure I'll be able to wait to claim you until the courtship period is over."

She let out a small laugh and shook her head. "I'm not sure it's a good thing you can read my thoughts."

He grinned and kissed her. "I thought the ability came in rather handy just a few minutes ago."

Her eyes widened at the realization she'd been directing him wordlessly the entire time. "Hmm... I'm starting to think you have an unfair advantage."

He chuckled. "Perhaps, but it goes both ways. You were reading me just as much."

Ariana leaned into him again and pressed a soft kiss against his lips. He was right. She could feel his intense pleasure at their shared connection. Her touch against his bare skin stirred something elemental within him. Feelings of desire, contentment, and adoration coursed through him. Alec had been telling the truth. She couldn't sense any doubts from him, only an intense longing for more.

He stroked her back in a soft caress as he trailed his

energy along the same path. The sensation was exquisite, and she shivered slightly, relaxing against him. She could easily stay in this moment forever, content to remain in his arms.

A chime interrupted them, and she lifted her head.

He frowned. "Are you expecting someone?"

She shook her head and bit her lip as a thought struck her. "Could anyone else have picked up on our energy in here?"

"Each family's quarters are reinforced for privacy from their neighbors. Depending on how your parents divided your wing, though, they may or may not be aware of what just happened between us."

Her eyes widened, and she scrambled off him. Snatching her bra from the floor, she paused for a fraction of a second to wonder when it had been removed. She fumbled to put it back on as the door chimed again.

"I think I'm going to die from embarrassment if it's my parents." She grabbed her blouse and pulled it over her head. "My father's going to have a heart attack. I mean, first, I yell at him, and then I announce to everyone within range that I had an earth-shattering orgasm. Fantastic."

Alec arched an eyebrow and grinned. "Earth-shattering, huh?"

"Don't think you're getting out of this, buddy. If I have to face my parents, you'll be right there with me." She glared at him and pushed off the floor, running a hand through her hair. "Oh, no. I have sex hair. I can't talk to my father with sex hair."

Alec tossed back his head and laughed. As Ariana grabbed his shirt to throw at him, he stood and ran a hand over her hair. A light band of air energy wafted over her, untangling and smoothing out her hair, and he pressed a kiss against her temple.

"Breathe, Ari. It's going to be fine."

"That's pretty useful." Ariana reached up to touch her hair in amazement. That talent alone would have come in handy all those times she'd found herself running late. Shaking off the wayward thought, she shoved his shirt in his direction and turned toward the door.

He chuckled and grabbed her arm. "Your shirt's inside out, love."

Ariana swore under her breath and yanked off her blouse, putting it to rights before heading to the door. Taking a deep breath, she tried to calm her thoughts. She was an adult who was in an adult relationship. She could handle this. It was probably just her parents wanting to make sure everything was okay. Yep. Right. She winced and tried not to squirm.

She was so screwed.

Ariana pressed the button to open the door, prepared to greet her parents, but her intentions fell apart at the sight of the man in the doorway.

"Hayden? What are you doing here? Are you looking for Jason?"

The tall, dark-haired man gave her a charming smile. He took her hand, placing a kiss against it, and sent a light trail of heated energy over her. The moment his power enveloped her, she felt Alec's irritation along their connection.

Uh oh. This might go badly.

"No, but I understand he'll be arriving shortly. I actually stopped by to see you. Do you have a few minutes to speak with me?"

She hesitated and glanced back toward the kitchen area where Alec had just emerged. He strolled toward the entrance appearing every inch of the High Council leader, exuding power and confidence. Ariana immediately felt her body respond, wanting to go to him. She swallowed and held herself back. Their connection was definitely stronger.

"Alec," Hayden said with the slightest hint of annoyance,

but he didn't release Ariana's hand. "I wasn't aware you were here."

Alec moved beside Ariana and put his arm around her waist in a possessive gesture. "Yes. Ariana and I have plans for dinner this evening."

"I see," Hayden replied, narrowing his eyes on Alec's arm before turning his focus back on her. "I apologize for my poor timing, Ari. If you don't mind, could I have a few moments to speak with you privately? There's a formal matter I'd like to discuss with you."

Her eyes widened, and she looked back and forth between the two men. They were both powerful *Drac'Kin* males. Having them in such close proximity when each was determined to claim her could potentially be disastrous. The strong scent of possessiveness tickled her nose and she rubbed at it absently. Their emotions were clashing against each other, and the tension in the air was quickly becoming stifling. Even her calming energy was doing little to combat it. She increased her output, sending more soothing threads to try to pacify them.

As though sensing her discomfort, Alec gave a curt nod. "Of course. It's your right to speak with Ariana if she wishes it."

Ariana hesitated but stepped aside to invite Hayden in. She couldn't rightfully deny a formal request, especially if Alec's suspicions were correct and her father had already given his permission. Although, she could strangle her father for not giving her fair warning. What had he done? Declared an open invitation for anyone to court her the minute she showed her talents?

"If you'll excuse me, I'll give you two some privacy," Alec said coolly to Hayden. His gaze softened slightly as he looked at Ariana. "Please let me know if you need me."

She gave him a small smile and nodded. Once he'd gone

back into the kitchen area, Ariana turned to face her brother's friend. Hayden glanced around the room, his eyes lingering on some of the plants and the fountain before turning back to her.

"Do you mind if we sit?"

"Um, no. That's fine." She gestured to the couch, completely at a loss as to the protocol in this situation. "Would you like a drink?"

"No, thank you," Hayden said, sitting on the couch and waiting until she was seated beside him. "Judging by your surprise at seeing me, I'm assuming your father hasn't had a chance to speak with you."

She shook her head. "No, I haven't yet had a chance to speak with him, but I think it's safe to assume you're not here about Jason."

Hayden took her hand in his, surrounding her with his heated fire energy. It was markedly different from Alec's, but it still reacted with hers. Alec's irritation flared to life again, and she clamped down tightly on their connection.

"No, I'm not here about Jason. After visiting with your brother yesterday in the medical ward, I spoke with your father about the possibility of courting you."

She swallowed and looked down at their entwined hands but didn't respond, unsure of what to say.

"I'm sure this is probably something of a surprise," he began, running his thumb over her hand. "I know we haven't had a chance to spend a great deal of time together. Most of the time, I've only been with you at family functions or when I've been with your brother."

When she made a small noise of agreement, he continued, "I've always been drawn to you, Ari. When I spoke with your father, he expressed his concerns about what happened when you went to the surface. The fact is, he's extremely worried. I can't say I blame him either. You're in a vulnerable position right now. Your abilities are evolving, and the bond you share with Jason is no longer sufficient. None of us want to see you in danger, and we don't know exactly how your abilities are changing."

Ariana frowned, irritated by her family's loquaciousness when they'd constantly encouraged her to remain silent about her talents. "I appreciate your concern, Hayden, but I'm not as vulnerable as you believe. While I may not possess traditional offensive or defensive abilities, I'm not helpless. I don't appreciate you insinuating I am."

Hayden's eyes widened a fraction, and he shook his head. "No, that's not what I meant." With a sigh, he admitted, "This is not going the way I'd hoped."

Ariana pulled away and folded her hands in her lap. "I'm flattered you asked to court me, but the truth of the matter is that my feelings have long since been engaged elsewhere. I don't want to lead you on or give you any indication I'm open to an arrangement between us."

Hayden was quiet for a long moment, studying her thoughtfully. "I understand Alec is courting you as well. I'm assuming that's why he's here now. Your father mentioned Alec had asked permission a few years ago, but I wasn't aware there was anything between you two back then."

She paused and shook her head. "No, there wasn't. Not really. It was... It was complicated."

Ariana looked down at her lap, wanting to be honest but not sure how to explain. What happened between her and Alec was private and not something she wanted to share with anyone else. He'd never made her any formal promises back then, but she'd thought they'd been heading in that direction.

"I think I understand," Hayden said, putting his hand over hers. His warm energy surrounded her once more, offering comfort and understanding. "You care for him, that much is obvious, but I think you should consider all your options before making a decision, Ari. A permanent bond is something that should be forever. I've never considered entering into one, until I met you."

She lifted her gaze, meeting his amber eyes. The warning in his words was unmistakable. Some people within the towers disapproved of the fact Alec's permanent bond with Kayla had been dissolved. It went against their basic core beliefs. She had difficulties wrapping her head around the idea herself. How could you love someone, commit yourself to them and fuse your very soul to theirs, only to just walk away?

Alec's explanation made sense, but she was still afraid. If he'd done it with Kayla, it was possible he could change his mind about her too. What if she gave her heart to him completely, embraced a permanent bond with him, and he broke it? It had hurt so much the first time he walked out of her life, she wasn't sure she could survive a second time.

"You don't have to make any decisions today," Hayden reminded her. "Right now, you just need to consider your options. Why don't you have dinner with me tomorrow? I'll take you out to a neutral setting. No pressure. It will just be two friends getting to know each other better."

Ariana hesitated. There wasn't much harm in what he was proposing. He wasn't pressuring her, and he was within his rights to insist since her father had already given his permission to court her. He wasn't doing that but simply asking instead. She owed him at least that much.

"All right. I'll go to dinner with you."

"Good," he said with a smile. Squeezing her hand, he stood from the couch. "How does seven sound?"

"That's fine," she agreed and stood.

Hayden leaned down and kissed her cheek, trailing a teasing band of energy over her skin. "Thank you for speaking with me, Ari. I look forward to tomorrow."

Ariana said her goodbyes and led him to the door. Once he was gone, she turned around and pressed her back against it. Squeezing her eyes shut, she cursed her father again and made the decision to speak with him first thing in the morning. He'd been avoiding her all day today, but she wouldn't give him the opportunity tomorrow.

"It's not your father's fault," Alec spoke from the opposite doorway. She opened her eyes to find him watching her, his expression guarded.

"No, but it doesn't make things any easier. He should have spoken to me before he did this."

"Perhaps," Alec agreed and walked toward her. She relaxed her hold on their connection, picking up on his tightly controlled hurt and anger. "Hayden's not wrong, Ari. Permanent bonds are supposed to be forever."

She frowned. "Do you really believe that?"

"Dammit, Ari, of course I do! If my bond with Kayla hadn't been dissolved during the duel with Lars, I would have stayed bonded to her for the rest of my life. I share the same beliefs you do. The only difference is I bonded with Kayla to save her. I don't regret that. If the situation happened again, I would do the exact same thing. The alternative could have killed her."

Guilt flooded through Ariana, and she hung her head. "I know, Alec. I shouldn't hold it against you. I think what you did for Kayla was honorable and selfless. It was a tremendous sacrifice, especially considering you barely knew her. But what happened between you two changed everything."

She turned away, walking over to the fountain in the corner of the room. She dipped her fingers in the water, needing to feel the cool and soothing energy around her.

"When you spend your whole life believing there's one other person who will complete you and be your counterpoint in every way, you hold on to that ideology. It shapes the way you view relationships. I know others have dated and experimented with energy outside of courtship, but I wasn't really interested to do the same. It wasn't just because my parents kept me isolated. Why would I want anyone else when my soulmate was out there waiting for me? Now that's all changed. I don't know what to believe anymore. Is everything we thought a lie?"

Alec sighed and moved to stand behind her. He wrapped his arms around her waist and pressed a kiss on the top of her head. "It's not a lie, Ari. I choose to believe it was the will of the gods."

Ariana turned in his arms to look up at him. "What do you mean?"

He lifted his hand to stroke her cheek. "Kayla wasn't meant for me, love. I wanted to believe we were meant to be together because we'd bonded, but it became clear that wasn't the case. I believe my purpose in Kayla's life was to protect her and introduce her to our world. Once that purpose had been fulfilled, we were both given another chance to find our happiness. Don't you think it's strange we've believed for centuries our bonds were permanent, only to find out they could be destroyed? Even now, we don't know how to duplicate it. All we know is it has something to do with spirit energy. Maybe it can't be done. Maybe it was the will of the gods." He lifted her chin with his fingers. "Maybe there's someone else who is meant for me. Maybe that person was always meant for me but we weren't ready to be with each other. Until now."

Ariana bit her lip, wondering if he was right. It couldn't be a coincidence that everything had lined up. The timing was too strange to be anything but part of Fate's design.

"I agreed to go to dinner with Hayden tomorrow," she said in a quiet voice.

Alec nodded. "I heard. That's your right and his, but it

doesn't change anything between us. You're mine, Ari. I'm not going to stand aside and let him convince you otherwise. Go to dinner with him, but I'd like you to come to me afterward and stay the night."

Her eyes flew open. "What? What about our connection? You said it wasn't a good idea."

"My intentions are innocent. Mostly." He took another step closer, trailing his fingers down the side of her face. "Will you do that for me? After you're finished with dinner, will you come to my quarters? I won't push you for anything, love. I just want to have you in my bed and hold you through the night. That's all."

She softened against him and nodded, wanting to embrace everything he offered and more. No matter what her head was telling her, her heart was determined to lead her down a different path. She just hoped she didn't end up falling too hard along the way.

"Yes, Alec, I'd love to spend the night with you."

CHAPTER NINE

SERGEI WALKED through the construction site the next morning, assessing the progress and quality of the work. They were still too far behind schedule, but the quality was better than he had expected. It was somewhat surprising, since most of the workers didn't possess the same amount of experience as the original tower creators.

"Our resource level is critical," Pavel, his second-in-command, advised in their native language. "Even if we receive additional resources from OmniLab, it is unlikely the construction will be completed before deadline."

"You will speak English," Sergei ordered, pausing to inspect a nearby column.

Pavel frowned at the rebuke. Sergei had insisted his people practice the language these Omnis used, since this was where they would be living for the next several years. However, many of them still frequently slipped into their more comfortable native tongue. Even he was guilty of it on occasion.

Pavel and some others resisted for an entirely different reason though. They made it clear they had no interest in integrating with OmniLab. Instead, they wished to return to one of their previous assignments. They'd been wary of the Inner Circle and OmniLab ever since they'd witnessed the profound energy displays during the attack on the towers.

If Pavel and the others were unable to overcome their fears, Sergei would have no choice but to remove them from their posts. Contrary to what they hoped, they wouldn't be welcome at their former assignments either. If there was one thing the Coalition prided themselves in, it was that unconquerable fear had no place among them.

Sergei halted, turning to regard Pavel. His second-in-command quickly hid his annoyance behind a blank mask. Good. At least that was something. Pavel repeated the construction and resource status, this time in accented English.

Sergei nodded. "Send me a full report on all deficits by tomorrow with the new projected completion date."

While Pavel made a note, Sergei lifted his head to study one of the overhead girders. He'd need to speak with Lars about enlisting more of these air channelers to assist in the construction efforts. It might help speed up production and also give his people a chance to work side by side with the Omnis. Perhaps if they worked together toward a common goal, they could overcome some of their reservations.

"Contact Lars and set up a meeting to discuss the construction progress," he ordered, resuming his progress toward his quarters. "We also need a full list of people requesting entrance into the towers when it is complete. I want names, ages, professions, medical information, and known facility affiliations."

"We will not use lottery?"

"Yes, but priority goes to highly-skilled workers," Sergei informed him. "If we cannot finish the construction before deadline, all our people will be at risk."

Sergei pressed his palm against the panel to his quarters, and the door slid open. He walked over to his desk and pulled out his notes. "Nikolai and Peter want to be updated on our status. Did Grigory and Sofia send their progress reports?"

When Pavel didn't reply, Sergei turned to find him staring at the plant Ariana had given him.

"I have seen this plant in our archives," Pavel whispered, slipping back into their native tongue.

This time, Sergei didn't reprimand him. He could understand Pavel's feelings of shock and awe. He'd experienced much of the same the day before. Answering in the same language, he replied, "Yes, it is from our homeland. It is called an Arctic Raspberry plant."

"Where did you get it?" Pavel asked, not tearing his eyes away from the plant as though it would disappear if he looked away.

"It was a gift," Sergei replied, turning back to his desk to review the notes he'd made on the surface camps they'd set up outside the towers.

They'd dispatched some of their people to harvest resources and offer support to the river excavation, while the remainder were assisting in the tower construction. Until they managed to finish mapping the underground river, he'd need to redirect some of his people back to the construction site. It was unfortunate Ariana and Jason hadn't been able to send the equipment down the river. He suspected if Ariana understood the urgency, she'd agree to try again.

Sergei lifted his head to find Pavel still gazing at the plant. Not bothering to hide his annoyance, he demanded, "Will you allow our people to die while you continue to stare at that plant?"

Pavel snapped to attention and approached the desk. He took the detailed instructions Sergei indicated and turned to leave.

"A moment, Pavel," Sergei called, deciding this could be another opportunity to show his people what could be gained by befriending the Omnis.

When his second-in-command turned around, Sergei said, "I've learned some of these Inner Circle members have the ability to grow their own food. The plant was a gift from one of them. With gifts such as these, it would be foolish to turn away their offer of friendship."

Pavel narrowed his eyes at the plant, regarding it with suspicion. "You trust them enough to accept one of their gifts? How do you know this is not a trick? Or poisonous?"

Sergei stared hard at the man in front of him, but he could not entirely fault the questions. Unless Pavel met Ariana, he would not understand. She simply did not possess enough artifice for even the most basic of manipulations. He'd spent years studying body language and the unspoken signals people choreographed to display their true intent. She was a breath of fresh air and far too sweet for her own good.

Sergei walked over to the plant and carefully pulled one of the berries off the bush. Popping it into his mouth, he savored the explosive burst of sweet flavor on his tongue. He swallowed and gestured to the plant, offering Pavel a challenge.

"They are not poisonous. You may try one of the berries, if you wish."

Pavel blanched, but after the slightest hesitation, he slowly reached out and emulated Sergei's careful removal of the fruit. He put it into his mouth, his eyes widening at the taste. Sergei nodded and headed back over to his desk. It was a beginning.

"I want Grigory and Sofia's progress reports on my desk by this afternoon. You are dismissed."

———

Ariana stood outside her brother's quarters and pressed the button for the third time. She tried to bury her panic, fearful he might have relapsed since his release from the medical wing the day before. She'd been trying to reach him all morning, but he wasn't answering his commlink or door. It was getting close to noon and she still hadn't heard from him. Hoping her brother would forgive the invasion of privacy, she pressed her palm against the panel beside the door and entered her override code.

A moment later, the door slid open. Ariana stepped inside the darkened room, a stale and sour smell wafting up from whereabouts unknown. She nearly gagged, covering her nose with her hand to ward off the smell, and reached over to engage the lights.

Jason's quarters were in complete disarray. Piles of dishes with half-eaten or forgotten food covered almost every surface. A thick, fuzzy film of something she didn't want to analyze too closely grew over many of them. Discarded clothing had been left in heaps all over the floor as though he'd stumbled in several nights in a row and disrobed as he headed toward his bedroom.

"Jason? Are you there?" she called out, listening for a response. There was nothing. She frowned, picking her way through the entry area and followed the trail of discarded clothing. She stopped outside his bedroom and knocked on the door. There was a muffled groan from somewhere inside. She reached out with her energy threads, sensing he was in pain.

Pushing open the door, she rushed inside and activated the lights by the entrance. "Jason? What's wrong?"

He rolled over in bed, throwing his arm over his eyes, and groaned again. At least he was fully clothed, even if he was in a foul disposition. "Fuck, Ari. Are you trying to kill me? Turn off the damn lights."

Ariana halted in her footsteps, sensing the distorted energy around him, and narrowed her eyes. "Unbelievable! I was going out of my mind thinking you might be in here dying, and you're nursing a hangover?"

She grabbed a pillow from the floor and walloped him with it. He yelped and tried to grab at it, but she yanked it back and swatted him again.

"You're an idiot, Jason. A complete and total idiot. You were just released from medical yesterday. How could you go out drinking last night? What were you thinking?"

"For fuck's sake, Ari, knock it off. I feel like shit," he groaned, grabbing another pillow and covering his face to block out the light.

She made a strangled cry of exasperation and threw the pillow aside. "I know you do! I feel it. The minute I stepped into your disgusting excuse for living quarters, it was very clear to me you were feeling like shit. That's why I thought you were *dying*."

"I feel like I am," he whimpered. "Please, Ari, my head is killing me."

"Oh no..." She shook her head, crossing her arms over her chest. "I am *not* healing your hangover. I'm not some little party trick you can just cart around whenever you make a stupid decision. Maybe if you suffer, you'll think twice about doing something so stupid next time."

"Please, Ari, I'm begging you," Jason pleaded. "You're right. It was stupid. I shouldn't have done it. I'm sorry. I don't want to end up back in the medical wing."

Ariana hesitated, knowing he was trying to manipulate her. If it were any other time, she'd leave him to his misery. They'd checked him out thoroughly when he was in the medical ward, but she'd seen too much to believe those machines were infallible. She'd felt the swelling in his brain. Those types of injuries could be tricky. What if he really did have a problem and it was masked because he got drunk? She'd never forgive herself for walking away.

Ariana sighed and walked over to him. "Close your eyes if the light bothers you. I'd rather not do this in the dark."

He did as she asked and removed the pillow that had been shielding him from the light. She placed her hands on his temples and used the contact to strengthen their connection. Drawing upon her power to explore and heal his ailments, a gentle warmth pulsed from her hands and spread into him. After a moment, he blinked open his eyes and gave her a huge smile.

"Thanks, Ari-bella. You're a lifesaver."

Ariana made a noncommittal noise and drew back. "That's your one freebie, Jason. If you're stupid again, you have to deal with the consequences. And you'd better clean up this mess. Some of the things growing out of these dirty dishes are starting to become sentient." She headed out of the room and toward the front door, calling over her shoulder, "I think whatever's in this bowl just waved at me."

Jason laughed. "Whatever you say, Ari."

———

ARIANA GLANCED DOWN AGAIN at the message from Sergei. She'd asked him if she could stop by to check on his plant, but he was outside the towers visiting one of the Coalition camps. He wouldn't be back until that evening, but he'd sent over the code to access his living quarters.

It was a little strange to go into his quarters while he wasn't there, but she wouldn't have another opportunity until tomorrow. Hayden was expecting her at dinner, and then she was supposed to spend the night with Alec. Her face warmed at the thought of Alec and what had happened between them the night before. She wasn't sure if she was more nervous or excited to see him again.

Her stomach fluttered in anticipation, and she shook her head to clear her thoughts. She needed to focus on attending to the small bush she'd awakened from seed. Plants needed a lot of care, especially in the beginning when they'd been encouraged to grow so rapidly. Given that she didn't have much experience with this particular type of plant, she wasn't willing to risk not checking on it.

Ariana entered the code to Sergei's quarters, and the door slid open. She froze, startled to see one of Sergei's men standing at his desk. He spun around, his hand reaching for his weapon.

She raised her hands and took a hasty step backward. Sending a strong wave of calming energy outward, she hoped it would work on a non-sensitive. Her heart thudded in her chest as she said, "Forgive me. I wasn't aware anyone was here. Sergei told me I could come by to check on his plant."

His cold eyes narrowed on her, studying her intently. "Who are you?"

She swallowed. The man's hand still rested on his weapon, but he hadn't drawn it. His suspicion permeated the energy threads in the air, and Ariana detected a trace of fear. It surprised her, but she couldn't afford to be distracted by it. She pulled some of the moisture from the air, using the water to reinforce her shields to block the man's strong emotions.

"My name is Ariana Alivette. I'm a friend of Sergei's."

He cocked his head as though evaluating her words and gestured toward the plant. "You gave him gift?"

Ariana nodded. "Yes, I gave it to him yesterday. I told him I'd need to stop by every day for a while to make sure it was growing well."

He removed his hand from his weapon and motioned for her to enter. "I remember. You are healer too."

"Yes," she admitted, now realizing where she recognized him from. He'd been in the control center during the Coalition's attack on the towers. Kayla's former camp leader, Leo, had been severely injured in an energy attack and Ariana had healed him. "I'm sorry, but I don't know your name."

"I am called Pavel."

He watched her closely as she walked over to the plant on the table. She could already feel her internal barriers straining against the threatening weight of his emotions. It was strange how certain people affected her differently. It was probably not a good idea to linger, but she needed to be polite.

She gave him a small smile. "It's nice to meet you, Pavel."

He didn't respond, but instead moved closer. She supposed his curiosity was to be expected. Sergei had been equally fascinated both times he'd seen her interact with plants. Maybe if she tried to engage him in conversation, she could alleviate his more potent emotions.

"Have you tried one of the berries?"

He nodded.

Ariana bit her lip. He wasn't much of a conversationalist. She decided to try again.

"Would you like to help me care for the plant?"

He appeared startled by the question and shook his head. "No. I will watch."

"All right." She wondered if his reticence in speaking was because he wasn't comfortable with the language. It didn't explain the fear she'd picked up, and she wasn't willing to lower her protective energy barrier enough to get a better read on him. She'd gotten used to Sergei's tight control and had forgotten how much his kind could affect her.

She sighed, brushing her fingers on the leaves of the plant. If they enjoyed this one, maybe she could see about harvesting the seeds and planting more of them for the rest of Sergei's people. It would be a wonderful way to generate more goodwill between them. She'd like to try some different types of plants too.

Ariana used her fingers to check the soil for dampness, sending out traces of earth and water energy toward the plant. While she went through the process, she launched into an abbreviated explanation about what she was doing. "The soil is a little drier than I'd like, and since this is a new plant, I'm going to add a little water to it."

Ariana pulled out the small hydrating pack she'd brought with her and showed it to Pavel so he could see it was just ordinary water. She poured a bit of it into the soil and tested it again with her fingers and energy. So far, the plant seemed quite content in its new home.

"It doesn't need very much since I just grew it yesterday. New seedlings always need more water at first, especially when they're encouraged to grow so quickly."

Pavel frowned. "You grow yesterday?"

She hesitated and then nodded. Sergei already knew about her skills, and Alec had assured her it wasn't a problem that the Coalition knew of their abilities. "Yes. Would you like to feel the soil so you can get an idea about how damp it should be? Different types of plants need different amounts of moisture."

Pavel approached her and placed his fingers against the soil like she showed him. She was careful not to touch him, wary of any contact which could break through her carefully crafted emotional barrier.

"You will grow more?"

She smiled at him, pleased by his interest and that he appeared a little more relaxed now. "Yes. When I chose this one, I spent quite a bit of time looking up the different edible plants from your homeland. There are a lot of different plants I'd like to try growing. I haven't tasted many of them, and I think it would be wonderful to try them."

He studied the plant thoughtfully before turning back to her. "You will come back tomorrow to care for plant?"

"Yes," she agreed, brushing the dirt from her hands. "It's a hardy plant, but I want to make sure it grows well. I'll come back every day around the same time to check on it. Once it's established, Sergei should be able to easily maintain it."

"Good."

She gave him another smile. "It was wonderful to see you again, Pavel. Take care. I hope to see you again soon."

He nodded, watching as she headed toward the door. "Yes, very soon."

CHAPTER TEN

ARIANA FINISHED FASTENING her earrings and smoothed out the silver dress. She regarded her reflection with a critical eye, not wanting to give Hayden the wrong impression but needing to give him the respect he deserved. The dress she'd chosen that night was one of her favorites. Its spaghetti straps supported a low, draped neckline, and it fell nearly to the floor in a shimmering column. It had just the right touch of elegance for dinner. She might have chosen something a little more conservative if it were just dinner with a friend, but she was wearing the dress as much for Alec as she was for Hayden.

A soft chime echoed throughout her living quarters, and she walked over to the door. Hayden's eyes warmed at the sight of her, taking the time to slowly peruse her from head to toe before meeting her gaze. His mouth curved in an appreciative smile as he took her hands in his, enveloping her in his heated fire energy.

"Ari, you're breathtaking."

She blushed and gave him a small smile, returning his energy with her own softer greeting.

"You look wonderful as well, Hayden." She admired the sharp lines of his dark tunic and how it hung on his trim physique. The darkness of his clothing complimented his nearly-black hair and made his amber eyes even more compelling.

He lifted her hand, placing a gentle kiss on it before tucking her against his side and leading her toward the priority elevators. "Thank you for agreeing to go out with me tonight. I promise, there will be no pressure. This will just be two friends enjoying dinner and getting to know each other."

She beamed a smile up at him. "Which restaurant are we going to?"

"Ah," he said, programming the elevator to take them to the designated floor. "I've been wanting to take you to my newest place, Club Sapphire."

She blinked, suddenly even more unsure about the evening. "The one that's open to Inner Circle members *and* non-sensitives?"

"Yes," Hayden replied, obviously pleased she'd heard of it. "Your father told me you occasionally have difficulties being around non-sensitives, so I have set up an isolated area where we'll be having dinner. Some areas of the club only permit Inner Circle members, but they have the option of mingling with the rest of the club. From our private area, you should be able to see the entire club, but you won't actually be in the middle of it."

"It sounds as though you've been speaking to my father more often than I have lately," Ariana acknowledged with a frown. "I'm sorry, Hayden. I truly appreciate you taking my feelings into account. I'm just a little upset with my father right now. He's been avoiding me ever since Jason was hospitalized."

He looked down at her, trailing a light thread of

comforting energy over her. "You mentioned he hadn't told you about giving me permission to court you."

"No," she said with a sigh. "He gave you and Alec permission, but he hasn't returned any of my messages. We argued in Jason's hospital room and haven't spoken since then. I don't like leaving things so unsettled."

"I understand, but you shouldn't worry. I'm sure he didn't intend to upset you. Your father has his hands full at the moment with a rather complicated issue," Hayden said as the doors to the elevator opened.

He placed his hand on her lower back and escorted her out into a busy thoroughfare with a wide assortment of restaurants and high-end shops that catered to the Inner Circle. They passed several known acquaintances, and Ariana gave them small nods in greeting. A few of their looks were more than covetous, and she had the sinking feeling they'd heard about the incident at the river. Thankfully, they didn't approach, but it was most likely because of her escort. She was going to have to be more careful when she ventured out alone.

"Do you know what my father's working on?"

Hayden nodded. "Yes. There have been several problems related to the influx of Coalition and surface-dwellers entering the towers. He's been working with a taskforce to resolve some of these issues."

Ariana frowned, wondering if Pavel's discomfort around her was related to these problems. Sergei hadn't said anything. In fact, he'd been much more understanding and open than most humans. "I wasn't aware there were any difficulties. What's going on?"

"Part of the issue is, we simply don't know anything about the people working on this new tower," Hayden explained, taking her down a different corridor. "We've had some conflicts since everyone comes from a different way of life.

They don't understand our ways, and most of our residents have never interacted with any of the surface-dwellers. We've been too isolated since the war." He paused for a moment. "To make matters worse, there are more rumors than ever about our abilities. Too many of our people used their talents to fight against the Coalition during the siege on the towers. It's not just contained to the surface-dwellers or Coalition either. Our human residents are being affected too."

"They're afraid of us," she murmured. This could be disastrous for everyone involved if they didn't find some way to alleviate these fears.

"Yes," Hayden agreed, slowing his pace as they approached another intersection. "With the creation of this new tower, we're going to need to integrate our people more with the non-sensitives. Ever since Kayla Rath'Varein returned from the surface, there's been even more curiosity about the Inner Circle. It's gotten worse since the Coalition occupation. I created this club in response to that demand. So far, it's been an extremely successful endeavor."

Ariana glanced at him, thoroughly impressed by not only his instinctive business sense but also by his philanthropy. Perhaps giving all of their people an opportunity to engage in a safe environment would help reduce any tensions. "What a wonderful idea, Hayden."

He gave her a small smile and gestured in front of them. "You'll have to let me know what you think."

Ariana turned to look at the exclusive club in front of them, a spill of sapphire-blue lighting against the black-and-silver design. Hayden led her inside, where thousands of blue crystalline shards floated from the ceiling, reflecting their light onto the walls and floor. He gave the receptionist and security officer a brief nod and took her into the main area.

Hayden had been accurate in his description, but it didn't even come close to captivating the experience of being there.

The club was laid out in three circular tiers, staggered in such a way a guest could watch what was happening from almost every location. A designated dance floor was set up on each level, allowing people to decide if they wanted to mingle or not.

He'd brought her through the middle-tier entrance and into a roped-off area separating them from the population. A table was set up on a dais, away from everyone but close enough they could watch all three tiers.

Hayden leaned close to her ear. "If you have any problems, let me know and we can leave."

Ariana nodded, grateful for the offer. The energy, ambiance, and music were exhilarating and exciting but more than a little overwhelming. There was a slight pounding against her temples, but it wasn't anything she couldn't handle. At least, not yet. They were far enough away from the throng that the tumultuous explosion of emotions shouldn't be too taxing, but she'd need to keep some water handy to be on the safe side. It was worth it for the experience, if nothing else.

Hayden led her to a private table and pulled his chair over to sit beside her. A moment later, a server appeared and poured them each a glass of wine. She glanced at it, deciding that a small splash of water in her wine probably wouldn't be enough.

"Would you mind if I also had a glass of water? It'll help with some of the stronger emotions."

"Of course." He motioned the server over again and indicated her request. As soon as the server disappeared, Hayden turned back to her. "I hope you don't mind, but I went ahead and spoke to the chef earlier. I asked him to prepare his specialty for us. Jason told me a few of your favorite dishes, and I think you might enjoy this."

Ariana tilted her head to study him. "I feel as though I'm

at a disadvantage here, Hayden. You know far more about me than I know about you."

He placed his hand over hers, sending a light flare of energy over her. "I'm hoping that might change tonight, Ari."

She didn't answer right away and took a sip of her wine before turning back to study the dance floor. Hayden was an incredibly attractive man, and his attention was flattering, but she didn't have enough room in her heart for anyone else. Even though he'd indicated this would be a friendly dinner and so far hadn't crossed any lines, the emotions she was picking up from him weren't exactly platonic.

The server placed a glass of water in front of her, and she took a long drink and used the water to weave her mental barrier even tighter. It wasn't fair to keep reading Hayden's emotions when he couldn't do the same.

"Most of what I know about you is from my brother," she admitted, deciding on a light and friendly approach. "He's told me a few stories about your antics."

He arched a brow, his eyes twinkling with amusement. He leaned back and rested his arm on the back of her chair. "I wouldn't believe anything he says. If it's your brother telling the stories, I was most likely the innocent bystander. Jason enjoys stirring up trouble whenever the opportunity arises."

"You know him well," she agreed with a laugh. "All right, I won't ask if the stories are true. I must admit, I'm not sure if I should be nervous or impressed anyway."

"Maybe one of these days I'll tell you," he teased. "I'd like to make it through one evening with you before scaring you away though."

"I don't scare that easily." She took another sip of her wine but kept the water glass close. "Now you have me very curious."

"No, I think you're right. You don't scare easily," Hayden replied with a thoughtful expression. "I thought for a long time you were just shy, and that's why you avoided going out with our social group. That's never been the case, has it?"

Ariana shook her head, unsurprised by his assumption. Sadly, many people believed the same. She enjoyed being around people, but certain circumstances made it uncomfortable, especially since no one had known about her talents for years. It's impossible to guard against something if you don't know it's a possibility.

"No. I wouldn't say I'm shy, but it's sometimes easier to be alone. Some people are more difficult to be around than others, and too many people in close quarters can become overwhelming." Ariana gazed out at the tiered dance floor. "They look like they're having fun, but I don't think I could ever join them."

"Would you want to?"

She took another sip of her wine and shrugged. "I've never considered it. In a way, I suppose I've missed out on a lot of experiences. I've been trying to make up for them lately, but there are some things that will probably always be out of reach."

He was quiet for a moment and then said, "I might have a solution."

She tilted her head, curious to hear his suggestion.

"How about dancing with me right here? You won't be out there with all of them, but you can still have the experience."

"Here?" She looked around in surprise.

"Yes. It's my club. I can make up whatever rules I want," Hayden said with a grin. He stood and held out his hand to her. "Come on, Ari. Dance with me. Let's give you another experience."

Ariana laughed and placed her hand in his. It was a little unconventional, but she'd had a lifetime of convention already. A little fun wouldn't hurt.

—————

SERGEI TOSSED BACK his drink and motioned for the bartender to refill it. He'd been sitting at the bar for almost an hour, listening in on various conversations. One thing had become perfectly clear: Omnis didn't know how to handle their liquor. He'd overheard some rather unusual conversations and received more than a few blatant sexual offers, but other than some hints at shady happenings, there was nothing concrete.

He eyed the strange bracelet they'd fastened on his wrist when he entered. It identified him as a non-sensitive, and he was beginning to suspect he'd need to remove it to find out anything significant. He'd watched more than a few Inner Circle members speak in hushed whispers to a staff member, pocket something they received, and disappear into one of the backrooms. When they emerged a few minutes later, their walk was a bit more buoyant and their eyes shone a little brighter.

A dark-haired woman approached him and leaned against the bar. She glanced over her shoulder before addressing him. "You're with the Coalition, right?"

He arched an eyebrow, studying the woman for a moment. Although she was dressed in a rather skimpy dress, her body language was rigid as though she were unaccustomed to wearing such clothing.

"I am," he agreed, alarm bells beginning to go off in his head. Something wasn't right.

She let out a relieved sigh. "Sorry. Charles couldn't make it tonight. He asked me to come instead. He sends his apologies. We've managed to get everything arranged—"

"Hey there," a buxom woman interrupted and sidled up alongside them. She giggled and trailed a fingernail down his arm. "You're that Sergei guy, right? The Coalition ambassador? I've seen you on videos. You're even hotter in person. I'm Lexi."

The other woman's eyes widened, and she backed away quickly, muttering something under her breath about having him confused with someone else. Sergei's eyes narrowed as he watched her retreat. It was tempting to investigate, especially since she'd obviously been meeting one of his people here, but he had other priorities at the moment. Besides, without any evidence of wrongdoing, he had no cause for suspicion.

Tabling his concern, he glanced down at Lexi's wrist, spotting her bracelet. Another dead end. He narrowed his eyes at her, making it clear he wasn't interested. If she'd been an Inner Circle member, he might have feigned interest long enough to see what she knew. The woman hesitated, blinking up at him through a drunken haze. Weaving slightly, she giggled again.

"You know, since you're new to the towers, maybe I should take you back to my place and give you an official OmniLab welcome."

"No," he replied in a cold, clipped tone and turned back to stare down the bartender who was taking a bit too long. The bartender refilled his drink, and Sergei picked up the glass, tossing it back and swallowing the cool liquid. The woman finally got the message and wandered away to try her charms on someone else.

"You've always been skilled at making friends," Lars observed from behind him.

Sergei scowled and placed his glass back on the bar, waving over the bartender again. He was tempted to insist the bartender leave the bottle behind. "She knows nothing. A drunken fool, nothing more."

"You're probably right." Lars leaned on the bar and looked over the room. He spoke in Russian, keeping his voice low enough to avoid being overhead by any translating devices.

"I've heard some whispered talk, but these people don't know me or trust me. I can't get anything useful out of them."

Sergei smirked. "*Now* who is skilled at making friends?"

Lars snorted but didn't disagree. "I called Brant. He says there are no security cameras in several key places, most likely by design. He's on his way here to show us which areas. Perhaps he'll have better luck getting someone to talk. At least these people know him."

"Perhaps," Sergei conceded, lifting the glass the bartender had just refilled. He'd tried engaging the bartender in conversation when he arrived, but one glance at his wrist had them moving on to serve the next patron. "The Shadows are not accepted either. We will need a regular Inner Circle member to discover what they are being given."

"Maybe we can get—" Lars cut off, straightening to peer over the crowd. "Oh, fuck. Is that Ari? I thought Hayden was taking her to dinner, not bringing her here. Alec is going to lose his fucking mind."

Sergei turned in the direction Lars was staring. It was. He narrowed his eyes at the sight of Ariana sitting with that *mudak*. He picked up his glass, tossed back his drink, and pushed away from the bar. This was not a place for one such as her. If she were in the slightest distress or had been harmed in any way, Sergei would make Hayden pay. For every step he took in their direction, Sergei thought of more than a dozen inventive ways to kill the man.

"We need to be careful," Lars advised, continuing to speak quietly in Russian as they pushed through the crowd. "This is his club. If we go storming over there, we're going to get tossed out on our asses."

"Can you get us into that area?" Sergei glanced at the roped-off area guarded by security.

"Possibly," Lars said. "If it's open to all Inner Circle, yes. If not, maybe we can get Ariana's attention."

"Do so," Sergei ordered, assessing the security officers standing nearby. "I do not want her here."

"You and me both," Lars agreed, moving forward to speak to the security officer.

Sergei stayed back several steps, waiting to intervene only if Lars couldn't handle the situation. When the security officer shook his head and started to motion for Lars to move back, Lars waved his hand toward Ariana and called her name.

Ariana turned her head in their direction, her eyes widening a fraction before a huge smile spread across her face. She stood, her delight at seeing them evident, but her companion was less than pleased. Hayden scowled at them, obviously debating whether he could get away with having them thrown out without upsetting Ariana. Sergei resisted the urge to smirk. No matter which option Hayden chose, his date with Ariana had just come to an end.

The security officer stepped aside enough for them to enter, and Ariana started walking in their direction, a radiant vision of shimmering silver that made her eyes even more striking. Her dark hair spilled over her shoulders in a tumble of midnight waves, drawing attention to the low cut of her dress. The silken material caressed her soft curves as she moved, leaving very little to the imagination. Sergei had taken several steps toward her before he even realized what he'd done, and he inwardly kicked himself for not taking the damn bottle from the bartender.

"Lars," she greeted, taking both his hands and pressing a kiss against his cheek.

Lars said something that was too low to overhear, and she laughed, a light, musical sound that warmed Sergei from within.

Ariana turned toward him next and whispered his name, her eyes lighting up at the sight of him. She held out her hands and he took them, taking the opportunity to draw her against him while Hayden glared at him from behind her. Sergei didn't bother to hide his smug grin and leaned down to kiss Ariana's cheek. He inhaled deeply, smelling the light floral scent that filled the air whenever she was nearby. It was a welcome distraction from the sweat and alcohol that permeated the air around the bar.

"You are stunning, *solnyshka*," he whispered near her ear.

She beamed up at him. "I didn't know you and Lars were going to be here. I thought you might still be on the surface at one of the Coalition camps."

"My business finished earlier than expected," he admitted, not wanting her to know she was the reason he was in this club. "I am surprised to see you here. Are you feeling well with so many people?"

"You were both worried about me?" she asked, her gaze softening.

"Of course," Lars answered.

Hayden approached and stood a little too close to Ariana for Sergei's liking. "You needn't have worried. I've asked her to let me know if she has any discomfort. So far, we've had a very enjoyable evening."

"Hayden's been very kind," Ariana agreed with a small smile. "It's not too bad right now, but I've been drinking a lot of water. I'm sure the server must think I'm severely dehydrated or something." She gestured to the different tiers. "I've always been curious about going to one of these clubs. My friend Kendra talks about them all the time."

"Indeed," Hayden said, putting his hand on Ariana's lower back. "Kendra is a frequent patron. If you'd like, we can invite her and Jason to join us next time."

Ariana nodded. "They would both love that."

Sergei's eyes narrowed on Hayden's hand as he slipped it even lower and began stroking Ariana's back through the thin material of her dress. There were twenty-seven bones in the human hand, and Sergei was about to double that number by breaking each one in half.

Ariana tilted her head to look at Sergei curiously, a small frown on her face. He forced himself to take a deep breath and slowly released it, focusing on centering his thoughts and releasing his emotions. Ariana had told him he was difficult to read. He needed to keep it that way.

A club security officer approached the group, trying to catch Hayden's eye. The nightclub owner paused for a moment, watching as the security officer gestured toward one of the back rooms. Hayden frowned. "Will you excuse me for just a moment, Ariana?"

"Of course," she replied, nodding.

Hayden and the security officer moved to stand a short distance away but not close enough Sergei could easily overhear them. Hayden's eyes narrowed as the security officer spoke, the tension in his shoulders making it clear that whatever news he was receiving wasn't good.

Ariana frowned as she watched the two men speaking. Sergei stepped forward and put his hand against Ariana's back. The back of her dress dipped low enough he could easily touch her bare skin. Now that he thought about it, he might have to triple the number of bone fragments in the man's hand.

"Tell me about this Kendra," Sergei suggested, hoping to distract her from whatever emotions she was picking up, either from himself or the argument happening nearby.

"Oh!" she said, turning back to them. "Kendra's a lot of fun and one of my dearest friends. I'll have to introduce you. She's a little flighty, but she has a wonderful heart."

Lars glanced over at Hayden and back at Sergei, catching on that he was trying to distract Ariana. "Kendra? Petite redhead with green eyes? Always getting into trouble?"

Ariana laughed and nodded. "Yes. It sounds like you know her well."

"Hmm. Yes. She set my parents' couch on fire when she was about ten because I didn't move quick enough," Lars said, his frown deepening. "When you were children, you two and my sister were thick as thieves."

Ariana bit her lip and lowered her gaze, trying to quell her laughter, but her eyes danced with amusement. "I want to say Kendra's changed since then, but that's not true. She just doesn't get caught as often anymore."

Hayden walked back over to the group. "My apologies, Ari. Something's come up, and I'm afraid it can't wait. If you'd like to accompany me to the back, you can relax in my office while I handle this matter. There's a viewing area where you can watch all three levels. It shouldn't take long."

She put her hand on Hayden's arm. "Is everything all right?"

Hayden put his hand over hers, but his smile didn't reach his eyes. "Just a small situation with an overly enthusiastic patron, I'm afraid." He lifted his head to regard Sergei and Lars more coldly. "If you'll excuse us, gentlemen, I'm sure you can find your way out."

"No," Sergei replied and crossed his arms over his chest, not about to let Ariana disappear with this man.

Lars shot him a warning look. "What Sergei means is, we're more than happy to keep Ariana company while you attend to your business. Besides, if she begins to suffer from any problems being here, we can escort her back to her quarters."

Hayden looked ready to argue, but Ariana lifted her head. "Lars is right, Hayden. I should probably head out in a few minutes. I'm afraid I may have overextended myself this evening."

"Sir, our guest—" the security officer began, but Hayden held up a hand to cut him off.

"Are you sure, Ari? If you'd like to wait here, I can finish up my business quickly and escort you home."

"That's not necessary," Lars advised. "You have my word I'll take the same level of care with Ariana as I would if she were my own sister."

Hayden regarded him skeptically but didn't argue. He lifted Ariana's hand and pressed a kiss against it. "Is that what you want?"

"It's probably for the best," she admitted and stood on her toes to press a kiss against his cheek. "I've had a wonderful time with you tonight, Hayden. Thank you for showing me your club and for the dance."

His eyes warmed. "I'd like to call upon you tomorrow, if you don't mind."

When she nodded, he gave her a brief bow and turned toward the back rooms with his security officer.

———

ARIANA FROWNED at Lars and Sergei, watching as they exchanged a meaningful look. They were both shielding so hard, she was amazed they could stand upright. It was even more impressive that Sergei was able to do it. But it just reinforced her earlier belief that they were up to something.

Lars walked over to the table she'd shared with Hayden. He picked up her water glass and handed it to her. "Are you feeling well enough to remain here a few minutes longer?"

She took a sip of the water, threading it through her mental barrier. "Yes. Will you tell me what's going on?"

"Wonderful," Lars replied, not answering her question. "I just need a few minutes to check something out."

Without another word, Lars walked out of the VIP area

and down toward the bar. Sergei put his hand on her back again and rubbed his thumb up and down her spine, sending a slight shiver through her.

She lifted her head to regard him, but he was busy watching Lars. Without looking away, Sergei said, "I have a request, *solnyshka*."

"What request?"

Sergei glanced down at her. "When I tell you to, smile and wave at Lars."

Her brow furrowed. "What in the world are you two up to?"

His thumb stopped its movement. "Now, Ari. Smile and wave."

Confused, but not seeing any harm in the request, she lifted her hand and waved to Lars, who was now gesturing toward her. The staff member nodded, pulled something out of his pocket, and dropped it into Lars's hand. Lars turned and trotted back to them.

"Got it," Lars announced and motioned toward the exit. Whatever the staff member had given him had disappeared into a pocket. "We need to get out of here."

Sergei plucked Ariana's glass from her hand and put it on a nearby table. He draped an arm around her shoulder, tucking her against his side, and ushered her toward the door with Lars walking on her opposite side. Once they were outside the club and halfway down the corridor, Ariana stopped in her tracks and put her hands on her hips, regarding them with suspicion.

"I'm not going another step with either of you until you tell me what that was about. What did that man give you? Why did I have to wave for him to give it to you?" Frowning, she demanded, "Is there a problem happening in Hayden's club? Does he know?"

Ariana wrinkled her nose. Emotions of guilt wafted up

from both men like the pungent odor of sulfur.

"Apologies, *solnyshka*. It is better you do not know too much. Will you trust us?"

She hesitated, looking back and forth between Sergei and Lars. Neither one had done anything to hurt her, and they'd even been concerned about her welfare that evening. Maybe it was foolish, but she *did* trust them.

With a sigh, she asked, "Will you eventually tell me the truth?"

Sergei's mouth curved upward. "You have my word."

"Then I'll try not to ask any questions," she agreed and pressed her hand to her nose. "But would you two mind relaxing or shielding your emotions? Guilt is a particularly offensive emotion. It smells bad. I've been picking it up since we were in the club."

The men exchanged another look, and Lars took a step toward her. "Ari, do you mean to tell us you can smell someone's guilt?"

She nodded. "If I'm not shielding well enough, yes. All emotions have different flavors. Love, hate, anger, desire, fear, and guilt are all very distinct. Most people experience a combination of emotions at once, so it can become more challenging to pick apart the different threads unless an emotion is particularly strong. Some are more pleasant than others, but guilt is one of the worst."

Lars's eyes widened. "I had no idea. How many people know about this?"

Ariana frowned. More people knew about her abilities now, but not many knew specific details. "Only a few outside my family."

"So much painful emotion," Sergei murmured, moving closer and taking her hand in his. "It hurts you."

She lifted her head to regard him. His compassion enveloped her thoroughly as if it were a band of energy surrounding her. Ariana put her hand on his chest and smiled up at him, spreading out enough power to fully encompass both of them with her soothing energy.

"Not always. If all I could do was experience the emotion, it might be different. But I have the ability to temper and heal the more painful ones. If I can alleviate even one person's suffering, I'll gladly accept all of it."

"I wasn't aware you could affect Shadows too," someone spoke from behind her. "I can feel your energy affecting me from here."

Ariana let her energy fall away and turned to meet Brant's considering gaze. She swallowed, suddenly uneasy. "I suspected, but I wasn't sure."

Brant took a few steps toward her. "Can you read my emotions too?"

She hesitated and then nodded.

He took another step toward her. "What about negating our abilities? Do you have the ability to break through our talents?"

Sergei pulled her behind him. "Enough."

Lars also stepped forward, putting himself between her and Brant. "Watch it, Brant. We're not friends, but our loyalties belong to Alec. He won't take kindly to you upsetting her."

Brant faltered, the strong odor of guilt making her nose itch. "I apologize, Ariana. That wasn't my intention. Having your energy affect me was something of a shock."

She placed her palm on Sergei's back to let him know it was okay. He took a half-step aside but didn't move away. "I understand. I'm still a little unsure about everyone knowing about my abilities. But to answer your question, I don't know. I suspect it's possible for me to circumvent your abilities, but I've never tried. I never wanted to draw attention to myself."

Brant studied her for a long time. "That's why your family

has never asked for our services and why your brother usually escorts you in public."

She nodded. "We couldn't risk it."

They fell silent for a moment, and Lars reached into his pocket to withdraw something. He handed it to Brant. "We managed a workaround, but I don't know what's in it."

Brant studied the small, brown vial and popped the cork to inhale it. Ariana gasped. All three men turned to look at her, but she couldn't stop staring at the familiar swirling and pulsating colors. The taste. She knew that taste. She took a few steps forward and held out her hand.

"May I see it?"

Brant hesitated, and Lars said, "That's not a good idea, Ari. I don't think it's safe."

Ariana shook her head. "If it's what I suspect, it shouldn't be possible. Please. I have to know for sure."

Brant held out the vial for her, and she gingerly took it. With almost shaking hands, she opened the cork once again. The emotions resonated deep inside her, and she closed her eyes, almost swaying at the symphony of sound that erupted around her as the emotions clamored for her to acknowledge them.

"This can't be," she whispered, blinking open her eyes and turning back to stare at the club in shock.

Lars frowned. "What is it? Do you know what's in that vial?"

She didn't answer. Instead, she turned back to Brant. "Where's Kayla? Is she still on the surface?"

"Yes," he replied, his mounting anxiety swirling through the air the moment Kayla's name was mentioned. "She's at the underground river site. Why?"

"Contact her, please. I need to know she's safe."

Sergei touched her arm, and she nearly jumped. Brant took the vial from her and closed it. She swallowed. It was just as well. Another minute and she probably would have dropped it. Her hands were shaking, either from anger or fear, maybe both.

"What is wrong, *solnyshka?*"

Ariana bit her lip, uncertain what her answer might mean but needing to tell them what she'd felt. "I don't know how it's possible, but there's energy contained in that vial—spirit energy. And as far as I know, Kayla's the only spirit channeler around."

CHAPTER ELEVEN

ALEC LOOKED over the reports from the underground river. They'd made more headway into the excavations, but they were still having problems with their equipment. Kayla and Carl were working on designing some sort of remote control speeder to try to navigate through the rapids. He sighed and pushed the tablet aside, wondering if he should ask Ariana again. So far, they hadn't been able to find anyone else or a bonded pair with enough power to accomplish the feat. If Kayla had a bit more training, there was no question she'd also be able to accomplish the task with ease.

He'd been trying to distract himself with various reports, but try as he might, his thoughts kept going back to Ariana. The idea that she was out right now with Hayden was making him crazy. Even when Kayla had been with Carl, he'd never felt this level of jealousy. His only calming thought was that Ariana had agreed to come to him tonight after she finished with dinner.

Alec suspected the fire channeler didn't have his level of strength from an energy standpoint, but Ariana's father wouldn't have accepted Hayden's courtship request if he wasn't powerful enough. Devan would have made sure Hayden had the strength to hold Ariana's bond before allowing him to court his daughter. The older man had always focused on hoarding power more than anything, especially when it came to his family's bloodlines.

To make matters worse, Alec had felt Ariana's concern that what was between them wasn't real. If Hayden tried to play on that fear, it might be enough to drive a wedge between them. She was nervous about being hurt again, and Alec couldn't blame her. From the moment he'd met her at Kendra's party years ago, Ariana had intrigued and captivated him. Unfortunately, she'd caught Hayden's attention too.

That was the whole reason Ariana was at that party. She rarely attended those types of gatherings, but Kendra was one of the few people Ariana socialized with regularly. When Hayden's initial efforts to make inroads with Ariana failed, Hayden had developed a close friendship with Jason. Ariana adored her twin brother, and everyone knew it. If nothing else, the fire channeler was annoyingly persistent and driven. Alec was somewhat surprised Hayden hadn't made a move before now, unless Ariana's father had previously refused him as well.

Alec drummed his fingers on the arm of his chair, wondering if he could have tried harder in the past. If he'd engaged the same ruse he'd used to keep the energy shackle off Kayla, maybe he wouldn't have needed to walk away from Ariana. Although, it could have easily backfired, and Alec wasn't willing to risk anything happening to her. It was too late for regrets anyhow. At least he had another chance to prove himself to her. He just had to convince her he wasn't going to walk away again, not for any reason.

The door chimed its arrival notification, and he glanced at the panel beside him. Anticipation flooded through him at her name on the screen. Finally. She was here. He stood and headed toward the door, relieved she was no longer with Hayden. He opened the door and froze, forgetting how to breathe.

Ariana was absolutely breathtaking, an angelic vision that made his heart skip several beats. Her long hair was swept over her shoulder, the inky darkness contrasting with the creamy expanse of her flawless skin. She lifted her gaze to meet his, and a tentative smile formed on her lips. He managed to relearn how to breathe and took her hands, drawing her into his quarters.

"Ari," he murmured, pulling her into his arms. She was all softness, and he breathed in the alluring floral scent that always seemed to tease her skin. "I see now that I made a mistake by not taking you out to dinner. You're breathtaking, love. I'm not sure if I should be jealous Hayden saw you like this, or if I should be thankful you came to me afterward."

"I wore this for you," she whispered, wrapping her arms around his neck.

A powerful surge of possessiveness and thrill rushed through him at her words. He lowered his head, capturing her lips with his. She tasted of wine, a hint of fruit, and underneath was the taste that was all Ariana, the most intoxicating of all. He pulled her closer, feeling her soft curves press against him. He could easily get lost in her forever, content to exist in this moment for eternity.

Someone cleared their throat, and he lifted his head, his eyes narrowing on Lars. He'd been so captivated by Ariana, he hadn't even noticed he'd accompanied her. "What are you doing here?"

Lars chuckled. "Enjoying the show."

An endearing flush colored Ariana's cheeks, and she lowered her head but didn't pull away. Alec turned her in his arms, angling her away from his cousin. "You've always been a tactless bastard, haven't you?"

Lars shrugged. "Apologies, Ari. I didn't intend to embarrass you, only my cousin."

She tucked her hair behind her ear and tilted her head to regard Lars. "It's all right. I suppose we got a little carried away." She looked up at Alec. "Would you mind if I use your shower? I think the emotions at Hayden's nightclub were a little strong for me."

A red haze coated his vision, and Alec clamped down tightly on their connection to keep his fury from leeching into it. "He took you to one of his clubs?"

She nodded, her brow furrowing at the unintended sharpness in his tone. "The Sapphire Club. It's very nice but a little overwhelming."

Alec forced himself to release her, even though his instincts were telling him to hold on even more tightly. He'd kill Hayden for taking her there. That must have been where Lars found her. Making a conscious effort to gentle his tone, he said, "Of course, Ari. If you'd like to go ahead and use the bathing area through my bedroom, your bag was delivered this afternoon. It's in there too."

She gave him a small smile and stood on her toes to press another kiss against his lips. "Thank you."

"Take your time," he said, watching until she left the room. Once the door closed behind her, Alec turned and headed for the bar. Yanking open a bottle, he poured two glasses. He paused, and then added a bit more. "That's where you found her? That bastard took her to his fucking club?"

Lars took one of the glasses and stepped away from Alec, as though wary of his mood. "Yes."

Alec downed the glass of liquor, barely tasting it, and resisted the urge to throw the glass. He poured himself another drink instead. "I'm going to kill him. He knows what she is, and he had the audacity to take her *there* of all places? She's a fucking empath. You don't take an empath to a place of debauchery and depravity. His fucking clubs are under investigation, and he knows it. Sex on the dance floor, drugs, gambling, and who knows what else, and he dragged her into the middle of it?"

Alec turned away from the bar and started to pace, his fingers itching to put a hole through the wall, or even better, Hayden's face. "For fuck's sake, it was bad enough when I thought he'd take her to some intimate dinner. If I'd known he would do this, I would have intervened. I'll burn his entire club to the ground with him in it before I allow him anywhere near her again."

Lars sipped his drink, eyeing him as he continued to pace. "If you do that, you'll lose her."

Alec turned, narrowing his eyes on his cousin. "I will *not* lose her."

Lars put his glass on the bar. "I know you're angry, but you need to hear me out. What would happen if you went after Hayden? You're both officially courting her. If Hayden provokes you and you intervene in his courtship, you know the end result."

Alec paused in his pacing, considering Lars's words. "You're suggesting he did this intentionally?"

Lars nodded. "That's exactly what I'm suggesting. If he can put you out of the running, it clears the way for him. Don't you find it strange that Ariana's father hasn't agreed to anyone else courting her? Only you and Hayden. I know her father has received several requests, but as soon as Hayden pled his case, no one else was considered."

"That bastard," Alec swore and threw his glass across the room. It shattered against the wall. "Either Hayden has something on Ariana's father or they've come to some sort of arrangement. Tell me you learned something while you were there tonight."

Lars flicked his wrist, and the shards of broken glass swept into the air, depositing themselves into the recycler unit. "We managed to get a sample of something called *Drakar*. They're distributing it only to select Inner Circle members, possibly as an incentive to get more of us to patronize the club. Brant and Sergei have taken the sample to the lab for testing, but Ariana said something puzzling about it."

"Do not test me, Lars," Alec warned, the energy threads around him snapping. "If you involved Ariana in this investigation, it will not go well for you."

"Don't threaten me, *cousin*," Lars retorted, crossing his arms over his chest. "You asked us to investigate the club because you couldn't take this to the Council. No one at the club was willing to engage me in dialogue, so I had to use my connection with Ariana. Hayden had taken her to the VIP area, where they had a very public dinner together. That was enough to convince one of the sellers to provide me with the sample. Sergei stayed with Ariana in the VIP area the entire time while I handled the transaction. She was never in any danger."

Alec slammed Lars against the wall with his wind energy. "You've implicated her. If word gets out, they may go after her."

Lars shoved back with his own air energy, struggling to break Alec's hold. "Dammit, Alec, I'm not your enemy here. Hayden wants her. He's not going to jeopardize that, not if he's intent on removing you from the competition. Ariana knows next to nothing about our reasons for going there. If he asks, she can tell him the truth. His surveillance system will protect her. She was never directly involved."

Alec clenched his fists and turned away, not faulting his cousin's logic, but it still grated. Ariana was his to protect. His need to keep her safe warred with his desire to give her the time she needed to accept his claim. Alec released the energy holding Lars in place and began pacing again.

"There's more," Lars continued with a sigh. "Ariana saw me hand off the vial to Brant. She claimed it contains the emotional energy of a spirit channeler and demanded we contact Kayla to make sure she's okay."

"How is that possible?" Alec shook his head. Inanimate objects didn't have emotion, unless Ariana was reading the echoes of emotion like she had in the ruins. "Did you do as she asked? Is Kayla all right?"

Lars nodded. "Brant reached out to her. Kayla's still at the underground river. The guards have been put on notice to keep a close eye on things. I don't know what Ariana sensed, but she seemed very confident that whatever was in the vial was tied to spirit energy."

"There has to be some connection," Alec mused, not willing to discount Ariana's comments simply because it didn't fit neatly into their perceived reality. Over the past year, he'd seen too much that was outside the normal realm of expectations. Besides, after seeing her dramatic display in the ruins and experiencing her energy firsthand, he'd be a fool not to trust her judgment. "I want to be notified as soon as the lab results come back."

"Of course," Lars agreed. "Brant and Sergei took the sample to the lab researcher you suggested. We need to keep our suspicions only within your most trusted circle. If Hayden learns you're investigating this, he can insinuate it's a setup to disqualify his claim on Ariana."

Alec glanced at the closed door to his bedroom. He wouldn't take any chances he could lose her. "That's why you and Brant are handling the investigation. I'll only step in if it's necessary. But I suspect you're right and Hayden's trying to force me into showing my hand. I'll need you to continue coordinating the efforts."

Lars nodded and headed toward the door. "I'll let you enjoy the remainder of your evening."

Lars paused at the doorway and turned back to him. "Alec, I know you cared for Kayla, but I hope you know she wasn't right for you." He gestured to the closed bedroom door. "Ariana's different, though, and you're different with her. When you're around her, it reminds me of how you used to be, before hell broke loose in these towers. Don't let her get away. She *is* the right one. She needs you just as much as you need her."

He'd known, but hearing the words loosened something inside him. He gave Lars a curt nod. "I have no intention of letting her get away. Ariana's mine. It's just a matter of proving it to her."

Lars chuckled and gave him a mock salute before the door slid shut behind him. Determined not to waste another minute, Alec turned and headed toward his bedroom. He opened the door, noting Ariana's bag had disappeared and the bathroom door was closed. There was no sound from the shower, so he guessed she'd finished.

He tapped on the door. "Ari? Do you need anything?"

She opened the door a moment later dressed in a similar lounging robe from the night before. It was partially sheer, the ivory color the same as the silken nightgown she wore underneath. The intimacy of her attire affected him more deeply than if she'd been standing nude before him. His mouth went dry, and he wondered how the hell he was going to keep his hands off her tonight. He'd promised to be on his best behavior, but he was now kicking himself for making that claim.

"No, I'm fine," she said in a soft voice. "Did Lars leave?"

"A few minutes ago," he managed, sending a small trail of energy over her skin and following the path with his eyes. Gods, she was beautiful. "Are you feeling better now?"

She nodded and walked into his arms. He pulled her close,

all of his earlier tension melting away at the sense of rightness in having her here.

"I missed you tonight," she murmured, leaning against his chest.

"I'm just glad you're here now," he whispered, running his hand down her back. He'd dreamed of having her here like this for so long. The reality was even better, and it only reinforced his decision to do whatever was necessary to convince her. "There's something I'd like to show you. I'm hoping you'll like it."

She lifted her head, a small smile on her face. "What is it?"

He took her hand in his. "Nope. I don't want to ruin the surprise."

She laughed, following him out of his room and down the hallway. He rarely came into this part of his family's quarters, at least until recently. Seara had been thrilled when he told her about his plan and gave him hundreds of suggestions about how to make the surprise irresistible. He said a silent prayer, hoping she was right.

Pausing outside the door, he turned to Ariana. "Close your eyes, and don't open them until I tell you."

"So mysterious," she teased but did as he asked.

Alec opened the door, activated the lights, and led her into the room. "Okay, you can open your eyes now."

He held his breath as she opened her eyes, a soft look of wonder coloring her expression. Ariana stepped off the raised platform and into the abandoned garden. Trailing her fingers over the planters that were full of soil and just waiting for her touch, she wandered over to the large reflecting pool in the center of the garden.

Alec approached her slowly. "What do you think?"

She turned around, still gazing at the garden with a dreamy look in her eyes. "It's beautiful, Alec. It holds so much promise. Have you decided what you're going to plant here?"

He took her hand, wishing he had a thousand more gardens so he could keep this look on her face. "I'm hoping you'll make that decision, Ari."

Her brow furrowed, and she shook her head. "I don't have the expertise yet. Seara would be much better suited to helping you."

He smiled. "No, you misunderstand. I want this to be *your* garden, Ari. It's been empty since my mother died. Seara helped me get it ready for you, but I'd like you to be the one who brings it back to life."

Ariana's mouth parted in surprise, and she gazed at the surrounding garden again before meeting his eyes. "You want to give me your mother's garden?"

"Yes, if you'll accept it," he replied, taking her hand once again. "I've already configured you to have entry into my family's quarters. You can come and go as you like. Seara left some recommendations about possible plants you might want to consider while you're learning the full range of your earth skills, but she also offered her assistance if you want help."

"Alec," she murmured, blinking back tears, "I don't know what to say."

"I'm hoping you'll say yes, both to the garden and to me," he said, praying he wasn't moving too soon. "Then maybe, one day, in the not-so-distant future, you won't have to walk all the way from your quarters to your garden. You'll already be here."

"Yes! A thousand times yes!" she squealed and threw her arms around his neck. "I can't believe you've done this, Alec. It's beyond wonderful. It's the most extraordinary gift I've ever received. I love it, and I love you for thinking of it."

His heart thudded as he pulled back, hoping he hadn't misheard. "Do you?"

"Stop shielding from me, Alec. You won't hurt me."

He lowered his internal shields, and his knees nearly buckled from the rush of emotion. A wave of love so powerful and pure flowed through their connection. How could he have been so blind? It had been too much to hope for, but the reality was more rewarding than his wildest dreams.

"Ari," he murmured, cupping her face and gazing into her eyes, "I love you too. I've loved you since the moment we first met, and I've fallen a little more in love with you each moment after that. I never believed someone such as you could even exist, much less return my affections." A tear trailed down her cheek, and he kissed it away. "I swear to you, here and now, I'll always love and protect you. From now until the last of the energy in this world is a memory, I'm yours."

"I'm yours too," she whispered. "I've always been yours. I love you, Alec."

He lowered his head, pulling her closer and capturing her lips with his. Gods, she was exquisite. Her lips were impossibly soft, and her taste was indescribable. She was everything he'd ever wanted and far more than he deserved. She wound her arms around his neck, and the heady aphrodisiac of her power cascaded over him.

"I want you, Alec," she murmured as her beguiling energy enveloped him in a magical spell. He groaned and pulled her tighter against him, struggling against his desire to claim her fully and his need to do what was right.

"Ari, I want you more than anything, but I don't trust myself not to lose control," he managed, burying his face against her neck and breathing in her delicious scent. "I don't know if I can be with you and not bind myself to you permanently."

She threaded her fingers through his hair. "I trust you, Alec. I want to be with you in every way possible."

He swallowed and lifted his head, cupping her face and looking into her guileless eyes. "Are you sure? If you have any doubts, we should wait. I won't be able to let you go after this. Even if we don't permanently bond, our connection will become even deeper."

Her answering smile was radiant. She pressed a kiss against his lips and nodded. "I'm sure, Alec. I've been waiting two years for you. Don't make me wait another night."

To hell with noble intentions. He'd be a fool to refuse her.

"Not here," he said, looking around the garden. If this was to be his first time with her, he wanted Ariana in his bed where he could take his time with her. He lifted her into his arms. She gasped in surprise, and he grinned. "You're mine now, Ariana Alivette. You've unleashed the dragon."

She laughed in delight, wrapping her arm around his neck as he carried her back toward his bedroom. Laying her down on his bed, he stepped back, wanting to always remember this image. Her robe had come unbound, the silken material of her nightgown clinging to the soft curves that lay beneath. Her dark hair fell around her, and she blinked up at him, those gorgeous, silvery eyes full of love and trust. The realization she was in his bed hit him like a punch in the gut.

"Do you have any idea how beautiful you are?"

Her skin flushed, a lovely rose color creeping over her cheeks. "I've always thought you were the beautiful one."

He paused in surprise and grinned. "Oh, Ari, you're not seeing yourself from where I'm standing."

She gave him a timid smile. "You make me feel beautiful, Alec."

"I want to make you feel so much more," he murmured, moving forward to join her on the bed. With an almost featherlight touch, he caressed her skin with his energy, and she quivered in response. He lowered his head, pressing his lips against hers, and nipped at her full bottom lip. Her mouth parted on a gasp, and he tasted her again, the rich ambrosia of the woman he'd wanted for so long finally on his tongue. Fuck, he didn't know how he was going to hold back claiming her in every way imaginable.

———

ARIANA DIDN'T WANT him to hold back. His thoughts were intermingling with hers, their connection making it almost impossible to know where he ended and she began. Not that it mattered. She'd wanted him for so long. He slid his hand along her side, the heat from his body surrounding her in a sensual cocoon.

He pulled the robe off her shoulders, trailing his lips down her neck and along her collarbone while his air energy caressed every inch of her exposed skin. He was driving her crazy with this slow, erotic teasing. Ariana felt his lips curve in a smile against her skin, and she knew that was his intention. Well, two could play that game.

She wriggled out from underneath him and pushed him down onto the bed, climbing on top of him. He raised his eyebrows and placed his hands on her hips, holding her against him.

"Why, Miss Alivette, what do you think you're doing?"

Ariana had no idea, but she'd figure it out. She tugged on his shirt, and he laughed but sat up enough to help her pull it off. Tossing it aside, she pressed her hands against his chest, staring in wonder at the man beneath her. His beauty wasn't just confined to his appearance. Admiration for his wonderful and caring nature surged through her, and she wanted him to know how much she treasured him.

She bent down, pressing a small kiss against his chest. He inhaled sharply, and this time, it was her turn to smile. Kissing him again, she trailed a mixture of water and earth energy over his skin. He groaned, reaching up to run his hands through her hair.

"Gods, Ari," he murmured, and she looked up to meet his gaze. His earlier mirth had disappeared, replaced by a much more heated expression.

She started to slide down his body, emulating his tactics as she kissed his skin and teased him with energy. When she got to his bellybutton and the small patch of hair that disappeared into his waistband, he hooked his arm around her and rolled her over, pinning her underneath him.

Yes! She wanted to crow in victory, pleased beyond all reason that her seduction attempt had worked.

"Oh, you have no idea, love," he murmured and covered her mouth with his.

A wave of his power washed over her, wiping away all her earlier thoughts until she was nothing but pure sensation. She matched his strength, her energy blending with his into a seamless transition of love and desire.

They rolled together, tossing their remaining clothing aside as they got lost in each other's bodies and energy. When he finally pushed inside her, Ariana gasped at the combined ecstasy and the strange sense of rightness. He began to move, and she moved with him in a passionate and primal dance. Their energies blended, fusing together in a blinding climax that had them both crying out their release.

Alec collapsed on top of her, resting his weight on her for a minute before rolling over and pulling her with him. She was out of breath, her heart still pounding in her chest, but she was more sated and content than she ever thought possible. Was this how it normally was between two people? If so, she wasn't sure why anyone would ever get out of bed.

Alec chuckled. Still trying to catch his breath, he threaded his fingers through her hair. "No, Ari. Only with you."

She ran her fingers over his chest, lightly tracing the movements with her energy. Alec's love for her flowed freely through their deepened connection, matching her feelings for the incredible man beside her. "I don't think I ever want to move again."

He laughed and pulled her even closer. " We're going to have to move eventually because I'd like to do that with you again soon."

"You would?" she asked hopefully, lifting her head to look down at him.

"Gods, woman," he murmured, running his fingers through her hair and sending another wave of his energy over her skin. "Do you think you can just give me an earth-shattering orgasm and not try for a repeat performance?"

She laughed. "Earth-shattering, huh?"

"Absolutely. I knew there would be definite perks to you being an earth talent." He kissed her again. "Definitely earth-shattering."

———

A LOW BUZZING noise awakened Ariana. She blinked, trying to focus on the dim room, noting the well-defined chest she was sprawled across. Alec's arm was wrapped around her and had been holding her while she slept. She smiled against his chest, once again reliving the events of the previous night.

Alec picked up his commlink from his nightstand and glanced at it before putting it back down.

"Is everything all right?" she asked, lifting her head a fraction to look up at him.

He threaded his fingers through her hair. "Hey, I'm sorry I woke you. That was Brant. I'll go speak with him in the other room. Why don't you go back to sleep? I won't be long."

"All right," she agreed with a yawn.

He gently extricated himself from her and pulled the blankets over her, pressing a kiss against her temple. "I love you, Ari."

Ariana smiled against the pillow. "I love you too, Alec."

She felt his soaring exultation at her response and listened to him quietly dress. A moment later, a small shaft of light filled the room as he exited and closed the door behind him. Ariana sighed dreamily, unable to remember a time when she'd ever been this happy. Alec was everything she'd ever wanted and more. He was the kindest, most compassionate, and sexiest man she'd ever met. And he was hers.

Ariana rolled onto her back to stare up at the ceiling. He'd already done so much for her, and she wanted to do the same for him. Alec was so self-assured and confident, but she knew he often second-guessed himself. It made sense considering he was still finding his way in his new responsibilities. When they were alone, he wasn't nearly so serious. He was playful with her, laughing, teasing, and frequently smiling. She sighed dreamily. He had such a sexy smile, and his eyes had a way of seeing right through her to expose all her secrets.

His large bed felt even emptier without him in it. A quick glance at her commlink let her know they'd only been asleep for maybe an hour. It was still the middle of the night.

Ariana pushed aside the blankets and sat up, reaching for her nightgown. If he was going to be a while, she might as well get up with him. At the very least, she could wander into the garden and look through the recommendations Seara had suggested.

She pulled on her robe and opened the door, halting at the sight of Brant and Alec. The cloud of tension that hung over the room was nearly stifling. She took a half-step backward, not wanting to intrude, but Alec walked over to her.

"Ari," Alec began and took her hands, leading her over to

the couch. "Come sit with me. I think you should know what's going on."

Alarm bells were ringing in her head as she studied both men. They were worried, tense, and wary of her reaction. It was causing her emotions to converge in a jumbled mix of nerves.

"What's happening? Is it my brother?"

Alec sat on the couch and pulled her beside him, taking her hands in his. "Your brother is fine, but he's in a little bit of trouble. How much do you know about what he's involved in?"

She frowned, looking back and forth between Alec and Brant. "What are you talking about? What trouble?"

Alec hesitated. "Jason's been taken to a holding cell in the security offices for causing a disturbance. He's extremely intoxicated and belligerent. This is the second time in the past week it's happened, but it's been going on for some time."

Ariana squeezed her eyes shut, cursing her brother's stupidity. She pulled away from Alec and stood, walking to the far side of the room to stand in front of the small fountain. How could he do such a thing? He'd promised her that morning he wouldn't drink again until he was healed.

She dipped her fingers in the water, the cool liquid offering a small measure of comfort against the onslaught of emotions in the room. It did little to help soothe her though. "How long has this been going on?"

"We've been getting complaints for the past couple months," Brant admitted. "It's been happening more frequently lately."

Alec walked over and wrapped his arms around her in a comforting embrace. "I'm sorry, Ari. Did you know he had a problem?"

She started to shake her head but then sighed and looked

away. "I want to say no, but I suspected something was wrong. He's been quick to anger lately and more difficult in general. I've been afraid something would happen when I wasn't around to calm him down."

"So you have been regulating his emotions," Alec murmured.

She nodded, still staring into the fountain and wishing it held the answers to all her problems. "I didn't realize Jason was drinking though, at least not until this morning. He's been very careful about hiding it from me. When he didn't answer my calls, I went into his room and found him badly hungover. I was worried the hangover might be masking a problem from his brain injury, so I agreed to heal him." She turned and lifted her head to meet Alec's gaze. "He promised me he wouldn't drink again until he was fully recovered. Why would he do this?"

"I don't know," Alec admitted with a frown. "I was hoping you might have some insight."

She glanced over at Brant. "Have you notified my father?"

Before Brant could reply, Alec said, "I asked him not to. After you and Jason came to my office the other day, Brant mentioned what had been happening with your brother. I asked the security offices to notify me next time instead of your father. There's something going on with him, and I'm worried about how it's affecting you."

"He's my twin, Alec." She pulled away from him. "We affect each other. It's part of our bond. I'll do whatever is necessary to help him."

Alec frowned. "This is wearing on you, Ari. He's taking more from you than he's giving back. You can't keep masking his problems. He needs to face this."

Ariana didn't answer right away and headed toward the bedroom. Maybe Alec was right. Covering for Jason hadn't helped the situation so far, but it was difficult to take a step back. She owed Jason so much. If it weren't for him helping to temper her abilities while they were growing up, she wasn't sure she would have survived. Regardless of his poor decisions, she loved her brother.

"I need to get dressed and go to Jason. My father needs to know. If he thinks you're keeping this from him, he'll be furious."

She heard Alec's footsteps following her back into the bedroom. Crossing the room, she opened her bag and pulled out some clothing.

Alec put his hand over hers, stopping her. "Ari, he was taken out of one of Hayden's clubs. Jason was out of control enough that he used his abilities to make one of the tanks on the wall explode. It caused a great deal of damage to the club. Fortunately, no one was hurt, but he's in a lot of trouble. I'll take you to him, but I need to speak with him before alerting your father. Jason may have information we need."

She blinked at him. "This was at one of Hayden's clubs?"

"Yes," Alec replied and motioned toward her bag. "Go ahead and get dressed. I'll take you to him. From there, we can discuss letting your father know what's happening."

She pulled off her robe, placing it back in her bag, and slipped off her nightgown. Alec's sharp intake of breath caught her attention and she blushed, reaching for the casual dress she'd laid out to wear. Alec moved behind her, placing his hands on her waist and running them up her side. She quivered at his touch and the intensity of his desire through their connection.

"I know we need to hurry, but you're just so beautiful, I can't resist touching you." Pulling her hair to the side, he kissed the nape of her neck. He ran his nose against her skin, inhaling deeply, and placed another kiss behind her ear. She dropped her hands against the dresser, unsure if she could support herself if he kept touching her.

He reached around to cup one of her breasts and ran a thumb over her nipple.

"Alec," she whispered, debating whether to beg him for more or ask him to stop so they could rescue Jason.

He groaned, lowering his head to rest on her shoulder. "I know, we need to go. I'm not terribly happy with your brother right now."

"You and me both," she said with a sigh, watching as he moved away to get dressed and feeling strangely bereft from his absence. "You and me both."

CHAPTER TWELVE

ARIANA WINCED at the pounding in her head. The harsh lighting, stark walls, and raised voices made this one of the more unpleasant areas she'd encountered in the towers. The accompanying anger and regret permeating the air made it difficult to breathe or even swallow.

Alec put his arm around her. "I'm sorry, Ari. I didn't realize it was like this. I'll take you out of here and come back."

She shook her head. "No, I need to see Jason."

"Do you want some water?"

She nodded, unsure if it would help, but the alternative would have her trembling in the corner and unable to stand. There hadn't been enough time between the nightclub and being in this situation now. But she couldn't walk away. Through the bond she shared with Jason, he had a muted version of her ability to pick up emotions. If Jason had been here for any significant amount of time, he had to be experiencing more than a little discomfort. As annoyed as she was with him, she wouldn't leave him suffering.

Brant walked forward quickly, issuing some orders to

other security officers. He brought over a glass of water and said, "They're arranging a private room for you to see Jason. It may help with some of the discomfort."

Ariana took a drink of the water, letting it sit on her tongue for a moment and using it to reinforce the protective energy surrounding her. The coolness of the water down her throat helped too. She'd need to completely submerge herself once she was finished in here. A strong wave of energy flowed through her connection from Alec, and she lifted her head to look at him.

The love in his eyes was staggering. He brushed the back of his fingers against her cheek. "Take whatever you need, love."

"Thank you," she managed, sending a gentle wave of gratitude and love over him. He pressed a kiss against her forehead, embracing her again with his power.

Brant cleared his throat and gestured down the hall. "Jason's in the center room. The adjacent rooms are empty."

Alec nodded, taking her hand and leading her toward the room. Jason was seated at the only table, his head resting on his hands. He appeared to be asleep, but the noise of the door opening made him look up with red-rimmed eyes.

Jason leaned back with a sardonic grin and drawled, "Well, if it isn't Alec Tal'Vayr. Shouldn't you be out trying to fuck my sister or something? Oh wait, it's Hayden's turn tonight, isn't it?"

Ariana gasped at the hurtful words and the wave of anger that nearly suffocated the room. She took a small step backward, but Brant had already closed the door behind them. Jason leaned over, narrowing his eyes on her. He jumped up, knocking his chair over backward. "You bastard! You brought my sister here? What the hell are you thinking?" He started to walk toward her but tripped on the leg of the table and fell to the floor in a heap.

"Jason!" Ariana rushed over to him and knelt beside him to see if he was hurt. He batted her hands away and collapsed against the floor laughing. She pulled back, thoroughly confused. She'd never seen him like this. Alec reached down and pulled her up and into his arms.

"I don't understand," she murmured. "Why is he acting like this?"

Jason looked up at her, alternating between laughing and crying. Tears ran down his cheeks, but his emotions were a chaotic swirl she couldn't even begin to decipher. The energy threads were jumbled and distorted, overlapping and intertwining where they shouldn't. It was almost as though the surrounding energy wasn't resonating with his anymore.

"I'm sorry, Ari-bella," he managed, wiping tears from his eyes. "You don't have to keep worrying about me. I'll be okay soon. I'll be as powerful as you, and I can protect you again."

She gripped Alec's arms and shook her head. "There's something wrong with him, Alec. He's not drunk. This is something else."

"I agree," he said and released her. He knelt beside Jason. "Did you take something?"

"Like you're trying to take my sister?" Jason stared up at the ceiling. "You can't have her, Alec. You'll break her, and I can't lose her. But Hayden wants her too. I promised him. He's going to save her."

Ariana clenched her fists and glared at her brother. If he wasn't out of his mind right now, she'd kick him. "What do you mean? What did you promise him, Jason?"

Her brother didn't answer. His head lolled to the side, and he squinted at Alec as though trying to focus on him.

Alec snapped his fingers in Jason's face. "What did you take?"

"Nope, I know the rules," he announced and then his gaze

shifted, focusing on her standing behind Alec. "Hey, Ari, I heard Hayden took you to his club. Whaddya think?"

"I think you're a fool," she hissed. "Look at you, Jason. I left you this morning nursing a hangover, and here you are, rolling around on the floor in a security office. Answer Alec's question. What did you take?"

"Is father here yet?" he drawled, his head rolling to the other side to stare at the wall. "I think it's time to go home."

"You're not going anywhere yet," Alec announced, walking over to Brant and exchanging a few quiet words with him. Brant entered something in his commlink.

While they were busy, Ariana decided to try again. She knelt on the floor near her brother. "Please, Jason. I'm worried about you. Tell me what you took. How can we fix this?"

He gave her a dopey smile and managed to shake his head. "It's already fixed, little sister. I just have to get used to it. It's not so bad. Not normally."

"Little sister? You're only three minutes older," she snapped. "Now talk. Get used to what?"

"I can't tell you," he said with a frown, reaching out to touch her arm. "You're too powerful. I can't protect you anymore. I failed you, Ari. I'm so sorry."

"I don't understand!" Her eyes started to tear up from frustration. What was happening to him? "You *do* protect me. You always have. You're not making any sense."

He squinted up at her as though she kept going in and out of focus. "You like Hayden, right?"

Ariana blew out a breath. She'd seen Jason drunk, but this went beyond his normal level of intoxication. "He's very nice, but what does that have to do with anything? Did he give you whatever you took tonight? Did he cause all of this? Jason, please tell me so we can fix this."

"You should be with Hayden," Jason slurred. "Stay away

from Alec. He can't have you. Hayden promised..." His voice trailed off as his eyes closed.

"Jason? Jason, answer me!" she cried, reaching down to make sure he was breathing. His heart was still beating, but it was thready. His breathing was shallow too. Brant was already beside her and checking his vital signs. She held her hands out, but the energy around him was too chaotic.

"I don't think I can heal him," she told Brant, panic beginning to flare inside her. "The energy threads aren't resonating with him. Something's wrong."

Brant spoke into his commlink, ordering an emergency medic to their location. He pressed a small cylinder injection against Jason's arm. It beeped a moment later and Brant pulled it away.

Alec knelt on the other side of her. "Try, Ari. They're going to be a few minutes, and I'm not sure what's wrong with him."

Ariana swallowed and nodded, reaching out to place her hands directly on Jason's clammy skin. She sent her senses outward, trying to discern whether she could encourage his energy to resonate with the surrounding threads. She knew Jason's energy signature as well as her own, so it should have been easy, but his energy was stunted and misaligned.

Why was it so different? She bit her lip, wondering if it were possible to change someone's base alignment. She looked over at Brant. "I know you can't manipulate energy without Kayla, but can you see the threads?"

"Yes," he admitted. "What do you have in mind?

She gestured to the surrounding threads. "I want to try bringing Jason's energy back into alignment, close to my own. Our energy is always shifting and changing, but his is especially erratic. Can you suppress or negate some of the outlying bands so I can work on the ones closer to him? I can't heal him until he's stable."

Alec knelt beside her and frowned. "I've never heard of such a thing being possible. You can bring someone's energy back into alignment?"

"I'm going to try," she whispered, hoping this would work.

Brant studied Jason and nodded. Lifting his hands, he said, "It may make it difficult for you to work around me."

"I guess we get to find out whether I can manipulate shadow energy," she replied, focusing once again on each of the threads around Jason. To her, energy had a wide variety of different characteristics, more than most of her kind experienced. For them, it was simply broken down into elements. But she saw thousands of colors, heard different sounds, tasted different flavors, and smelled hundreds of scents to go along with those elemental alignments. If she could manage to sort them correctly, maybe she could heal him.

For over an hour, she worked around Brant's shadow energy and picked apart each thread, humming softly as she reset the alignment back to Jason's. The world became a sharp focus of color, harmony, and emotion, all intertwined to reside inside her brother. As she finished the threads closest to him, she moved outward, this time working directly through Brant's energy. It was more difficult to manipulate the threads, but Brant was keeping them stable and that's what she needed. She continued to hum, trying to determine which energy thread reacted to the tones in her wordless song.

It was at least another hour before she was close to being finished, and she could barely keep her eyes open. Alec tried to hand her some water, but she shook her head, not willing to tear her gaze away from her brother.

"Can I give you some of my strength, Ari? I don't know if it'll interfere."

"No, I can't risk it," she replied, determined to get

through this. The alternative was unthinkable. "I'm almost finished. I just need to do a little more."

She blinked her eyes, trying again to focus on the energy threads. They were so close to her signature now, and her brother was breathing much easier. She hummed again, watching to see which energy thread reverberated, and then she plucked it out of the mix, twisting and aligning it with hers. Once she finished the remainder, she was barely able to sit upright.

Alec put his hands on her shoulders. "I can help you heal him."

Ariana nodded, and Alec's power swept through her, supplementing her weakening strength. She'd need to sleep for several hours, possibly in the bottom of a pool, but she could handle the rest. Placing her hands once again on Jason's skin, his warmer skin under her fingertips was a reassurance she'd been more than moderately successful.

Taking a deep breath, she sent her senses outward once more, shifting and aligning his energy until he was healed. With a relieved sigh, she announced, "It's done. He'll probably sleep for a while though. You won't be able to get any useful information out of him until then."

She started to stand but stumbled, the drain from using her abilities more than she expected. Alec wrapped his arm around her before she fell, holding her against him. He helped her into a chair and handed her the water she'd refused earlier. The drink didn't help nearly enough. Her strength was too depleted. She needed rest more than anything.

The medics were now checking Jason out and arranging to take him back to the medical ward where they'd monitor him until he recovered. Once he was better, she was going to hurt him again for pulling such a stupid stunt. But that would have to wait until later. Unable to keep her eyes open, she lowered her head against her arm and slipped into a deep slumber.

"I WANT at least two security officers and one Shadow with him until we get some answers," Alec ordered as the medics took Jason out of the room and down to the medical wing. "You took a blood sample from Jason?"

Brant nodded and showed him the vial. "I'll send it over to the lab and have the analysis expedited. I'll also have it compared to the vial Lars acquired from the club. Do you want me to notify Devan Alivette that his son is in medical?"

"I don't believe we have much of a choice," Alec replied, not particularly pleased with the idea. He might have more flexibility if Devan wasn't already furious that he'd taken Ariana and Jason to the surface. "Notify him but have a security officer present to serve as a reminder of the severity of the situation when Devan arrives. I want answers, but I suspect Devan will be reluctant to allow any sort of interrogation involving Jason. We need whatever leverage we can get. He controls too many votes on the High Council."

"Understood," Brant replied, entering some commands into his commlink.

Alec looked through the glass door at Ariana sleeping with her head on the desk. The stark setting of the security office was almost offensive compared to the peaceful serenity surrounding her. In a low voice, he asked, "She was able to circumvent your energy, wasn't she?"

Brant looked over at Ariana and nodded. "Yes. I didn't have a chance to tell you earlier, but her abilities affect me as well. She was sending a calming wave to Lars and Sergei earlier, and I stepped into the area of effect."

Alec's eyes widened a fraction. "Like Kayla? Ariana can

use her energy to influence Shadows and avoid your negating effects?"

"It appears so," Brant admitted. "I don't know what it is about the two of them, but it makes me wonder if there are others in the towers who are able to do the same. Our abilities may not be as reliable as we once believed. This could have widespread repercussions."

Alec glanced around to make sure no one was within earshot. Kayla's announcement about her abilities to affect the Shadows had caused an uproar within the Inner Circle. He wasn't sure the towers could withstand another announcement so soon, or what it could mean for Ariana's more sensitive nature. If people realized she had the ability to manipulate an entire room and turn them to her way of thinking without restriction, it could be disastrous.

"You're right. This can't get out. Ariana may be willing to conduct some tests to determine the scope of her abilities, but we need to proceed cautiously. Any investigation involving her should be strictly controlled. If the wrong people found out how easily she can read them or manipulate their emotions, she'll be a target."

"I agree," Brant said, tapping another order into his commlink before closing the device. "She's strong but also fragile. Kayla's more like a steamroller, but it was only Kayla's inexperience that made her susceptible to outside influence. Ariana is far more skilled than I ever imagined, but she's still vulnerable." Brant paused for a moment. "With your permission, I'd like to wire Hayden's living quarters."

"I can't risk it yet," Alec replied, keeping an eye on the hallway to make sure no one was approaching.

Hayden was somehow tied up in this mess, but Lars was right. They needed to be careful so Hayden couldn't make any accusations against him. Until Ariana publicly accepted his claim, he had to tread lightly around the fire channeler.

"I want Jason's medical room monitored though. I'll speak with him once he awakens and hopefully get some information from him. Otherwise, we may be able to learn something from one of his visitors. Have the results from the vial come back yet? Do we know what the substance is?"

"Not yet. It's proving challenging. Based on Ariana's earlier comments, I believe we may have to enlist some trusted Inner Circle members to assist with the analysis."

"Very well, I'll reach out to some of my contacts," Alec agreed with a sigh. There were too many questions and not enough answers. The number of Inner Circle members he trusted with sensitive information was getting smaller every day.

"Alec," Brant began and then hesitated. "I don't want to overstep myself, but I would be remiss in not saying something."

Alec arched an eyebrow. Brant was one of the few people he trusted implicitly. The fact his half-brother was apprehensive about saying something was more than a little curious. "You know I value your opinion and thoughts, Brant. What is it?"

Brant sighed. "I've known how you felt about Ariana for a long time. When the bond with Kayla broke, I'd hoped it would be an opportunity for you to pursue something with Ariana."

Alec nodded. He'd suspected as much.

"But I have some concerns," Brant explained, glancing in Ariana's direction again. "I know Hayden has more than a passing interest in her, but Sergei does as well. Earlier tonight, I saw her and Sergei together, and then I reviewed the surveillance feed from Hayden's club. Sergei is extremely protective and solicitous toward her. I believe it goes far beyond a mild interest. I suspect she may reciprocate some of his feelings."

Alec frowned, and he glanced again at her sleeping form. "I'm aware. She told me of her attraction to him. She's curious about non-sensitives, and Sergei is a way to alleviate that curiosity. Other than a kiss the other day, I don't believe anything of consequence has happened between them."

"What?" Brant's eyes widened a fraction. "I apologize. I wasn't aware you knew about their interactions."

Alec shrugged. "I'm not happy about it, but I'm not overly concerned about it either. She's been more than forthcoming about her interest in Sergei. She cares for him, but then again, I've never met anyone she doesn't care about in some way. It's just who she is. I don't believe her interest is serious."

"I see, but that brings up another concern," Brant said with a frown. "If she rebukes him, it may cause problems with our alliance. We're already behind schedule with the construction, and I'm not sure what will happen if we're unable to meet our deadline. If Sergei becomes angry that Ariana's chosen you over him, it could affect the outcome. We've allowed the Coalition a great deal of access to the towers, but we haven't sent our people to their satellite camps. I'm afraid we're at a strategic disadvantage."

Alec clasped his hands behind his back. "The Council has discussed sending an envoy to some of their camps for specifically that reason, but we're still deciding who should go and when. I was hoping you would be one of the people to go when things settle down. There are few in the towers that I would trust to act on my behalf."

Brant blinked, the only indication Alec's words had caught him off guard. "Thank you, Alec. I appreciate your trust."

"As far as Ariana is concerned," Alec began, glancing at her again through the glass, "Lars doesn't seem to think the situation with him will be a problem. I don't know Sergei well, and I'm not overly fond of him, but I believe his first loyalty is to his people. I don't believe he'll do anything to jeopardize that."

"I've heard that, but I don't know him well enough to comment," Brant admitted. "How do you intend to handle the situation with Hayden? It sounded like some promises were made regarding Ariana."

"Yes, I gathered that too," he replied, not bothering to mask his irritation. "That's one of the things I intend to discuss with Jason. Lars also brought up a concern about how Devan hasn't given permission for anyone else to court her. I suspect they came to some sort of arrangement."

Brant nodded. "For what it's worth, it didn't appear Ariana was aware."

"No, she's made it clear to me she's not interested in Hayden, not that it would matter at this point," Alec said with a small shrug. "I appreciate your candor, Brant, but you're right about Ariana. She's always been my biggest regret. I don't know if I've ever thanked you for your involvement in breaking the bond with Kayla. Ariana is..." He trailed off, not sure he could put into words how important she was to him.

"You love her," Brant said with a grin.

"I do," he admitted with a small smile.

Brant clapped Alec on the arm. "Then go to her. I'll walk with you two up to your quarters and then check on the situation with Jason. As soon as I hear something, I'll let you know."

"I appreciate it," Alec said and turned to retrieve the sleeping beauty that had awakened his heart.

————

ARIANA WOKE to the sensation of a hand stroking her back.

She made a small noise of contentment as Alec's enticing air energy traced the path of his hand, making lazy patterns as he held her.

"Good morning." Alec's warm breath tickled her ear as he spoke.

Ariana blinked open her eyes to find she was sprawled on top of him again, pinning him to the bed. She'd spent the last two years keeping her distance from him, but it appeared her subconscious was determined to make up for lost time. She started to move away, but he wrapped his arms around her, refusing to let her go.

"Not just yet," he murmured.

She gave up, content to remain his willing captive. "Mmm. We could just stay in bed all day."

Alec chuckled, the sound vibrating underneath her. She lifted her head a fraction, unable to resist seeing him smile. He rolled them over together, propping himself on his elbow to look down at her, and brushed a strand of hair away from her face.

"You have no idea how long I've imagined seeing you like this, here in my bed, with your hair spread out over my pillow and those gorgeous eyes looking up at me. Waking up with you in my arms is better than anything I could have ever dreamed."

She gazed up at him, his words sending those delicious butterflies in her stomach soaring.

He cupped her face and murmured, "You're so beautiful, Ari, inside and out. I want this life with you more than I've wanted anything."

"Alec..." she whispered, trying to blink back the tears that threatened to spill over. "If you're trying to keep me in bed with you, it's working."

He laughed, burying his face against her neck.

She reached up to run her fingers through his hair, marveling at the silky texture. "I love it when you laugh."

She felt his mouth curve against her skin. He pressed a kiss just below her ear, sending a small shiver through her. "You're the only one who makes me laugh like this, Ari."

Alec sighed in contentment, resting his hand on her hip and nuzzling her neck. Ariana started to close her eyes, entranced by the gentle swirl of his fingers against her hip and the trail of energy that followed. She definitely wouldn't mind spending the day lounging around with him. She was still so tired. Last night had really taken a lot— Her eyes flew open, and she sat up, looking around in a panic.

"Last night, what happened? How did I get here? Where's Jason?"

"Shh, it's all right, love," Alec urged, sitting up beside her. "Your brother's fine. He was released from medical about an hour ago. They wanted to make sure whatever was affecting him was completely out of his system. You fell asleep after healing him, and I brought you back here."

She let out a sigh of relief and frowned, remembering Jason's obnoxious behavior. "What do you think would happen if an empath decided to strangle her brother?"

Alec laughed again, his eyes sparking with amusement. "I don't think I want to risk it. I'm in love with that empath, and I'd rather not have anything happen to her, especially since we have so much to look forward to."

She couldn't help the smile that spread across her face at his words. Interlacing her fingers with his, she said, "We do have a lot to look forward to, don't we?"

"Mmhmm," he agreed, lifting her hand to press a kiss against it. "We'll deal with your brother some other way."

She tilted her head. "Did you find out what was wrong with Jason?"

"Actually—" A loud chime interrupted them. He frowned,

glancing over at a display screen beside the bed. He turned back to her, his earlier mirth gone. "It's your brother, along with your father."

Ariana felt her face pale. Nothing good could come of their visit.

Alec grasped her hands and enveloped her in a strong wave of energy. "Ari, breathe. It's going to be fine."

"They're not here to wish you well, Alec," she said, unable to hide her concern.

Reluctantly pulling away from him, she went over to her bag to retrieve her clothing. Alec must have dressed her in her nightgown after he brought her back last night because her dress had been carefully folded and placed on top of her bag. She was touched by his actions, and it only irritated her further that her family was intruding. Her father was probably livid for not being notified immediately that Jason had been detained.

"You're probably right," he admitted, pulling on his clothing. "But you don't need to worry. I'll handle it."

Alec disappeared into the bathroom, and Ariana slipped on the dress she'd worn to the security offices. She grabbed her brush and ran it through her hair before tossing it aside and searching her bag for her hair clips.

She was grumbling to herself when Alec emerged from the bathroom. Her hair clips had disappeared into another vortex and were nowhere to be found. There was nothing to be done about it. It would just be one more sign she'd spent the night with Alec. After everything that had happened over the past few days, her father would be less than thrilled.

She started to head into the bathroom, but Alec stopped her with a quick kiss. "Take your time, Ari. I'll speak with them and find out what's going on. Come join me for breakfast whenever you're ready."

She nodded but had no intention of leaving him to deal

with her family alone. Her father was bound to be out for blood. She finished quickly and slipped on her shoes, deciding she was more or less presentable. Steeling herself, she exited Alec's bedroom to confront her family and froze at the scene in front of her.

The jagged and brittle energy in the room nearly stole her breath. Her father was staring Alec down, his wrath a chilling force pummeling against the younger man. She spared Jason the briefest of glances. Her brother, in typical fashion, was sprawled out on Alec's couch, content to watch the unfolding argument. Physically, he didn't appear any worse for wear, but after everything he'd done, Ariana was tempted to change that.

"How dare you involve yourself with my family's personal matters," Devan snapped, the chill in his voice plunging the room into frigid temperatures. "Your interference has gone beyond all parameters of your position."

"You're incorrect, Devan," Alec replied evenly, clasping his hands behind his back and ignoring the emanating chill. Although on the surface he appeared calm and collected, the emotions surrounding him were fraught with tension. "This latest incident with Jason just happened to coincide with another investigation. In conjunction with my orders, he was detained until he could be properly questioned to determine whether he had any knowledge relevant to the investigation."

"What investigation?" Devan demanded.

Ariana took a step forward, and Jason's gaze turned toward her. His eyes widened, and he stood, running a hand through his dark hair. His gaze darted between Alec and their father, and then back to her. "Fuck, Ari. I thought I'd imagined seeing you last night. What the hell are you doing here?"

Her father turned in her direction, his eyes narrowing on her appearance. She lifted her head, prepared to tell her brother off, but Alec intervened before she could say anything.

"She exhausted herself trying to heal you last night, Jason. After she passed out, I ordered you to be taken to medical for observation. I brought her back here because I wasn't willing to leave her unattended."

Jason had the grace to look chagrined. He scrubbed his hands over his face and muttered, "Dammit. I'd hoped you were just my imagination." He lifted his head, his expression pained. "I'm so sorry, Ari. I shouldn't have put you through that."

The bitter scent of his remorse filled the surrounding air, intermingling with the icy chill of her father's anger. She lowered her head, resisting the urge to comfort and soothe with her energy. Alec was right. Sometimes things needed to play out naturally. Otherwise, they'd just continue to be caught in this perpetual loop.

"Ariana," her father addressed her, and she lifted her head to regard him. "It would be best if you returned to our quarters. Jason will escort you."

She blinked at him, darting her gaze to Alec who was observing Devan with a frown. Through their connection, she could tell he was apprehensive about something.

Ariana turned back to her father. "I'd prefer to remain here, if you don't mind. Alec and I have breakfast plans this morning."

"There's been a change," Devan informed her. "I've decided to rescind my earlier agreement to allow this courtship. I don't believe Alec is a good fit for you."

Her heart dropped into her stomach, and the world turned a sickly gray. In a strained voice, she managed, "What? Why?"

Alec's anger was lightning-fast and furious, causing the air to crackle with hints of ozone. "What's the meaning of this, Devan?" he demanded.

"After careful consideration, I don't believe you are the best choice for my daughter," Devan announced in an impassioned tone. "You've proven to be unreliable, as evidenced by your fractured bond with Kayla. We have no way of knowing whether you're even capable of maintaining a permanent bond with my daughter."

Alec's jaw clenched, and his entire body stiffened.

Ariana shook her head, detecting the pungent aroma of deception. Her father was hiding something. "If you truly believed that, why did you agree in the first place? What's changed?"

He didn't answer.

Jason approached her and said, "Ari, we want what's best for you. Hayden is a better choice. He's never entered into a bond, and he wants that with you. He can give you a future."

She glared at her brother. "Why do you keep pushing Hayden on me? What promises did you two make to each other? What is going on?"

"I can't tell you," Jason whispered, reaching for her hand. "I'm sorry, Ari. Please trust me. This is for the best."

Ariana jerked away from him and straightened her shoulders. "No. This is *not* for the best." She turned toward Devan. "I love Alec, Father. I've loved him for a long time. I won't walk away from him. Do not ask this of me."

There was a trace of pity in Devan's eyes, and he sighed. "Ariana, sometimes sacrifices need to be made. There are reasons for my decision, but we will speak of them in private."

"No," Alec declared, walking over to her and putting his arm around her shoulder. "I swear to you, here and now, that I am fully capable of holding a permanent bond. What happened with Kayla was an aberration, most likely a result of her spirit energy. I agreed to walk away from Ariana once before because it was in her best interest. I will not walk away from her again."

"Ari, please," Jason urged. "You don't understand."

"Then make me understand," she snapped and turned back to her father. "Alec and I have every right to know why you're making this request. While your approval of our courtship would mean a great deal to me, it is ultimately our decision."

A surge of pride and hope flowed through her connection with Alec. He squeezed her shoulder and said silently, *"I love you, Ari. We will get through this, I promise."*

"Yes, we will." She was more determined than ever not to lose the second chance they'd been given.

"Very well," Devan finally replied. "A union with Hayden Gavron will strengthen our family's line. I would not see the cumulative efforts of our ancestors diminished because you chose love over duty."

Ariana gaped at her father. "How can you possibly believe that? Love *strengthens* a bond. I don't love Hayden. I barely know him. Besides, Alec is an extremely strong air channeler. He holds the one element I don't."

"You can hold fire too," Alec murmured, his surprise coloring the energy in the air. "That must be the tie that binds your earth and water abilities together. That's the link to your empath abilities."

She nodded at him. "Yes. I'm not a traditional fire channeler, but it's enough to fuse the two together."

"Ariana," Devan snapped, "that's enough. You will not discuss your abilities."

"Alec has a right to know," she insisted. "He has a right to know all of this. He's never betrayed me in all the years he's known about me, and now you're asking us to walk away from each other simply to secure your power base."

Jason frowned. "Ari, Father wasn't talking about your power strengthening our family line. He was talking about mine."

She jerked her head back toward her brother. "What are you talking about?"

"Jason," Devan warned.

"No, she's right," he said. "She has a right to know."

Despair, dark and unyielding, permeated the energy around her brother. Ariana rushed over to him, gripping his hands tightly. She'd never seen him like this before.

"Jason, what's wrong?"

"Hayden's been working on developing a serum. He believes it will strengthen my abilities."

Her mouth dropped open. "That's what you took yesterday? You took something to try to make yourself more powerful? For heaven's sake, why? How could you do such a thing?"

"To protect you!" He turned away and began pacing. "Your abilities are changing and growing even stronger. I can't be your strength anymore, Ari. There's no guarantee a bondmate will help. Hayden promised to continue working on this serum in exchange for exclusive courtship rights. It's the only way to make sure you're protected."

She blinked at him and pulled her hands away, looking back and forth between Jason and her father. "Both of you planned this? You agreed to this courtship with Hayden because it'll make you more powerful?"

"What is this serum?" Alec demanded.

Jason sighed and rubbed the bridge of his nose. "He calls it *Drakar*. There's a lesser version being marketed at his clubs. He uses the credits from the sale to continue researching a more powerful and customized version for me. I tried the latest batch last night. It didn't go well."

"The vial," Ariana whispered, understanding dawning. "This serum was created from Kayla's blood, wasn't it?"

"Yes," Jason admitted. "They took her blood when she was in medical. Hayden bribed someone for a sample and has his own researchers working with it. They've been trying to tweak it to match with my energy signature. Something went wrong last night."

Her heart clenched at the thought of what might have happened if she hadn't been there. "How could you put yourself at risk like that, Jason? It could have killed you."

"I'd do anything to protect you, Ari," he whispered, his expression pained.

Her heart broke a little at his words. She turned to her father. "You knew about this? Why would you let him do it?"

"I knew," Devan acknowledged. "It was a calculated risk. I wasn't aware they were attempting a new version of the serum last night. They finished it earlier than expected."

She shook her head. "You shouldn't have done this. He almost died last night. If I hadn't been with Alec when Brant contacted him, he wouldn't be here right now."

"If Alec hadn't interfered," Devan began, glaring again at Alec, "I would have been at my son's side and been able to transport him to the research team. The healing you did last night has negated any effects the serum had on your brother. He'll have to attempt another dosage, this time with full twenty-four-hour monitoring."

"No," Ariana gasped, horrified by the thought. "You will not do this. Not for me. I won't be the reason he's endangering himself. Can't you see this is wrong?"

"I will not lose the most powerful empath in generations simply because she's headstrong and willful," Devan snapped. "Your brother shares a bond with you, so he can supplement your strength and protect you. He will continue to do what is necessary to fulfill that role, as will you."

"No," she whispered, taking a step back and bumping into Alec.

Wrapping his arms around her, he spoke over her head. "Devan, this is unacceptable. We do not tolerate this sort of testing or genetic manipulation. This is what took us down the path of those bracelets. The cost is much too high."

"When you asked to court my daughter, you claimed you cared for her," Devan said, crossing his arms over his chest. "What price would you put on her life? The last empath who lived wasn't nearly as powerful, and she was the same age as Ariana when she died. The only difference was she didn't have a twin who could help share the burden. Jason and Ariana admit their bond is failing. Her powers are continuing to grow and soon their bond won't be enough. What other choice is there?"

Alec tightened his arms around her but didn't reply. She swallowed and pulled away from him. Pain, raw and unfiltered, shone in his eyes and cascaded through their shared connection. She knew. She knew Alec was willing to do just about anything to keep her safe.

"Ari," he began, reaching for her.

"No," she told them, backing away from all of them. "This is wrong. You cannot put Jason at risk for me."

"It's my choice, Ari," Jason said, taking a step toward her.

"It's not," she pleaded. "What do you think it would do to me if you died, Jason? I can't— I *won't* be the reason for this. I would rather die than be responsible for your suffering. This will break me. I know it in my heart."

She squeezed her eyes shut, swaying from the emotions swirling throughout the room. After everything at the night-club and healing Jason, the assault was brutal. No wonder they'd kept this a secret. All the secrecy, Jason's weird mood swings, everything made sense.

"Dammit," Jason said. "This is too much on her. Ari, you need to leave."

Alec wrapped his arm around her again, sending a strong wave of energy through their connection. It wasn't enough to help insulate her from the volatile emotions. "Do you want to take a shower or go to the pool? Tell me what you need, beautiful."

Ariana leaned into his touch, closing her eyes as his exquisite energy flowed over her. "I need to be alone for a little while. There's too much emotion. I just..." Her voice trailed off, and she frowned. "I'm sorry, Alec. I don't want to leave you right now. I know things need to play out naturally, but I can't stay here and protect myself against all the emotion."

"I understand," he replied, pressing a kiss against her forehead. "I'll be here for you whenever you need me. I love you, Ari."

"I love you too," she whispered, sending a wave of gratitude and love over him. "Thank you for understanding."

"We'll fix this," he promised, squeezing her hand. "I won't lose you, and I won't let anything happen to your brother either. Trust me, Ari."

She nodded and lowered her gaze, not wanting him to see the doubt in her eyes. Turning away again, she walked out of his quarters, her heart breaking all over again.

CHAPTER THIRTEEN

ARIANA WRAPPED her arms around herself as she walked through the silent corridor. How could everything have changed so quickly? Just last night, her world had been full of color and hope. Now that precious future was being threatened by the dim reality that her brother was jeopardizing his health and happiness for the remote possibility she would survive her evolving powers. To make matters worse, her father had tried to sell her off to Hayden in exchange for this serum.

Tears pricked the corners of her eyes, and she blinked rapidly to keep them from falling. She wouldn't cry. Her commlink beeped, and she glanced at it before shutting it off. Jason wanted to know where she'd gone, but she couldn't deal with him right now. Not until she got her head around everything. More than anything, she wanted to get lost in the soothing waters of her pool, but that would be the first place Jason would look. She didn't want to listen to any more of his justifications, even if she were immersed in the protective barrier of the water.

Ariana hesitated before pressing her palm against the

panel by the priority elevator. She programmed in one of the lower levels and the elevator shot downward. Leaning against the glass windows, she sighed. There was only one place she could think of where Jason wouldn't intrude on her thoughts. He knew all the other places she frequented.

Stepping out when the doors opened, she crossed the breezeway into the construction tower and headed toward Sergei's room. She trusted him not to betray their secrets and hoped he'd have some insight into the situation with her brother. His calm practicality would be refreshing. At the very least, she needed to take care of his plant.

She pressed the button beside his door and waited, hoping she wasn't interrupting anything. Maybe she should have contacted him first. There was always the possibility he'd gone back to the surface again. She pulled out her commlink, but the door opened before she could turn it back on. She blinked up at Pavel and managed a small smile.

"Hi again. Is Sergei here?"

"No," he replied in his accented voice, stepping aside and motioning for her to enter.

"Oh," she murmured, not bothering to hide her disappointment.

"Sergei is busy today. You are here to care for plant?"

His sharp eagerness at her arrival was a little disconcerting, but she plucked some moisture from the air to insulate against his emotions. A headache was already beginning to form behind her eyes. Maybe she should have gone to the pool instead and risked dealing with her brother.

"I was hoping to speak with him, and yes. I only have a few minutes, but I should check on his plant while I'm here. I didn't bring any hydrating packs with me. Do you know where he stores them?"

Pavel slid the door shut behind her and motioned toward a small cabinet in the corner. She opened it, selected a hydrating pack, and walked over to the plant. Pushing a small amount of earth energy toward it, she determined it was still doing well. She added a touch of water, smiling at the eagerness of the hardy little bush. If only everything could be so simple.

Feeling a sharp prick at her neck, she lifted her hand to swat at it. Dizziness engulfed her, and she staggered. Pavel caught her before she fell, and she blinked up at him, trying to understand what was happening. Dark malevolence and greed swirled through the energy in the air, and she shuddered against the onslaught. Her thoughts were growing fuzzy, and she couldn't focus enough to reinforce her internal shields to resist his emotions.

He was speaking, but the words were too confusing. Was he talking into a commlink? She couldn't understand, and it was becoming harder to focus. Ariana blinked again, her eyes growing heavy, and then the world faded away into darkness.

———

ALEC DISCONNECTED from his commlink call and rested his head in his hands. After Devan and Jason had left, he'd gone into his office and spent the last hour dealing with the *Drakar* situation. Now that he knew the purpose of the serum, he needed to stop its distribution to the public. There was only one person with access to all the information they needed, and Hayden was on his way there right now.

"Using the security feeds, we're compiling a list of the potential users right now," Brant explained, entering something into his tablet. "Three more establishments have been identified as distribution sites. All of these are operated by different individuals."

Alec watched as a map of the locations within OmniLab populated on his wall screen. One of them was a gambling hall and the other two were nightclubs, but he couldn't see the connection. One of the clubs was a rather upscale establishment, while the other was decidedly not.

Alec frowned. "What do these places have in common?"

"Other than an active nightlife?"

When Alec nodded, Brant said, "There's a small overlap of clientele, but not much. We're running the comparison now, but there are no other connections between Hayden's establishment and these others. Our surveillance cameras identified the same two individuals making sales at these other locations within the past few days."

In a dry tone, Alec replied, "I find it a remarkable coincidence that we caught these sales on surveillance in other clubs right after Devan agreed to Hayden's courtship request. Hayden had to know I'd investigate him and his clubs. I wouldn't be surprised if this was an effort to circumvent suspicion of his involvement."

"I agree," Brant said. "Up until then, the distribution of *Drakar* had been contained to only a few of Hayden's clubs and out of sight. We're arranging to have the sellers brought in for questioning, but they've likely been heavily compensated to act as a diversion. I doubt they'll be forthcoming with information."

"Do what you can," Alex said with a sigh, leaning back in his chair. "I also want the name of the person responsible for selling the serum crafted from Kayla's blood. See if you can connect them to the researchers working on modifying this serum. If Hayden doesn't give us information, we need to find it another way."

Alec drummed his fingers on the desk, his thoughts going back to Ariana. On the off chance they needed Hayden's continued cooperation, Devan and Jason had refused to give any other information about the serum. The idea that Hayden was using this potential life-saving serum to force

Ariana into a bond enraged him. Alec had felt her shock and horror at the thought her brother was using himself as a test subject in an effort to save her. Although, if he had been in Jason's shoes, he might have done the same.

Devan had admitted to looking into ways to strengthen the bond between Jason and Ariana for the past two years, ever since it began failing. This serum was just the latest in a long string of attempts to protect his daughter. Alec refused to believe this was the only solution. There had to be another way. He wouldn't lose her, not to her abilities and definitely not to Hayden.

Alec pressed a button on his desk and said, "Sheila, I want you to locate any and all files we've accumulated on empaths and their abilities. If possible, trace their elemental alignments."

"Of course, sir," came her polite reply. "Do you want case studies or information about specific individuals?"

He paused for a moment. "Both. I want specific names, genealogy charts, birth and death dates, whatever information you can locate. In particular, I want their bond status, including the alignments of the mate. Focus on the most recent, then go back through the pre-war archives."

"I'll get started right away, Master Tal'Vayr."

Brant looked over at him when he disconnected. "You're hoping to find something?"

"Devan said most empaths don't survive into their early twenties," Alec explained. "There has to be some way to protect Ariana. I refuse to believe this godsforsaken serum is the answer." No matter what, he wouldn't lose her. If he had to move heaven and earth to keep her safe, he'd find a way to do it.

Brant lowered his tablet. "You think there might be a connection with their bond status?"

"Devan and Jason believe so. The bond with Jason has

protected her up until this point. He's been buffering some of the negative effects since they were children. If there's a connection between an empath's bond status and their premature demise, I want to know what it is."

"I can put some of my people on this too," Brant offered.

Alec nodded. "Go ahead, but only enlist the assistance of people you trust. I don't want them to make the connection between Ariana and her ability to circumvent shadow energy."

"Of course," Brant agreed, typing a few commands into his tablet.

There was a small chime and Sheila's voice came over the speaker again. "Excuse me, Master Tal'Vayr, but Hayden Gavron is here to see you."

"Send him in."

The door opened, and the dark-haired man who was competing for Ariana's affections entered. Alec had a momentary flash of anger at the thought of him touching her. He'd reviewed the available security video and had to force himself not to hunt down the bastard right then and there.

"Hayden," Alec acknowledged, keeping his tone cool. He gestured to the chair in front of his desk. "Please, have a seat."

Hayden inclined his head and sat down, taking a moment to survey the office. "Well, Alec, I must admit I was surprised to receive your meeting request. Other than Ariana, I'm not sure what business we have in common." He paused for a moment, his expression becoming calculating. "Unless, of course, you wish to inform me you're no longer courting her?"

Alec leaned back in his chair, feigning nonchalance. "On the contrary, I am still courting Ariana and have no intention of conceding." *And I love her, you arrogant prick.*

Hayden's mouth curved downward a fraction, but that was the only indication he was displeased. "I see. Devan indicated to me that he planned to rescind his permission for you to court his daughter."

"Yes, you're quite mistaken," Alec replied and pressed a button to display each of Hayden's clubs. "I asked you here because we've had a number of disturbing reports about something called *Drakar* being distributed in your establishments."

Hayden put his elbows on the arm of the chair and tapped his finger idly against his chin. "Ah, yes. It's unfortunate, but drug use and clubs have a rather sordid past. I'm not sure why this would warrant the interest of our esteemed Council leader." He shrugged. "Of course, I'll have security monitor the situation more closely. After all, it wouldn't be prudent to expose Ariana to such things. We had a rather enjoyable evening last night at Club Sapphire. She is remarkable, isn't she?"

"Oh, I'd say remarkable is far too tame of a description," Alec returned, unable to resist smirking at the fire channeler.

You'll never know how tame. After waking up with her in my arms this morning, remarkable doesn't even come close to describing her. So yeah, you can have the memory of your evening with her because that's all you'll have, you stupid fuck.

Hayden's eyes narrowed. Alec motioned toward Brant, who pushed forward his tablet and said, "Up until a few days ago, *Drakar* had only been distributed at your clubs and only to Inner Circle members. We believe this 'drug' originated from your club, and specifically, was funded from your pockets."

Hayden ignored the tablet and Brant, instead focusing directly on Alec. "Are you accusing me of something, Alec?"

Before he could respond, a sharp chime alerted him to an urgent call. He held up his hand to ask Hayden to wait a moment and took the call.

"Is Ari with you?"

Alec frowned. "Jason? What are you talking about?"

"I can't find her anywhere," Jason said in a rush. "Fuck. She's just disappeared. Something's wrong. I feel it."

"You checked the pool?"

"Of course I checked the fucking pool. I checked with Kendra, I checked her favorite spot in the library, I checked every place she goes when she's upset, and she's not in any of them. I need to find her. When did you last see her?"

"This morning with you," Alec replied. "She wanted to be alone, but I'll check with security and let you know what I find out."

"Hurry," Jason urged, the anxiety in his tone evident. Alec disconnected from the call and reached out toward Ariana through their connection. It wasn't strong enough yet, but he managed to get a dim sense of her. Something wasn't quite right, but he wasn't sure what was wrong. A small sense of worry coiled in his gut.

Hayden frowned and leaned forward. "Is it Ariana? Is she all right?"

Alec lifted his gaze to regard Hayden. He'd momentarily forgotten about him. Annoyed, both with himself and Hayden, he said, "Jason's trying to locate her and wanted to know if I'd seen her. To answer your earlier question, no. I'm not accusing you of anything. I am, however, going to make a demand."

Hayden arched an eyebrow. "Enlighten me."

Alec stood and leaned forward, narrowing his eyes. "You will immediately cease all distribution of *Drakar*. You will turn over all related research of the serum as well as all information on the attempts you've made to strengthen the bond between Ariana and Jason. And you will back the fuck off from Ariana and her family and stop trying to capitalize on saving a young woman's life."

Hayden's face remained carefully blank. "You make a lot of presumptions, Alec."

"I'm not playing this game with you, Hayden," Alec snapped. "I want the names of the researchers and their notes sent to my office in the next hour or I will see you imprisoned and your clubs shut down indefinitely while I drag you through a long and arduous investigation."

Hayden stood, pressing his hands against the desk. "You think you can meddle in my business affairs and threaten me? This can be construed as an act of interference with a potential claimant. If you won't take Devan's warnings of withdrawing your claim seriously, I'll take this matter before the Council."

"I don't give a fuck what you do. You've been made aware of my demands and the consequences of your actions if you don't comply. Now, get the hell out of my office."

Hayden glared at him, barely suppressing his fire energy, but a brief flash of the flames reflected in his eyes. Without another word, Hayden turned and stormed out of his office.

Alec sat back down and pulled up Ariana's security profile to track her movements.

"Are you sure that was wise?" Brant asked in a low voice.

"Ariana's missing," Alec retorted, ignoring his question. He leaned forward to study Ariana's recent expenditures while the biometric scanner ran in the background. There were no purchases from this morning. He checked the biometric scanner and frowned at the warning message that appeared on the screen. "How could she not be in the towers?"

"Perhaps she went to the construction tower," Brant suggested. "We can track her movements from when she left your family's quarters. Do you know what time she left?"

"Around eleven," Alec replied as Brant pulled up the video.

A moment later, an image of Ariana appeared on the screen. She was obviously distraught, her arms wrapped around herself in a protective gesture. His heart clenched as he watched her walk down the corridor alone. He should have gone with her. He'd known she was upset, but she looked so lost.

She hesitated at the priority elevator before stepping inside. Alec frowned. "She's not going to her quarters. Where did she go?"

Brant entered a few commands and the video resumed in the lobby. Dammit. Brant was right. She'd taken one of the breezeways to the construction tower. What the hell was she doing there?

Brant glanced down at his tablet. "She exited at the floor to Sergei's quarters."

Oh, hell no.

Alec pushed away from his desk and headed out of his office. Brant jogged after him to catch up, still checking his tablet. "We don't have that area under adequate surveillance yet. According to Sergei's calendar, he has a meeting with Lars right now."

The door to the priority elevator slid open and they stepped inside. Alec programmed in their destination and glanced over at Brant's tablet. "Where are they meeting?"

"A conference room on that same level. It's a few doors down from his quarters."

Alec pulled out his commlink and called Lars. His cousin answered almost immediately. "Hey Alec, how's it going?"

"Are you with Sergei?"

Lars hesitated, apparently picking up on his tone. "Yeah, he just got here. We're trying to figure out a workaround for the construction delays. Why? What's going on?"

"Is Ariana with you?"

"What? No, why would she be? Alec, what's going on?"

Alec frowned, the worry in his gut coiling even tighter like a serpent prepared to strike. "Ask Sergei if he's seen her."

The elevator doors opened, and they stepped out, heading down the noisy corridor.

Lars replied a moment later. "No. He hasn't seen her since last night. What's going on?"

"Ariana's missing. Her brother can't find her, she's not in the tower, and her last known location was the construction tower."

There was a lengthy pause and then Lars said, "We're on our way to Sergei's quarters. She may have gone there. He gave her the code yesterday so she could check on the plant."

Alec disengaged his call and shoved it back in his pocket. She'd been gone for two hours. It didn't take that long to check on a plant. "Check to see if Ariana used an access code to enter Sergei's quarters."

Brant glanced down at his tablet again and shook his head. "She didn't. Shortly after she arrived on this level, the door was opened from the inside."

Alec's jaw clenched. What the hell sort of game was Sergei playing and why would he deny seeing her? He approached Sergei's quarters and entered his override code. The door slid open, and he cast his gaze around the empty room.

Sergei and Lars entered a moment later, and Alec whirled around. He flicked his wrist, slamming Sergei against the wall with his air energy.

"Where the fuck is she?"

"Control yourself, Alec!" Lars shouted. "You can see she's not here. Sergei wouldn't hurt her."

Brant grabbed Alec's arm, his shadow energy swirling through the air and coaxing him to calm. He pointed to a hydrating pack lying on its side near the plant, most of its contents spilled in a small puddle on the floor. Alec released the air energy holding Sergei, letting him fall to the ground.

"Your cousin is correct," Sergei asserted coldly as he stood, his hand brushing against the weapon at his side. "I will forgive your lapse in control this once. However, if you use energy against me again, our treaty will be finished."

Alec ignored him and approached the spilled pack, the gnawing worry growing larger. "If she had been here, Ariana wouldn't have left the water like that. Every drop is precious to her."

Sergei strode toward the plant and pressed his fingers against the soil. "She was here."

"Who else has access to your quarters?" Alec demanded. "She didn't use the code to enter. Someone let her in."

Sergei scowled at him. "Your people have codes to enter. Some of my people do too."

"Brant, contact security and have them analyze this room," Alec ordered. "I want the names of everyone who has been here. Backtrack and find out which of our people accessed this floor within the past twenty-four hours." He turned back to Sergei. "I want your people questioned as well."

Sergei ignored him, sweeping his gaze over the remainder of the room. He moved beside the table and knelt to pick up something off the ground. He studied it for a long moment and murmured, "This belongs to Ariana."

Alec frowned and walked over to Sergei. In his hand was a small ring with a deep-blue stone. He swallowed, the fear in his gut becoming a living thing. He took it from Sergei and managed, "She was wearing it this morning. She never takes this off."

Sergei's eyes narrowed, and he walked over to his desk, scanning the contents. He picked up a tablet and swore in his native tongue.

Lars turned to him and demanded, "What is it?"

"Pavel," Sergei snapped. "He was in my quarters yesterday to deliver progress reports. He must have met her and realized she was responsible for the plant."

Alec clenched his fist around the ring and took a step forward. "Are you saying one of your people abducted her?"

Lars's eyes grew wide as he glanced back and forth between them. "Sergei, are you sure? Pavel's your second-in-command."

Sergei tossed the tablet aside in disgust. "Yes. He accessed my notes on Ariana and the instructions she gave me to care for the plant. If he knew she would return, he could have waited for her. Ariana is too trusting. She would not have considered him to be a danger."

"Would he hurt her?" Lars asked, a trace of fear creeping into his voice.

Sergei was silent for a long moment and looked over his desk again. "I do not know. I was planning to release Pavel from service at the end of the month. He and some others are afraid of your people. Fear makes them unpredictable."

"If this is true and he's taken her," Alec said, his tone sharp, "our alliance is forfeit."

Sergei met his gaze evenly. "I understand. We will discuss this after we locate her. I will not endanger my people because of a rogue agent."

"Very well," Alec conceded. "However, if this Pavel has harmed her in any way, I will kill him."

Sergei inclined his head. "If he has harmed her, I will help you."

———

PAIN, sharp and stinging, lanced over her cheek as someone slapped her. Ariana groaned, trying to move, but her body wouldn't cooperate. It was heavy and sluggish, and the pounding in her head was competing against the brutality of someone slapping her again. She whimpered, trying to move away, but her limbs wouldn't work.

"Wake up," a man demanded.

She blinked open her eyes, trying to focus on the dark shadow looming over her. So much anger and rage—it overwhelmed the room, suffocating her with its onslaught. Ariana cringed, reaching for her energy to soothe them, but they slapped her again. She cried out, her eyes now wide open, the throbbing in her head from the cacophony of emotions outrivaling the physical pain in her cheek. It was a migraine of emotion pounding against her—so much fear, fury, and desperation coming from everywhere all at once.

A sharp object was jabbed against her side, the tip of it piercing her skin. "If you use energy, you will die."

"Please," she managed, her voice hoarse. "I need water."

A moment later, water splashed over her face. She coughed and sputtered but managed to weave some of the water energy into her shields. It wasn't enough. The emotions were too strong and there were too many of them, all clamoring for attention. Her awareness sharpened a fraction, but the images wavered as she tried to focus on the room. Pieces began to solidify before going blurring again. Why couldn't she focus? Was it from the emotions?

She managed to get a few impressions of the small room. A dirt floor, a small table and chair, and beyond that, she could make out a textured wall. The wall wasn't like anything she'd seen in the towers. Pavel was standing over her with an ugly sneer on his face, holding a dripping hydrating pack in one hand and a knife in the other. A wave of nausea washed over her, and she squeezed her eyes shut trying to keep herself from being sick.

"Sit up," he ordered.

Ariana blinked again from her prone position on the floor, but her arms still wouldn't work. She was bound, with her hands behind her back and her ankles tied together. Impatient, Pavel put down the hydrating pack and grabbed her arm, jerking her upright. She cried out from the burning agony of his touch and the emotional pain surrounding her.

"This pathetic creature is who you were so interested in?" a woman spoke from somewhere behind Pavel. "I am not impressed, Pavel. If she is of no use to us, you will dispose of her. But do it away from here so her people will not find her."

"She grew plant in Sergei's room," Pavel snapped. "We will use her to grow more."

Ariana swallowed, her throat dry, and glanced at the hydrating pack. If she were going to figure out how to get out of this, she needed clarity of mind. "Can I have some water to drink?"

"You will grow plant first," he demanded, gesturing to a pot on the floor near her.

She stared at it and frowned. A plant? That was why they'd brought her here? It didn't make any sense. If Sergei had wanted her help, all he needed to do was ask.

"Where's Sergei?"

Pavel's eyes narrowed, and he raised his hand, bringing it down with a sharp *crack*. The force of the blow sent Ariana reeling, knocking her back down to the ground. Her eyes welled with tears, the pain in her head a hot and stabbing lance. He grabbed her again, this time by her hair, and forced her upright.

"Begin," he ordered and raised his hand, threatening to strike her again.

She flinched and tried to focus on the pot, but her vision kept wavering. The fury emanating from Pavel wasn't the only emotion surrounding him. Ariana caught the pungent aroma of guilt too. There was no way to tell if the guilt was from abducting her or if her question about Sergei had triggered it. Whatever it was, Ariana had no doubt Sergei was ignorant of Pavel's plans.

Ariana licked her lips, trying to retain some of the moisture that had splashed on her skin. It wasn't enough to insulate her from the relentless emotions. She hesitated, wondering if he'd strike her again for speaking. "I—I'm not a fully-trained earth channeler, but I can try to grow your plant. I'll need my hands free though."

Suspicion crept over Pavel's face, but he leaned forward to remove her wrist bindings. His movements were brisk, but he never turned the weapon away from her.

"Is that wise?" the woman asked.

Ariana tried to rub life back into her wrists. They were red and raw where the metallic bindings had dug into her skin.

"Sergei made notes about her. She does not have offensive abilities."

Ariana's heart fell into her stomach. Sergei couldn't have shared that information with him. Sergei was difficult to read, but she should have been able to tell if he were planning to hurt her. Had she been shielding from everyone so much that she'd crippled herself? She'd known there was something off about Pavel, but she never suspected this. She hung her head, ashamed she'd suppressed her abilities to such an extent. In trying to protect herself, she'd make things far worse than she'd ever imagined.

"I want to see these notes." A tall, dark-haired woman with streaks of gray in her hair stepped out of the shadows. She was handsome but possessed a callousness in her aura Ariana found unsettling. There was a connection between her and Pavel, some sort of compact that bound them together. Ariana had no doubt that this woman would hurt her if given the opportunity.

Pavel motioned toward a tablet sitting on a small table. The woman picked it up and read over the contents before replacing it. When she turned back to Ariana, there was a calculating gleam in her eye. "You are a healer too?"

"Yes. I saw her heal," Pavel said before Ariana could answer.

"Indeed," the woman murmured, taking several steps toward Ariana. She bent down, grasping Ariana's hair and jerking her head upright. "A healer who can grow plants? You may be very valuable to us."

Ariana's eyes watered, the pain from this woman's touch even more brutal than Pavel's. There was so much hatred, so much envy, so much of everything. It was too much. Ariana unwillingly flinched at the woman's critical assessment.

The woman released her suddenly with a sharp laugh and stepped away, gesturing to the pot. "Make it grow. If you succeed, we will allow you to live. For now."

Ariana swallowed and studied the pot beside her. There were a few handfuls of dirt thrown into it, but she had no idea what they wanted her to grow.

"Did you have a seed?" she asked, trying to see if she'd missed it somewhere.

"You will use this," the woman said, thrusting a strange object at her.

Ariana took it, studying the relatively hard, brownish vegetable with several lumps and small sprouts. She leaned forward and took a sniff, the earthly aroma strangely soothing. It had slumbered under the soil, still retaining its preference for the dark.

"You will grow it," Pavel reiterated.

She blinked up at him and studied the vegetable again. Seara had only taught her how to grow plants from seed. She knew it was possible, the plant was already beginning to sprout without her assistance, but her experience was too limited.

"What is it?"

The woman scoffed and turned away, heading toward the door. "She does not even know what it is. This is a waste of time. Kill her and be done with it, Pavel. I have better things to do."

"No, please," Ariana urged, panic rising sharply within her. She clutched it to her chest and added, "I'd like to try."

Pavel regarded her for several heartbeats. "It is a potato. You will grow it now."

"Oh," Ariana murmured, looking down at the vegetable again. She'd eaten potatoes but had never held an uncooked one in her hands. There was so much potential in this small vegetable. Why had she ignored her earth talents for so long?

Ariana took a deep breath and closed her eyes, reaching out to the surrounding energy in the room. They were in some sort of compound. The echoes of the emotions of dozens of other people overlapped, but she didn't recognize any energy signatures.

I must be in a Coalition camp.

She took another deep breath—pretending to be focused on the potato—and reached out farther, trying to sense the bond with Jason or even her connection to Alec.

There were sharp tugs from both of them, and she gasped. Their worry and desperate fear were nearly overwhelming. They knew she was missing. She had to stall to give them time to find her.

"What is it?" Pavel demanded, taking a step toward her.

She shook her head. "I'm sorry. I'll try again. It might help if I had a little water though. That's more of my element. I'm not used to working with earth energy"

"Give it to her," the woman demanded, obviously growing impatient with the whole ordeal.

Pavel scowled but handed over the hydrating pack. Ariana took a large sip, gathering the energy threads inside her and using them to fortify her strength. Pavel snatched the hydrating pack from her hand, and she lowered her gaze. Maybe it would be enough.

She closed her eyes again, reaching out across her connections, and sensed Alec. Although her bond with Jason was stronger, Alec had the unique ability to communicate telepathically.

"Pavel, Coalition camp, Prisoner." She sent the thought outward, along with the mental images of her captors. There was no way to know if he picked up on the message. She could only hope he was listening.

Ariana turned her focus toward the potato, uneasy about how much energy she'd already used by sending the message. It was taking almost everything she had to keep from being overwhelmed by the emotions in the camp. If she wasn't able to grow the potato, though, it might be for naught. Neither Pavel nor the woman seemed overly troubled about exterminating her if she didn't live up to their expectations.

She sent a trace amount of energy toward the potato, trying to get a sense of the vegetable and what it would demand in exchange for growing. Its requirements were relatively modest. Hopefully, they wouldn't require more than this one demonstration. She blinked open her eyes and studied the pot in front of her. Sending another small amount of energy outward, she checked the composition of the soil. It wasn't ideal, but she didn't think they'd take kindly to her asking for something different.

Ariana placed the potato in the deep pot, carefully covering it with a layer of dirt. Spreading her hands over the soil-covered vegetable, she sent her power outward and into those small little sprouts just beginning to emerge. The roots began to unfurl beneath the soil, reaching outward, but it hesitated.

She paused and glanced up at Pavel. "I need the hydrating pack again."

He handed it to her, and she poured it over the soil, feeling the moisture permeate the roots beneath the surface. When it had enough, she placed the hydrating pack beside her and moved her hands over the vegetable again. Wiping her brow with her elbow, she sent out more energy. She needed to hurry. Her remaining strength was dwindling too quickly. The sprouting plant reached outward, breaking through the surface and forming small leaves. Underneath, the roots were becoming even more established. The growing excitement from Pavel and the woman were overpowering, and Ariana slumped forward, barely catching herself before she fell.

Pavel's expression was smug. "I told you, Sofia. She will be of great use to us and easy to manage."

"Well done," the woman declared. "It appears Pavel was correct. We may keep you for a while." She motioned toward the plant. "Pavel, come. I want our scientists to look at our new plant."

Pavel moved forward and refastened the bindings tightly on her wrists. She winced as the metal once again bit into her skin, but she didn't object. He retrieved the plant and followed the woman out the door.

Ariana's eyes fluttered closed, unable to find the strength to even try to pick up the abandoned hydrating pack beside her.

———

ALEC CLOSED his eyes and inhaled sharply. He kept repeating Ariana's words over again in his head. *Pavel, Coalition Camp,*

Prisoner. Underneath, he could sense her exhaustion and pain. What the fuck were they doing to her? He pressed his hands against his desk, reaching out to her again and cursing himself for not solidifying their bond. So much for noble intentions. If he'd bonded with her, he'd be able to share his energy with her. As it was, he only had a dim sense of her—just enough to know she was still alive.

They'd all returned to Alec's office as a central base to organize their efforts to locate Ariana. Jason had joined them and was now sitting in a nearby chair, resting his head in his hands. Ariana's brother was picking up on some of her emotions, too, but so far hadn't been able to locate her. He was still trying, but Alec didn't have much hope he would be successful.

At least he'd convinced Ariana's father to lead the investigation searching the construction tower for any trace of Ariana. Devan had been a whirlwind of icy fury when he learned Ariana had been taken. He'd demanded they launch an immediate attack against the Coalition and only reconsidered after someone pointed out that an attack against them might put Ariana's life in even more danger. If they didn't find her soon, Alec was tempted to launch the attack himself. Someone had to know something.

"The drones are in the air," Brant advised. "We've employed the new devices to track energy manipulation, but they're still not completely reliable. Hopefully, Ariana's still emitting her usual low-level energy current."

"She's exhausted." Alec curled his hands into fists. "She can't keep this up much longer. I want several squads on standby. As soon as we find something, I want them ready to move out."

Brant nodded. "We have an aircraft already waiting for you. Kayla's on the surface at the underground river location, and she's trying to find Ariana based on the description of the clothing you provided her. Her ability to locate objects is still unpredictable, but she wants to try."

Alec started pacing. It wasn't enough. There had to be something else they could do. He couldn't just sit here and wait while Ariana was out there suffering. He glanced over at Sergei, who was arguing hotly via commlink with someone in his native language. Lars was hunched over a digital map of the surrounding area and occasionally interjected a comment in the same language.

Sergei ended the call and tossed his commlink on the table in disgust before leaning over to view the screen in front of Lars. "Pavel is not in Grigory's camp either, but he will thoroughly question his people to be sure."

Lars grimaced as though the idea of Grigory's version of questioning was something decidedly uncomfortable. He pressed a few buttons, graying out part of the map.

Alec stepped over to view the map, wondering if there was another way to go about this. So far, none of Sergei's people had admitted to seeing Pavel that day.

"Perhaps we're asking the wrong questions. If they're holding Ariana in one of the camps and there's no trace of Pavel, it's likely he's working with someone." Alec looked over at Sergei. "Which of your people would be willing to risk harboring him?"

Sergei was quiet for several minutes and then said, "Few would risk my wrath, but desperation may make them bold." He picked up a tablet and entered a few commands. A list of over two dozen names appeared on the screen. "I am releasing these people from service soon. If they suspected I intended to release them, any of them may be tempted to betray me, especially for a prize such as Ariana. My superiors still do not believe in your energy, but Pavel may wish to use her to prove these claims."

Lars nodded. "I recognize a few names on that list. Some

of them are in a position where they could effectively hide Pavel and Ariana from the rest of the camp without raising suspicion."

Sergei pressed the screen, eliminating several names. When he finished, there were at least ten names still on the list. "These people have access to secure areas within our camps. I'll put them under surveillance immediately, but I will need to question them directly. I do not trust anyone else to handle their interrogation."

Alec leaned forward, studying the names. They didn't mean anything to him, but he didn't know any of the Coalition forces. "How well do these people know Pavel?"

"Well enough," Sergei replied. "Pavel has been acting as my second for several months. I have some contacts who may know more."

He picked up his commlink again, but before he could make a call, Jason lifted his head and demanded, "How do we know you're not behind this?"

Sergei's expression was an unreadable mask, and he didn't respond.

Jason stood up and snarled, "We're just going along with whatever he says, but how much do we *really* know about him?" He pinned Sergei with his glare. "Ariana trusted you. I warned her away from you, but she wouldn't listen. Now *your* people have taken her. She's out there somewhere, in pain and hurting. He's done something to her. I fucking feel it."

Lars stood and held up his hand. "Jason, you need to calm down. Sergei is doing everything possible to work with us to try to find her."

Alec wasn't overly fond of Sergei, especially given his previous interest in Ariana, but he was inclined to believe he was innocent of any wrongdoing. Right now, he was their best chance of finding her. They couldn't risk alienating him.

Alec walked over to his desk and pressed a button

signaling Sheila to come into his office. "I understand your worry, Jason, but we need you to keep trying to locate her through your bond. No one else can do what you can. We'll handle the rest of the search."

Sheila entered a moment later, waiting expectantly for direction. Alec gestured to Jason and said, "Sheila, can you show Jason into the conference room next door? He needs quiet to concentrate, and I'm afraid we're being a little disruptive. Be sure he has everything he needs."

"Of course, Master Tal'Vayr," she replied. "Please, let me show you to the conference room, Master Alivette. Would you care for a drink?"

Jason frowned. "I don't appreciate you trying to get rid of me, Alec, but I get it. I can't look at Sergei and not wonder. I'm not going to be much help in here as long as he's involved." He paused and took a deep breath. "Just... do what you can to find her. I can't lose her."

Alec walked over to him and clasped his shoulder. A frisson of awareness went through them at the contact, and they both stared at each other.

"Oh, fuck!" Jason cried out, jerking away from him. "You slept with my sister? What the hell, Alec?"

Lars choked on his drink. Alec's jaw clenched, and he glanced over at Sheila, who was staring open-mouthed at them.

Alec cleared his throat. "Sheila, I believe we're going to need another minute."

"Of course, Master Tal'Vayr," she managed and quickly rushed out the door.

"I'm sure your sister will appreciate your discretion," Alec told Jason in a dry tone.

"Fuck discretion," Jason retorted. "You've been courting her for all of two minutes. You drag her down to the ruins, convince her to form a connection with you, fuck her, and then let her get abducted in some Coalition powerplay? If you were any sort of potential bondmate, you would have protected her from all this shit."

"You're right," Alec agreed. "I should have protected her better."

Jason crossed his arms over his chest and glared at him. "You're a bastard. If anything happens to my sister, I'm holding you partially responsible." He turned his cold gaze to Sergei, letting him know without words who else he'd hold responsible.

Lars put his drink aside and walked over to them. "How did you know Alec slept with her, Jason?"

Jason sighed and scrubbed his face with his hands. "I felt it. When he touched me, it was like I felt Ariana through him."

Alec froze. He'd also had a flash and sensation of Ariana when he touched Jason, but was it possible? He frowned, wondering if the bond connection between Jason and Ariana could act as a conduit for communication. He thought back to the research he'd asked Sheila to gather on empaths and bonds. She was too far for him to reach through their shared connection, but maybe with Jason's help...

"I need to touch you again, Jason," Alec said.

Jason's eyes narrowed. "Fuck you, Alec. You think I want to feel that again?"

"Yes, if it'll help us find Ari."

Jason paused, his expression skeptical. "What makes you think you'll have any sort of connection with her?"

"Because I fucking love her!" Alec shouted, at the end of his patience. "I've loved her for two years, ever since I met her at Kendra's party. Do you honestly think she was alone all that time she spent in the library? While you were out fucking most of the towers, I was with your sister."

A stunned silence met his announcement. Alec grimaced,

realizing how that sounded. Before he could explain, Jason reared back and punched him in the face.

"Fuck!" Alec yelled as pain shot through his jaw. He rubbed it and said, "Dammit, Jason. I didn't sleep with her back then. I've always wanted to court her. That's why I went to your father years ago."

"I know you didn't sleep with her back then," Jason returned, rubbing his hand and shaking it out. "If you had touched her back then, I would have done a lot more than punch you. That was for fucking her last night and because you're still a bastard."

Lars glanced back and forth between them. "Alec, you have an idea?"

"Yes," he replied, still smarting from Jason's well-placed hit. "I felt Ariana too. I believe she's too weak to hear me through our connection, but I might be able to piggyback off Jason's bond."

"That might be how she sent the message to you earlier," Jason mused, flexing his hand. "I caught something through our bond, but I didn't hear her words. She must have used the last of her strength to send that message."

Alec held out his hand and waited for Jason to accept his connection. Jason eyed him warily for a moment and then connected with him psychically. A moment later, it was almost as though Ariana was in the room with them and only separated by a thin sheet of glass. He could sense her, but it was blurry and unfocused.

"Ari?" Alec urged, worried about the strange disconnect. *"Can you hear me? We're trying to find you, but we need your help."*

Ariana didn't respond right away. Alec had a growing sense of unease. He reached out to her again, trying to get a better sense of her. She'd withdrawn, trying to do what she could to block the emotions surrounding her. Dammit. She hadn't even had time to recover from healing Jason, and now she was surrounded by non-sensitives and their intense emotions. She was fading. Fast.

He sent a surge of energy through Jason, trying to target her with it. Even if she only retained a fraction, maybe it would be enough to get her through this until they located her.

"Come back to me, Ari," he urged. *"We need you to tell us where they're keeping you."*

"Alec?" she asked, her presence becoming more solid in his mind's eye.

He blew out a breath of relief. *"Yes. I'm here, love. We're trying to find you. Can you tell us where you are?"*

"A Coalition camp. Pavel drugged me. I don't know where I am," she replied, her mental voice shaky and still too weak. They had to hurry. He wasn't sure how long she could keep communicating.

"Have you seen anyone else? Heard any names? We know he's working with someone."

She paused, and Alec had a vague image of a woman form in his mind. *"I think he called her Sofia."*

"Good. That's very good. We're coming for you soon. Are you all right?"

"I—" she began, but there was a sharp flash of pain and the connection was gone.

Alec doubled over, pain radiating from his abdomen. Jason was in a similar state.

Lars put his hand on Alec's shoulder. "What happened? Alec, are you okay?"

"I'm calling for a medic," Brant announced.

"No," Alec managed. "It was a rebound effect. It was Ariana."

"I'm going to kill that bitch." Jason groaned, his eyes tearing up from the pain. "She kicked her. Ari was on the floor, and some woman fucking kicked her."

Sergei's eyes narrowed as he approached them. "You saw this woman?"

"Yeah. Alec sent energy to Ariana, and I was able to see the room. This woman was speaking to her, and Ariana didn't respond fast enough."

Alec swallowed. He hadn't seen, but... He squeezed his eyes shut. They had to find her now. "Sofia. She said Pavel was with a woman named Sofia."

Sergei's gaze flew to him, and he began swearing loudly in his language. He stalked over to his commlink. "I know where they are keeping her. We must go now before Sofia kills her."

CHAPTER FOURTEEN

PAIN EXPLODED in Ariana's ribs as her breath was knocked out of her, and Alec's comforting presence was ripped away. Tears flowed down her face as she fought to breathe.

"Get up," Sofia demanded, taking a step forward as though preparing to kick her again.

Ariana cringed away from her, struggling to push up from the floor with her bound wrists. Each breath was a brutal torment, but she managed to succeed.

A dozen more pots had been placed in the room. Pavel dropped a small bag of potatoes beside her.

Sofia gestured to the bag. "You will begin."

Ariana swallowed, trying to suppress her panic. Even if she were at full strength, it would be almost impossible to accomplish this feat. "It's too much. I can't do all of them. I need to rest."

Sofia wrapped her hand around Ariana's neck, her nails digging into her skin as she squeezed. Malevolence and hatred seeped through Ariana's skin, poisoning her with its toxicity.

"I heard what you did at the river. For someone who can

move earth and water, this is nothing compared to that," Sofia sneered. She released her abruptly and gestured to the pots again. "Begin, or I'll reconsider whether we have any use for you."

Ariana scooted forward and grasped the memory of Alec's energy embrace to sustain her. She just had to hold on a little bit longer until they found her. Pavel leaned forward and removed her bindings once again. She winced at the tingling in her fingers as the blood rushed back into her hands.

Ariana rubbed her wrists and picked up a potato, cradling it in her hands. She closed her eyes to center her thoughts and took a deep breath. This potato wasn't as eager to cooperate. She placed it in the closest pot, dismayed once again by the composition of the soil. It would require even more power than the last one to grow. She covered the potato with the soil and lifted the hydrating pack Pavel provided, pouring some of the precious fluid over the soil.

She sent out her earth energy, surrounding and calling forth the small sprouts within the potato. They stretched and unfurled, breaking through the soil's surface as though reaching for her hands. She slumped forward, the movement causing the pain in her chest to radiate outward. Each breath hurt as though her chest were on fire.

"Good," Sofia announced and gestured toward the next pot. "Continue."

Ariana pressed her hands against the ground, trying to gather strength from the earthen contact. It wasn't the same. She'd relied almost exclusively on water energy for most of her life. It required much more concentration to try to use the earth energy to do the same.

A banging on the door interrupted her concentration. Sofia turned and opened the door, her entire body stiffening at the sight of the person on the other side. "What are you doing here?"

"Now, Sofia," a woman gently chided, her voice almost musical, "someone might think you weren't glad to see me."

"I'm not," she snapped. "Why are you in my camp, Valentina?"

Although Sofia was partially blocking the door, Ariana caught a glimpse of a young woman in the doorway. Her chestnut hair was pulled back in a high ponytail, with the delicacy of her features contrasting sharply with her military-style clothing. Clear, blue eyes met hers, a flicker of amusement in her gaze. The woman's mouth curved upwards in a smile. She shoved open the door, forcing Sofia to take a half-step backward, and entered the room.

"Who is this?" Valentina asked, and then her gaze swept the room, pausing on the plant in front of Ariana. "And what do we have here?"

"This is not your concern," Sofia hissed, crossing her arms over her chest.

"No?" Valentina once more regarded Ariana thoughtfully. She knelt in front of the plant, brushing her fingers over one of the leaves.

Ariana frowned. The tightly coiled energy surrounding this woman reminded her of Sergei. Her emotions were difficult to read, and she moved with a competent grace. Ariana had the sense she was a predator, a highly-skilled hunter who would kill just as easily as she saved a life. Who was this woman and why was she here?

Valentina winked at Ariana before standing. Turning back around to face Sofia and Pavel, she leaned casually against the wall. "I heard you've been getting into trouble, Pavel. There are some rumors you're going to be released from service at the end of the month."

Pavel's entire body went rigid, his wariness at the young woman's arrival evident in his body language and the choking emotional energy threads surrounding him. "That will not happen."

Valentina made a noncommittal noise. "Do you really think Sofia intends to take you in? If Sergei releases you from service, the Coalition will wash their hands of you. She won't risk herself to save you."

"Really, Valentina? You seek to drive a wedge between me and Pavel?" Sofia scoffed, crossing her arms over her chest. "You could have come up with something a little more original."

Valentina tilted her head. "Oh, I don't know. Pavel looks like he's having doubts about your loyalty. Maybe he's remembering what happened to your last associate."

"Why are you here, Valentina?" Sofia demanded. "If Nikolai thinks he can send you here to interfere—"

Valentina dropped her hand to the weapon on her belt, all earlier traces of humor gone. In its place was a dark, swirling emotion that clouded the surrounding air. "Watch your tongue, Sofia. You would do well to remember what happened last time someone chose to insult Nikolai in my presence."

Sofia stepped forward, refusing to back down. "You're in *my* camp, Valentina."

"Last I checked, this was a Coalition camp, and I'm an agent of Chairman Nikolai," Valentina said in a low voice, as though daring Sofia to contradict her. "Pavel has taken this young woman from the towers without authorization. By harboring him, you're in direct violation of the terms of your agreement."

Sofia floundered for a brief moment and gestured toward Ariana.

"She has skills we need," Sofia argued, glancing over at Pavel. "OmniLab has not been honest with us about their abilities. Several other chairmen are interested in seeing proof of her skills. She's being kept here at their request."

Ariana lifted her head, the pungent odor of a lie emanating from the older woman.

Valentina threw her head back and laughed. "Oh, Sofia, you cannot possibly expect I would believe such a story."

Ariana stared at the young woman, wondering how she had guessed. Their kind couldn't read energy, could they?

Sofia straightened, feigning indignation. "You're calling me a liar?"

Valentina's mouth curved upward. "Yes, I absolutely am."

The room became thick with tension. Sofia glanced again at Pavel and gave him a brief nod. He drew a small weapon, the blade glinting in the light, and flung it in Valentina's direction. Ariana had the briefest realization the knife had hit her, but the young woman was already in motion.

Valentina dove to the side, drawing her electrolaser gun and firing at Pavel. He crumpled to the floor in a heap. Sofia leapt toward Valentina and the two women collided, falling to the floor, wrestling for control over the weapon. They rolled, crashing into the pots. Valentina slid the gun in Ariana's direction and she grabbed it.

Ariana lifted the unfamiliar weapon, trying to aim at Sofia. They were still grappling, and she couldn't risk hitting the wrong person. Valentina managed to get on top of Sofia, and Sofia wrapped her hands around her throat. Valentina slammed the other woman's head against the ground. Sofia's hands fell away, and she reached down for the knife sticking out of Valentina's abdomen. Twisting it sharply, she shoved Valentina off her.

Ariana fired the moment she had a clear shot. Sofia fell backward, hitting the ground with a *thud*. Valentina clutched the hilt of the knife and blinked up at Ariana. She managed a grimaced smile and said, "Well done. You are tougher than Sergei said you were."

Ariana swallowed, lowering the weapon with shaking hands. "Sergei sent you?"

"Yes," she confirmed, squeezing her eyes shut. "Your towers have been looking for you. They'll be here soon."

"Thank you," Ariana whispered, worried about the woman's pallor. She was in a great deal of pain. The knife had embedded in her abdomen, and Ariana had seen enough injuries to know this one was potentially fatal. She pushed herself along the floor toward the young woman and placed the electrolaser gun beside her. "I'd like to try to heal you. Will you allow it?"

Valentina opened her eyes. "You can heal too?"

Ariana nodded. "It's more difficult to heal your kind, but I'd like to try."

"Sure," she managed, reaching for the weapon as though not willing to be parted from it. "Why the hell not? It's not like I have many options at the moment."

Ariana smiled at the woman's abrasiveness. She reminded her a great deal of Kayla. Ariana spread her hands over the woman's abdomen, trying to get a sense of the severity of her injury. As she suspected, the knife had nicked Valentina's abdominal aorta. She wasn't willing to risk withdrawing the knife right away. This was going to be tricky.

With one hand hovering over Valentina's midsection, she grasped the handle of the blade with the other. She pulled the knife out a fraction, swathing Valentina in a healing wave of energy. Valentina's eyes were squeezed shut, her breathing growing labored. Ariana swallowed and took a deep breath, ignoring the pain in her ribs.

She pulled the knife out a bit more, sending more healing energy into Valentina's abdomen. The blood loss was slowing, but Ariana couldn't risk stopping to check on Valentina's condition. The young woman had already lost too much blood. She had to keep going or it would be too late. Valentina wouldn't survive.

Bit by bit, Ariana worked the knife out of Valentina. She dropped it on the ground and spread both hands over Valentina once again. Her breathing was beginning to normalize, but she was still too pale. Ariana couldn't do much to replenish blood loss, but her chances of survival were much better now.

A wave of dizziness crashed over Ariana, and her vision swam. She'd done too much. Whatever energy Alec had provided was long gone. The emotions in the camp pounded against her psyche as she slumped forward, hoping help would arrive soon. For all her abilities to heal others, she couldn't heal herself.

———

ALEC PULLED off his helmet the moment they entered the compound. Jason had wanted to accompany them, but Alec had refused. Jason was unpredictable when Ariana was threatened, and the situation was already too volatile.

"She's here," Alec murmured, detecting the subtle trace of Ariana's energy.

"Which way?" Sergei demanded.

Alec took a deep breath, trying to pinpoint Ariana's location. Her energy was faint and growing weaker by the second.

"That way," he pointed and ran, unmindful that he was racing through a Coalition camp. His only thought was of Ariana and his desperation to reach her before that light faded completely.

He pushed open a door to reveal a disturbing scene. Four people were lying unconscious on the floor amid broken crockery and dirt, but he only had eyes for Ariana.

"Ari," he whispered, rushing to her side and pulling her into his arms. She didn't respond. There were bruises on her face and neck, as well as lacerations around her wrists where she'd been bound. Sergei shouted something in his language and rushed over to the young woman on the ground, dropping to his knees beside her.

"The medics are coming in now," Brant said in a low voice. "Lars just went out to meet them."

Alec nodded, unable to tear his eyes away from Ariana. She was breathing, but that's all he knew. "Water," he croaked. "She needs water."

Brant reached over to grab several nearby hydrating packs and ripped them open before handing them over. Alec began pouring the water on Ariana's arms and face and anywhere he saw exposed skin. It wouldn't help if she wasn't able to use the water energy, but it might help revive her enough if she sensed the comforting presence of her element.

"Is she all right?" the young woman beside Ariana asked, wincing as Sergei helped her sit up.

Alec scowled, glancing over at her. If this was one of the people responsible for hurting Ariana...

Sergei held up his hand. "This is Valentina. She is one of mine."

The woman's eyes flashed in anger. "I am *not* one of yours."

Sergei grinned. "Ah, I see you are feeling better, Valechka."

"Bastard," she muttered, rubbing her stomach as though it pained her. She glanced down at Ariana, her gaze worried. "She saved me. Pavel got in a lucky shot, and Sofia took advantage."

"You should not have been here," Sergei chided.

"Nikolai was busy," she snapped. "Give us a bit more notice next time your second falls into bed with a *suka*."

Sergei scowled. "How badly are you hurt?"

"I will live." She gestured to the water. "What are you doing to her?"

"Water helps her," Sergei said by way of explanation and removed Ariana's bindings. He stood to check on the other two unconscious people in the room, fastening the bindings around their wrists.

"Her energy is still fading." Alec frowned, panic growing with every heartbeat. He reached outward through their connection, but she was still and silent. He could sense her, but she wasn't responding.

"Brant, I need you to stand guard. She's slipping farther away from me. If I wait any longer, I'll lose her."

Brant nodded, drawing his weapon.

Sergei paused. "What is wrong?"

Alec shook his head. There was no time to explain. The sense of urgency within him was growing. Alec cupped Ariana's face, tracing her features with his hand. He closed his eyes, reaching out to her through their connection.

"Ari? Can you hear me, love?" he asked, floundering in the darkness.

There was no response.

He tried calling out to her again, but everything remained dark and silent. The strange darkness was disturbingly familiar, but he'd never invaded her mind before. As a general rule, he avoided it, except for that time when Kayla had been unconscious...

That was it! Their energy must be more similar than anyone had realized. He thought back to the research files on empaths. Most of them had entered a comalike state where they remained until they died. It wasn't a true coma, though; it couldn't be. Just like Kayla, Ariana must have found a way to protect herself from outside attacks. Her energy levels must have depleted themselves to a point that her mind imprisoned itself as a last resort to shield her from further harm.

He sent out a small stream of strengthening energy, trying to coax her back to awareness. *"Ari, please, love. Come back to me."*

She didn't respond.

He increased his energy, flooding her with his power. *"Ari, come back to me now."*

She began to stir, her mental voice sleepy as she said, *"It hurts, Alec."*

His relief at hearing her voice was almost overwhelming. She wasn't gone. He caressed her cheek, trailing his fingers against the softness of her skin. *"I know, love. Please come back to me. We'll fix this."*

Alec felt her mental sigh, and she started to slip farther away. He grabbed hold of her tightly, increasing his energy to the full capacity of their connection. *"Ari, no. You must come back now."*

He could sense her confusion, but she was struggling to resurface from the prison she'd created. It was too much for her. She was so tired. Releasing him again, she slipped back into those dark depths. *"No! Ari, bond with me right now. Please, love, I can't lose you."*

Why hadn't he formed a complete connection with her? Damn his foolish sense of nobility. He reached outward and completely encircled her with his energy threads, silently begging her to hold on to them.

Her usual grace was gone, replaced by an exhausted fumbling. He kept up his steady stream of energy, trying to direct her as best as possible to gather his remaining threads. With every additional connection, he amplified his energy. *"That's it, love. Just a little more."*

"I'm so tired, Alec."

"I know, beautiful. You can rest soon, I promise. Once we have a

complete connection, I can bond with you and share my energy with you." He leaned down and pressed a kiss against her lips. "*I love you, Ari. Please try for me.*"

Her mouth curved in a small smile, and hope welled within him. She was even closer now.

"*I love you too, Alec,*" was her whispered reply as he felt the last of her energy threads connect with his.

———

ARIANA WAS STILL FLOATING, somewhere dark and safe, but Alec's pull was irresistible. Through their connection, she could feel everything. He was terrified of losing her, furious with the people who had hurt her, and above all, irrevocably in love with her. All façades fell away, and their emotions and thoughts were laid completely bare to the other.

This was the gift of their kind, this potential for complete love and acceptance through holding a bond.

"*Will you, Ari? Will you bond with me and allow me to claim you forever?*"

His words brought to life her greatest hope and most precious dream, and now it was within her grasp. When she'd first met him, he'd charmed her with his wit and humor. But it was in the days afterward—during secret meetings at the library and laughing over whatever latest antics their friends had gotten into—that she'd fallen in love with him. Try as she might, she'd never been able to stop loving him, and now he was offering to be hers forever.

Her heart overflowed with joy. "*Yes, from now until the last of the energy in this world is a memory, I'll be yours.*"

He opened his heart even wider, enveloping her with the full force of his energy. It was beautiful and exquisite, more alluring than she'd ever imagined. This was Alec, all of him, the very essence of his being. She reached outward, the darkness falling away, and embraced him with her energy, caressing him and chasing away his darkness.

"Ari," he murmured as their bond blossomed between them like a new plant emerging from the soil.

She blinked open her eyes, staring into his with a sense of wonder. There were thousands more colors in the world now, with each strand of energy containing the promise of all the possibilities of the future. She lifted her hand to touch his face, his rough whiskers tickling her fingers as she traced his jawline. He was hurt. Had someone hit him? It was a minor injury, but she'd never allow him to have a moment of pain ever again.

Weaving a band of healing energy around him, she eased away the slight hurt. Alec turned his head, kissing her fingertips. She smiled up at him, wanting to feel his lips on hers. His eyes darkened with desire as his gaze lowered to her mouth. He dipped his head, his kiss gentle with an undercurrent of barely restrained passion. Ariana threaded her fingers through his hair, getting lost in his touch and his kiss. Memories of the night before flooded back to her, and she begged him silently to claim her once again.

He pulled her tighter against him, and she cried out as pain shot through her ribs. Alec froze, his horror evident as his eyes scanned over her. He lifted his head to address someone standing nearby and snapped, "Check her ribs. I think they're broken."

Ariana recognized the medic as a man named Paul. She'd worked with him on occasion in the medical ward. He had an adorable little girl who occasionally visited him at work.

She managed a strained smile. "I don't know if they're broken, but at least two of them are cracked."

Paul's expression was worried, but he nodded and glanced at Alec. "With your permission?"

Alec nodded at him to go ahead but didn't release her.

Paul lifted her shirt to reveal dark, mottled bruises. He pulled out a small handheld scanner and began running it over her midsection. Ariana winced, wondering how bad the rest of her looked. She could feel the swelling in her neck and cheek, but it paled in comparison to the pain in her ribs.

"You're beautiful, Ari."

She flushed. It was going to take a while before she was accustomed to having Alec read her thoughts.

He smiled and lifted her hand to press a kiss against it. *"I've spent so long without you that every intimacy is another gift."*

"You make it difficult to object," she admitted. *"It's an adjustment, but I like having you only a thought away."*

"I promise, Ari, I'll always be here for you. I'm never leaving you again."

The medic tucked away his device. "You're correct. Two of yours ribs are cracked. There's significant bruising too. We can stabilize you for now and put you into the bone molds as soon as we get you back to the towers."

"Do it," Alec ordered.

Paul nodded and reached into his bag to pull out the supports. He gently began winding the bracing around her midsection. When he finished, he turned to Valentina. "You should also return with us to the towers for observation. Mistress Alivette is a skilled healer, but that was an extremely dangerous injury. We need to check to make sure there are no other internal issues."

Ariana glanced at Valentina, who was scowling at Paul. Sergei spoke up and said, "She'll go."

Valentina glared at Sergei. "I do not report to you."

Sergei reached into his pocket and pulled out his commlink. He pressed a button and spoke into it in a steady stream of Russian. He paused for a long moment, listening to someone, and then held out the commlink to her. "Nikolai wishes to speak with you."

She snatched the commlink out of his hand and listened for a long time. The voice grew louder, and she pulled it away from her ear. When he finished, she answered with one word and thrust it back in Sergei's direction with a scowl. "Bastard."

Sergei chuckled, slipping the commlink back into his pocket. Ariana sat up and Alec stood, helping her to her feet. The air in the room shifted slightly, and Pavel made a soft groaning noise. He was waking up.

Alec turned toward him, the surrounding air energizing with his fury. He flicked his wrist and slammed Pavel into the wall, a deadly wind whipping through the room. A strange vortex surrounded Pavel, stealing the air around him so he couldn't breathe. He choked, twisting against his restraints, fully awake now and unable to breathe.

Ariana shook her head and gripped Alec's arm. "Alec, please. Don't do this."

"He hurt you," Alec said, his voice almost unrecognizable in its fury.

She lifted her hand, cupping his cheek and turning his head back in her direction. Embracing him with her soothing energy, she said, "Yes, but you saved me in more ways than one. The emotions aren't hurting me anymore."

Alec abruptly withdrew his air energy and Pavel crashed to the ground. Alec ignored him and drew her into his arms, searching her expression. "You're not shielding, are you?"

She shook her head and smiled up at him. "No. I didn't realize it until Pavel woke up. You sensed him wake up through our bond too. The emotions in the camp aren't hurting me anymore."

"Are you sure?" Alec asked, hope and worry intermingled in his eyes.

Ariana nodded. "I feel... whole. Maybe you were right and this was all part of Fate's grand design. You're holding the one element I've always needed. Between the two of us, we carry all four elements and have the ability to draw upon them through our bond." She paused, reaching up to touch his face. "You saved me from myself, Alec. We're the perfect counter-balance to each other."

He pulled her against him, burying his face in her hair, and inhaled deeply. "Thank the gods. You really are safe then, from all of it. I was so worried I might lose you. I love you, Ariana."

"I love you too, Alec." She rested her head against his chest and inhaled the alluring scent of earth and incense that always surrounded him.

He held her tightly and ran his hand along her back. "Now that we don't need the serum, this means I can torch Hayden's lab."

Ariana pulled back, staring up at him in shock.

Alec shrugged. "What? I wasn't proposing doing it with him inside." He paused as though considering it, and Ariana smacked him lightly when she sensed his silent laughter. He captured her hand, studying the marks on her wrist with a frown.

Brant approached them. "Do you want us to transport the prisoners back to the towers?"

Alec's frown deepened, and he eyed Pavel and Sofia with barely restrained fury. They were both awake now, watching the occupants of the rooms with wary expressions.

"Alec," Ariana said in a soft tone, placing her hand over his heart. "Vengeance can wound the soul. I'll always be a healer, but there are some things which aren't healed easily. If you hurt, I'll hurt along with you."

"I'm sorry, but I can't let this stand." Alec wrapped his hand around her wrist. "I love your sensitive heart, but I cannot and will not ignore what they've done. A message needs to be sent that their actions will not be tolerated."

She hung her head, knowing he was right but hating that he would carry this burden.

"Leave them with me," Sergei demanded. "They are my people and must be held accountable in accordance with our laws."

Alec and Sergei exchanged a look. Ariana glanced back and forth between them, but more was being communicated beneath the surface. They were suppressing their emotions, preventing her from reading them. She frowned but decided it was better she didn't know.

Alec inclined his head. "Very well. I'd appreciate your assistance with this matter. We'll see you back at the towers when your business is concluded."

Valentina rubbed her stomach where Pavel's knife had entered. "I will stay long enough to help you deal with Sofia and Pavel."

Sergei frowned at her. "Get on the aircraft or I will put you on it."

"Do not threaten me, Sergei," she snarled, putting her hands on her hips.

"Then stop acting like a child."

She jabbed her finger against his chest and spoke rapidly in Russian. He grabbed her finger, shouting back at her. Ariana's eyes widened, watching the uncharacteristic display. She'd never seen Sergei lose his temper before. He'd always been so calm whenever he'd been around her.

Brant cleared his throat. "Excuse me, Valentina? My name is Brant Mason, and I'm a security officer within the towers. I'd be honored if you allowed me to escort you out to our aircraft."

They paused in their fighting, and Valentina turned to stare at Brant. She blinked at him as though seeing him for the first time, assessing him with a critical eye. An amused smile crossed her lips. "I think I might enjoy a trip to the towers after all."

With a cheeky wave to Sergei, she headed out of the room with Brant. Sergei frowned after her and hesitated as though undecided about something. Finally, he shook his head and sighed. Turning back to Ariana, he studied her for a long moment and his gaze softened. "How are you feeling, *solnyshka*?"

She gave him a shy smile. "I'm okay. Thank you for sending Valentina to help me. I'm not sure what would have happened if she hadn't shown up."

Sergei took Ariana's hand. "Thank you for healing her. She is stubborn and difficult but beloved by many."

"You didn't look happy with her a minute ago," Ariana admitted.

Sergei shrugged. "She takes many risks she should not. It is sometimes difficult to get her to see reason."

"Who's Nikolai?"

Sergei frowned. "Nikolai is one of our leaders. Valentina is his... She is very important to him."

"Oh," Ariana murmured, glancing at the door. "She seemed taken with Brant."

Sergei's expression darkened, but he didn't reply.

Alec put his arm back around her. "We should go. The sooner we get you back to the towers, the sooner we can reassure your family you're safe."

She nodded and stepped forward, standing on her toes to kiss Sergei's cheek. "Thank you, Sergei. For everything."

He lifted her hand and pressed a kiss against it. "You are bonded with Alec now, correct?"

She nodded shyly. They didn't normally announce such things right away, but it had happened rather publicly. Nothing seemed to be going in accordance with tradition as far as they were concerned, but she didn't really mind. Alec was hers, and she was his. That was all that truly mattered.

"Good," he murmured. "He cares deeply for you."

Alec tightened his arm around her waist. Looking up at the man she loved, she nodded. "Yes, he does."

"If he ever hurts you," Sergei warned, his eyes glinting with unmistakable meaning, "you will come to me. We will figure out how to break this bond."

Alec's jaw clenched, but Ariana sent a soothing wave of energy to ease both men. "I don't think you have anything to worry about. Alec would never hurt me."

"No," Sergei relented with a small grin. "If I believed he would, I would not allow you to leave with him."

Ariana smiled and leaned against Alec, a sense of rightness filling her as his energy surrounded her. There was no question in her mind she'd managed to find the one person who had always been destined as her bondmate. This had been part of Fate's plan the entire time, and she'd never doubt again.

"I feel it too, Ari," Alec whispered and pressed a kiss against her lips, his eyes overflowing with love and adoration. "Will you let me take you home?"

She nodded and slipped her hand in his, letting him lead her out of the Coalition camp and back to the towers where they belonged.

CHAPTER FIFTEEN

"You're *what*?" Devan demanded as the surrounding air plummeted several degrees.

"We're bonded," Alec repeated firmly, wrapping his arm around Ariana's waist and pulling her closer. "Ariana's my mate. I know this isn't in accordance with our usual courtship traditions, but circumstances—"

Devan took a step forward, his eyes cold and unyielding. "Do you think you can just steal away my daughter without consequences? You manipulated Seara's daughter into forming a bond with you and now you've had the audacity to so the same with Ariana? This won't stand, Alec. I'll see your dead and broken body at my feet before I allow this."

Alec opened his mouth to argue, but Ariana stepped in front of him to face her father. She wasn't about to let Alec keep taking the brunt of his anger. Not now. Not ever again. Alec was hers just as much as she was his. She'd protect him, even against her own flesh and blood.

Lifting her chin, she announced, "I'm not shielding anymore, Father."

Devan froze. His eyes focused on her, but his gaze became

suspicious. "If this is some sort of attempt to prevent me from seeking vengeance on Alec for doing this..."

Ariana shook her head. The whirlwind of emotions surrounding her father was quickly dampening her indignation. Now that she wasn't shielding, she could sense her father's deeper emotions and the ones he kept hidden from most of the world. He truly did love her. Maybe Devan's actions were misguided and he put too much emphasis on retaining the purity of their bloodlines, but she understood his intentions. He simply wanted to protect their family lineage, especially his children. The stronger they were, the better able they would be in protecting themselves.

Gentling her tone, she said, "No, there's no trick. No deception. I haven't felt the need to shield myself since we bonded."

Ariana looked up at Alec, telling him without words how much she cared for him before turning back to her father. "Alec holds the one element I've never possessed. For the first time in my life, I've reached a perfect balance. Alec is everything I've always wanted and more than I ever dreamed was possible. He completes me, and I do the same for him."

Alec moved forward, putting his arm around her waist and drawing her against his side once more. "I love your daughter, Devan. I intended to wait out of respect for her, but I wasn't willing to risk losing her. You asked me before what I was willing to do for her. The answer is anything and everything. I may not deserve her, but I'll gladly spend the rest of my life trying to earn the right to stand by her side."

Devan frowned.

Ariana walked over to her father and took his hands in hers. Pressing a kiss against his cheek, she said, "Without Alec, I wouldn't have survived what happened at the Coalition camp or the evolution of my abilities. My heart's been telling me all along that I'm meant to be with him. Our bond was formed out of love, and his love saved me and brought me back to you. I want you to be happy for us, Papa."

"You haven't called me that since you were a little girl," Devan said, his voice choking with emotion. He stared at her for several heartbeats, and she felt his emotional barriers beginning to crumble.

She bit her lip, looking up at her father. "Tell me you'll accept him—and us. Alec's a good man. You know that. He kept my secret all these years and protected me, just like you've done. You'll always be my family, but Alec's part of that too. I don't want this to cause a divide between us."

Finally, he nodded and lifted his head to look at Alec. "It seems I owe you an apology, Alec. Ariana's right. I knew you suspected the scope of her abilities. You could have used her secret for your own ambitions, but you never did. Even when I refused your request to court Ariana years ago, you gracefully stepped aside to protect her. I'm sorry for trying to stand in your way now."

Devan swallowed and looked down at Ariana again, squeezing her hands gently. "Thank you for saving my daughter and bringing her back to me. She means more to me than I can ever say."

Ariana beamed a smile at her father and hugged him tightly. Devan ran a hand over her hair and murmured, "I'm glad he makes you happy, Ari."

She released him and nodded, brushing away a tear that had escaped. Alec put his arm back around her waist and she leaned against him.

"Thank you, Devan," Alec said quietly.

Devan nodded. "Just... take care of her."

"I will," Alec promised, his eyes filled with tenderness as he looked down at her.

Ariana smiled at Alec, part of her still in disbelief that he really belonged to her. More than anything, she wanted to show him exactly how she felt, but there was something they needed to do first. Turning back to her father, she said, "I'm sorry, Papa, but there's someone we need to go see."

"Of course," he agreed and then hesitated. "Perhaps— After things have a chance to settle down, I'd like to extend the invitation for both of you to have dinner with your mother and me. A family dinner, if you will."

Ariana's heart soared. "Yes, I'd like that a great deal."

"Good," he agreed, his expression softening a fraction in the barest trace of a smile. "I'll wait to hear from you."

Ariana watched her father walk away before taking Alec's hand and walking with him down the corridor. Alec squeezed her hand as they approached the breezeway.

"I wish you'd reconsider," he said with a sigh. "I understood the need to tell your father, and it went far better than I hoped, but you don't owe Hayden an explanation."

She shook her head. "I need to, Alec. It's the right thing to do."

Alec frowned, glancing down the breezeway toward the figure waiting at the other end. "I don't like it. I don't trust him around you."

Ariana lifted her hand, pressing it against Alec's cheek, and sent out a soothing band of energy to surround him. His frown deepened, creating an adorable 'v' between his eyebrows.

"I know what you're doing, Ari. It's not going to work. Our bond is still too new, and he still hasn't relinquished his courtship rights. You were taken from me just yesterday. I'm not ready to let you out of my sight."

"Alec," she began, taking a small step closer to him and closing the distance between them. "I'm bonded to you. You're the only one I want, the only one I've ever wanted. Hayden's family is powerful, and it's not wise to offend them."

Alec sighed. "Will you let me listen through our bond?"

She shook her head. "No, you need to trust me."

"You're not the problem, love," he murmured, taking her hands in his and teasing her with a light trace of energy. "I don't doubt your feelings or intentions. But now that I can sense other people's emotions through you, I'm even less fond of Hayden. He's a little too covetous when it comes to you."

She laughed, standing on her toes to press a kiss against his lips. "Give me ten minutes. I won't be long."

"Very well," he agreed, his reluctance coursing through their connection.

Ariana turned away and headed down the breezeway, missing Alec's closeness almost immediately. It was the newness of the bond, in part. She wanted to spend every minute with him, deepening their connection and exploring all the nuances. He felt the same, and it thrilled her on an elemental level. Their bond would eventually settle down, but until then, she had every intention of exploring all these new and exciting feelings.

He hadn't been happy when she insisted on seeing Hayden so soon after their return from the Coalition camp, but it was necessary. Prolonging the inevitable would only cause more problems.

Hayden was standing at the end of the breezeway with his hands clasped behind his back. His dark hair ruffled slightly, and his amber eyes warmed at the sight of her. She bit her lip. Alec was right. Hayden's feelings weren't platonic in the slightest.

"Ari," he murmured, taking her offered hands. He sent a light trace of fire energy over her, and she felt Alec's irritation from the other end of the breezeway.

"Hayden, thank you for coming," she began and withdrew her hands.

He glanced down the breezeway in Alec's direction and frowned. "I wasn't expecting you to bring company."

She lowered her head, trying to figure out the best way to tell him. Unfortunately, there was no delicate way to say it. "Alec and I are bonded."

Hayden froze, his eyes narrowing. "When?"

"Yesterday. He saved my life," she explained. "For the first time since I can remember, I'm able to breathe without having everyone's emotions threatening to drown me. I can feel my emotions and recognize them as my own, independent of everyone else. His strength is my salvation. I owe him everything."

Hayden stiffened. "Ari, if the reason you bonded with him was because of your empath abilities, you know I've been working on a serum for Jason. We're closer than ever to making it work. We can figure out how to dissolve this bond. You don't need to tie yourself to him."

"No," she insisted, wanting to make him understand. "I love him, Hayden. I've loved him for a long time." She lowered her gaze and added, "I can't tell you how much it means to me that you were willing to develop that serum. I had no idea you cared for me to such an extent."

She really had crippled herself by suppressing her empathic abilities. If she had known how Hayden felt in the beginning, maybe she could have spared him this hurt by making her position clear. Although she knew she'd needed to protect herself against the surrounding emotions, it saddened her to know how long she hadn't been living up to her full potential. There were so many people she could have helped over the years.

He sighed and took her hand in his once again. "That's my fault, I suppose. I thought you were shy. I had no idea your abilities kept you away from everyone, or I would have made my intentions known sooner."

She lifted her head. "I don't want to lose your friendship, Hayden. You gave me my first dance, and I'll always treasure that memory."

He chuckled. "I took you there to make Alec jealous. I wanted to protect you by keeping you away from the crowd, but I was worried about him as competition. I thought it would make him lose his temper and he'd lose his chance with you."

Her eyes widened. "Hayden! Shame on you."

He shrugged and grinned. "What can I say? All's fair in love and war, right? Besides, Alec won the war. He has the best reward possible."

She bit her lip. In her mind, Alec was *her* reward, not the other way around. "You're not angry the month was cut short?"

Hayden paused, searching her expression. "Are you happy, Ari? Does he truly make you happy?"

She nodded, letting him see everything she felt for Alec in her eyes. "I'm happier than I've ever been. He means everything to me."

He gave her a sad smile. "Then no, I'm not angry. But if you ever change your mind, I'd gladly challenge him for your bond. It would be unfortunate to do away with the High Council leader, but it would be for a good cause."

"No," she whispered, horrified by the thought. "Please don't. I couldn't bear to have anything happen to either of you."

"Then I'll console myself with that thought. I'll speak with your father and officially announce my concession."

She took a step forward and kissed his cheek. "Thank you, Hayden."

He put his arms around her, drawing her close, and whispered, "Be happy, Ari."

"You too, Hayden," she whispered and pulled away from

him. He really was a good man, just not the right man for her. But one day, he'd find the person he was meant to be with. After all, Fate had a way of giving them a nudge in the right direction.

As she headed back down the breezeway, her heart felt lighter. Each step she took forward was one step closer to her future. At the end of the breezeway, Alec was waiting with a worried expression on his face.

"Are you okay?"

She nodded. "Our courtship is over. He's conceded to you."

Alec's shoulders relaxed, and he pulled her into his arms. "Thank the gods. I didn't want to have to kill him."

Ariana frowned. "He said the same thing about you."

Alec scowled, glancing down the breezeway again. "Did he? It's been a while since I last dueled..."

"Don't even think about it," Ariana warned and then giggled at the mischievous glint in his eyes.

Alec grinned. "I have something for you."

She tilted her head, watching him curiously as he reached into his pocket to withdraw a small object. He held it out in his hand, and she gasped. It was her ring, the same one with the stone that reminded her of Alec's eyes.

"You must have dropped it in Sergei's room," he murmured, taking her left hand and sliding it on her finger. "It got me thinking though. What do you think about having a claiming ceremony at the end of the month?"

Her eyes widened. "A wedding?"

"Yes," he murmured, tracing the ring on her hand with his finger. "I want everyone to know you're mine, Ariana Alivette. Humans and *Drac'Kin* alike. We could even have it in Seara's gardens, if you want."

She blinked back her tears, wanting everything he offered. He really was the man of her dreams, and even more importantly, the man of her future. "Yes, Alec, I'd love to marry you."

"My bondmate, soon to also be my wife," he murmured, his eyes filled with adoration and love. He lowered his head, claiming her mouth in a passionate embrace that sent her heart soaring. When he pulled away, he cupped her face and sent a strong wave of love-infused energy over her. "I'm not sure I can wait to have you move in with me. I don't want to spend another night without you in my bed."

Ariana smiled up at him, embracing him with her energy and her heart. "You don't have to wait. From now until the last of the energy in this world is a memory, I'm yours."

ABOUT THE AUTHOR

Jamie A. Waters is an award-winning science fiction and para-normal romance author. Her first novel, Beneath the Fallen City (previously titled as The Two Towers), was a winner of the Readers' Favorite Award in Science-Fiction Romance and the CIPA EVVY Award in Science-Fiction.

Jamie currently resides in Florida with her two neurotic dogs who enjoy stealing socks and chasing lizards. When she's not pursuing her passion of writing, she's usually trying to learn new and interesting random things (like how to pick locks or use the self-cleaning feature of the oven without setting off the fire alarm). In her downtime, she enjoys reading, playing computer games, painting, or acting as a referee between the dragons and fairies currently at war inside her closet.

You can learn more by visiting: www.jamieawaters.com

Made in the USA
Columbia, SC
03 January 2025

51137594R00186